The Ballad of the Low Lifes

By the Author

Rossenotti

Enrico Remmert

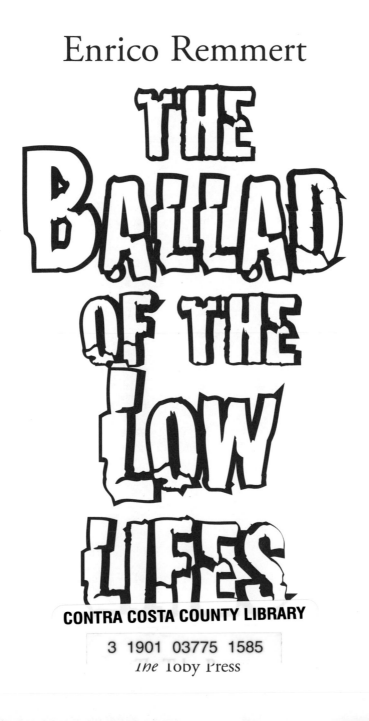

THE BALLAD OF THE LOW LIFES

The Toby Press

First English language Edition 2004

The Toby Press LLC

POB 8531, New Milford, CT. 06676-8531, USA

& POB 2455, London WIA 5WY, England

www.tobypress.com

Originally published as *La ballata delle
caniglie,* Venezia, Marsilio Editore, 2002

Translation © copyright Aubrey Botsford, 2003

ISBN 1 59264 054 0

A CIP catalogue record for this title is
available from the British Library

Typeset in Garamond by Jerusalem Typesetting

Printed and bound in the United States
by Thomson-Shore Inc., Michigan

To my father

The fact is that we are all losers, with a glorious penchant for self-destruction.

W. Somerset Maugham, *The Summing Up*

Translator's note

The currency used in this novel is the Italian lira (plural lire). In January 2002, Italy joined the "euro zone" and its currency became the euro (€). The lira ceased to exist, and the rate at the time of the changeover was fixed at 1,950 lire = €1.00. To give an idea of the scale of the characters' ambitions, it may help to think of 1,000 lire as being roughly $0.50/£0.35, and 100 million lire as being a bit more than $50,000 or a bit less than £35,000.

Author's note

This is a work of fiction. All the characters, events and conversations are imaginary. Any reference to actual events or real people is purely coincidental, with the exception of James Addison Reavis (whose story is part the history of the United States of America) and Martin Frankel (whose story was part of American news in the 1990s).

Part One

It's a hot Sunday in early summer, no flies.

You're standing in the middle of this vast open pit, surrounded by old warehouses and disused factories. Everything around you is deserted: walls and concrete as far as the eye can see, mounds of rubble, rusty containers, empty cans, weeds, plastic bags, the bodies of two cars dumped in the undergrowth.

Your eyes are fixed on a broken windscreen that is reflecting the fiery golden rays of the sun like a pool of water, when Milo leans out of the window of his old blue van and breaks the silence.

"HOW'M I DOING?" he yells.

You look around for the umpteenth time—to confirm that you're the only human beings for miles around—then concentrate on the white Punto parked forty-odd yards behind the van.

"JUST A MINUTE!" you yell back.

You take a few steps over to the car, lean down along the line of the hood and start pretending to take visual measurements in the direction of the van.

"YOU'RE LINED UP PERFECTLY," you yell. "GO!"

The starter motor struggles for a few seconds, then you hear a roar as the engine catches. A moment later, with a grinding of gears, Milo engages reverse: the van jumps and starts moving backwards.

"CARRY ON LIKE THAT," you yell, moving aside. "THAT'S FINE!"

Milo checks his mirrors and presses the pedal to the floor, the engine screams, gravel sprays up under the van, and it gathers speed, lurching about on the dirt, raising a cloud of dust, faster and faster, until it slams into the front of the Punto with an impressive crash.

The whole thing seems to have gone rather well.

You go over to check and yell to Milo to move forwards. The van slowly moves a couple of yards, then stops: a moment later, preceded by a screeching noise, the Punto's bumper crashes to the ground.

3

Milo jumps down, covered in sweat, and you assess the situation: the front of the Punto is almost completely wrecked, while the rear of the van is unmarked but for a small dent in the bumper.

"Damn," you say, "we'll have to do it ourselves."

Milo climbs into the van and soon reappears with two large hammers. He hands one to you, smiling conspiratorially, and you start furiously banging away at the back of the van until there are some obvious marks on the panels. When you finish, Milo tries to open the rear door, but it's jammed.

"Perfect," he says. He looks up and you follow his gaze: the sky between the warehouses is a long blue rectangle.

Milo lights a cigarette, satisfied. "To sum up: whiplash, at least three million. Plus another for the damage to the van...making four...less two hundred thousand rental for the Punto... and another million deductible on the damage. Result: we get to keep at least two and a half million."

Chapter one

In which the story moves to the following year, we get to know Vittorio and Milo better, and our subjects are Jan Potocki, individual responsibility, ecstasy and starfish.

Hey Milo, I'm reading a book by some guy called Jan Potocki, from the eighteenth century... or maybe the nineteenth.... Anyway, a while ago...."

"What's that got to do with anything?"

"Wait. Just listen."

You reach out to get a cocktail stick from the bar and almost slip off your stool.

The barmaid looks over absently as Milo jokes, "I'm listening. That's if you manage to stay upright."

You don't rise to it. "So, this Jan Potocki... I think he was Polish...."

"What do you mean, you think? You don't know if he's eighteenth or nineteenth century, you don't know if he's Polish.... You don't know anything."

You twiddle the cocktail stick around in your beer glass. "True, true... but that's not the point... something else struck me."

"And that would be?"

"Okay, listen carefully: one day this Jan Potocki—nobody

knows why—takes the silver handle off the lid of a salad dish. You get the picture? A solid silver ball. And he pulls it off."

You stop and look at Milo for a few seconds, until he loses patience. "So?"

"So he starts to polish it—but gradually, every now and again."

Milo glances at you, puzzled, then takes a cigarette from the pack you left on the bar. "What kind of stupid story is this?"

You smile. "No, it's amazing. Keep listening. After three years, after lots of gradual polishing, the ball has become much smaller: it's exactly the right size to be used as a bullet. So this Potocki takes his pistol—this was in the days when you still loaded them down the barrel—puts in some gunpowder, drops in the bullet and then fires it into his brain."

"And kills himself?"

"Of course he kills himself," you say enthusiastically. "Isn't that incredible?"

Milo makes a face.

"Try to imagine it," you go on. "Three years of gradual polishing…. Three years…. Who knows what it was really like. Maybe on bad days he polished like crazy, but when times were good he didn't touch it at all…. And as a *gesture*, it's almost artistic—basically, he shot himself in the head with his own sculpture."

"Well, it doesn't seem such a big deal to me," Milo mutters.

"And then," you interrupt immediately, "there's another side that fascinates me: the idea of *starting* to commit suicide…. I mean, one day you reach the decision that you're going to kill yourself but you don't shoot yourself until three years later. I don't know about you, but I think it's an incredible story."

The bar is filling up. Milo shrugs, looks around pensively, then remarks, "You know, Vittorio, I don't give a damn about your Potocki. At the moment, the only situation that interests me is my own."

Oh God, you think, here we go.

He reads your expression. "Christ, Vittorio, you just don't understand. It's an important subject. Look, sometimes I think, if you reduced my whole life to a single day… well, waking up was great, generous breakfast—just about everything you could ask for:

6

all in all, a good morning. But now…roughly lunchtime (I'm twenty-seven, right?), it's about time for a comfortable house and some good home cooking. And what have I got instead? I'll tell you: nothing. I've got nothing."

God no, you think, now he's going to start on the usual tale of woe: he's done a thousand jobs, all of them badly paid and under the table, and how come a mediocre second-division footballer, without an original idea in his head—just listen to the interviews—earns in a couple of weeks what I earn in a year?

Milo goes on. "I've done a thousand jobs…all of them badly paid and under the table…always the worst kind of slavery. And how come a mediocre second-division footballer, without an original idea in his head—just listen to the interviews—earns in a couple of weeks what I earn in a year?"

He stops, downs a big gulp, and goes on. "You see? It's not acceptable. I have to do something. And given that I can barely dribble a football, I'm forced to do something illegal…or rather: something against the law but not against my morality."

You look at the people around you. It's like being in the bar in *Star Wars*: the only thing missing is the freaks with the blue faces and proboscis-like noses; actually no, when you look more carefully they're here too. You'd like to change the subject, for example to continue with your idea of the Big C, or else re-examine the latest shifts in your feelings about Cristina, but she's his fiancée, so what's a guy to do?

"Christ, Vittorio, you're not listening…." Milo gloomily puts down his beer, then goes on. "Fine, I'm just going to the men's room."

Two girls, dressed up as fortune tellers, perhaps, are sitting on stools at the bar next to you, talking hard and sipping at martinis. You notice four other people behind them: an indifferent him, a thoughtful her, chatting with another couple likewise. Actually, the two men are doing all the talking; the two women are staring at their fingernails and twisting their rings. All around you, there are a good number of young Italians dressed like refugees and a few real refugees dressed like young Italians. Your guardian angel ought to appear on your right shoulder and say something like: you're wasting time, go on, run along home and tomorrow I'll wake you up and you'll go find a proper job. Instead, you hear only the chorus of your three magico-animistic demons, who don't say much but are always persuasive: you stay where you are because *this is where life is.*

A deranged-looking young man goes up to the two fortune tellers and they greet him, "Hey, Heart Attack!" You smile at this nickname and look at him curiously, but he gives you a nasty look so you turn round to the barmaid and order another beer.

Milo takes up his place on the stool next to yours and starts up again. "What I ask myself is, like, how come I haven't managed to do anything at twenty-seven? No permanent job, no career, no monthly salary…. Nothing. I'm just some poor schmuck living by his wits…."

This is too much. You point your finger at him and declaim, theatrically, "I'm just some poor schmuck living by his wits! But that's Shakespeare, *King Lear*, Act Four, Scene One!" and then you laugh.

This has always been a favourite line of yours, to point out a particularly banal or pretentious phrase: the immediate response, often in chorus, is to repeat the phrase in question as if it were a quotation from *King Lear*. This time, though, you've picked the wrong moment. Milo glances at you irritably and carries on. "And, Vittorio, it's all because of—"

A young man unexpectedly interrupts him, resting a hand on Milo's left shoulder. You turn to look at him: he can't be more than sixteen.

"I was told you two might be able to help me out," he mumbles.

Milo looks him up and down carefully, then glances around cautiously and whispers, "What do you need, pal?"

The kid thinks for a moment, looks at you shyly and says, "Starlight."

Milo raises his glass and drinks with studied slowness. The kid starts nervously massaging the back of his neck.

"No. I'm sorry, pal: no starlight," Milo says finally, putting his glass down.

"But tonight you're in luck," you add quickly. "We've got some limbo coblatz."

The kid seems unimpressed. He stares at you silently.

"M-D-M-A," Milo spells out by way of explanation. "Pure ecstasy."

So the kid decides to ask, "How much?"

Milo looks at you for a second, then murmurs, "Fifty thousand."

The kid turns to you, perhaps wondering what you have to do with all this, then back to Milo. "What? The others sell it for thirty…."

"The others, pal," says Milo smoothly, "have strange pills and you don't know what the hell is in them, whereas we," and here he claps his hand on the pocket of his denim jacket, "we have nice little capsules with this magic powder inside, pure MDMA. So if you want something that'll make you feel good, trust me: this stuff will have you out of your skull in paradise. If you don't, go somewhere else and buy your thirty thousand's worth of pure anxiety…get them to mix you up the usual amphetamine shit and spend the next five hours worrying and palpitating."

The kid stands there, not saying anything. He looks at Milo for a couple of seconds, then looks at you for a couple of seconds, then looks at Milo for another couple of seconds. "Okay, give me a couple," he says.

Money and capsules change hands with a quick handshake.

"One last thing, pal," says Milo, putting on his earnest face. "No, two things," he corrects himself. "First: drink nothing but water on top of this, absolutely no alcohol, no Coca-Cola, only water…I mean it. Second: watch what you swallow, pal, because there are people going round selling stuff that kills."

The kid shrugs, then says, "See you around," and disappears.

Milo smiles contentedly and orders another beer.

"Limbo coblatz? Where did you get that from?" he asks, shaking his head.

"Come on, Milo," you explain complacently, "nowadays it's all about marketing and communications, and we have to adapt

9

too. These kids used to be happy with ecstasy, but now they're more demanding, now they want names: 'starlight,' 'fish,' 'superman,' 'UFO'.... The bottom line is, these capsules in our pockets are worth more if they have a special name. That's the simple truth, so we have to be quick about choosing a name for our merchandise. We're giving them what they want, that's all. I can just see our young friend: he'll be so happy opening up his fist in front of one of his little friends and saying, Look what I've got: two 'limbo coblatz,' and the other one saying, Cool, hot shit...."

Milo laughs and raises his glass. "Let's drink to limbo coblatz. By the way, what the hell is it?"

"I don't know...a cartoon character or something...who cares?" you answer, raising your glass.

The barmaid is graceful as a sapling. You stare at her long, graceful neck and its snowy skin, then look up at the ceiling, which is covered with fake starfish made of red plastic. Milo says the barmaid has an enchanting, harmonious and very white neck. Somewhere in the world, someone is paying five thousand dollars for a miniature animal made of crystal. Somewhere in the world, someone is lovingly bathing an old man who is no longer capable of doing it himself. Somewhere in the world, someone is even reading what you write. Isn't it amazing how dazzling and miraculous it is, this reality ticking away from one second to the next?

You head towards the men's room, and when you get there you find to your delight that it's empty, so you take the opportunity to turn on the tap and put your face right under the jet of water. When you straighten up again, some time later, you discover that you've soaked your whole shirt, so you take it off and turn on the electric hair dryer. That's when you notice, catching sight of your upper body in the mirror, that a strange red mark—about the size of a penny—has appeared on the patch of skin between your left shoulder and collarbone. You don't pay too much attention to it, put your shirt back on and go back to your stool.

As soon as you sit down, Milo orders more drinks and starts complaining again. You don't say anything for a quarter of an hour, part listening to him, part looking around, part fiddling with the cocktail stick. All the while, you're carefully aiming for just the right state of inebriation, or rather, of ecstatic appreciation of the multi-faceted beauty of the world.

Milo lights a cigarette and continues, somewhat the worse for drink. "Society's basically to blame for our situation, wouldn't you say?"

"No, I wouldn't," you say.

Milo looks at you like you've insulted him and then repeats, "Well, in my opinion, society's to blame."

You look at the time: twenty-four minutes past midnight. You can't hold back: "Milo, please stop this. I can't take any more of these lectures on what society does wrong. I've been hearing them for too long, and always from the same kind of person: they've never grown up, they've always got some cult book in their pocket (writ-ten by some member of an ethnic minority in Iceland), they go to outrageous concerts, they own fifteen thousand CDs, they eat in the most expensive restaurants, they have beautiful homes...in short, they don't do a damn thing all day, but they spend every minute telling you society's killing us all. You want to know the truth? The truth is, society must be a terrible shot, because people like that are still alive, and stronger than ever."

Milo laughs. "But I've got to blame someone, surely? And if not society, who?"

"Simple." You spread your arms wide. "Individual human beings are to blame—" and you interrupt yourself to take another gulp. By now you're half drunk. You have no idea what comes next.

"Go on," Milo prods.

"I'll give you an example," you continue. "Okay, just for a start, our parents allow us to study trivia instead of training us for useful jobs like...I don't know...molecular biologist...DJ...and that's not all: they let us join a totally useless faculty, instead of making us study important and lucrative subjects like dentistry...or computer science...or arms dealing. So, do you still think the fact that we never have a lira in our pockets is society's fault?"

"No," laughs Milo, raising his glass in a mock toast, "it's our parents', obviously!"

And you raise your glass—isn't it amazing how dazzling and miraculous it is, this reality ticking away from one second to the next? —you drink and carry straight on. "I'll give you another example. At university I fooled around the whole time, that's all I did, and now the only jobs I can do are illegal. Is that supposed to be society's fault? Of course not: the fault lies with friends like you, who led me astray—"

"Hear hear! I'll drink to that!" says Milo, raising his glass. He takes a gulp and goes on, amused. "This is good stuff, Vittorio, go on."

"I'll give you another example," you say, smiling. "I've had six or seven job interviews, and each time they've told me 'my experience does not match the requirements of the position they wish to fill.' So, whose fault is that?"

Milo raises his glass with shining eyes and repeats, laughing, "Whose fault is it?"

"Society's, maybe? Absolutely not: the fault lies with the cretins in the personnel office who think studying Ovid makes you unsuited to a job on the switchboard...."

"Hear hear!" laughs Milo again. "I'll drink to that!"

"And I'll give you another example. Is it society's fault I'm not interested in politics any more?"

"Is it?" laughs Milo, by now flushed and sweating.

"No. The fault lies with the politicians themselves, because they insist on appearing on TV every night. Come on, you only have to look at their faces: I wouldn't trust them with the keys to my toilet."

And Milo promptly raises his glass. "Shakespeare, *King Lear,* Act Four, Scene One," and you laugh, you're in high spirits.

At this point you notice out of the corner of your eye that the barmaid is leaning on the bar and listening in, amused. So you go on, turning in her direction. "There's plenty to go round, Milo, just think about it. Why is the Church having such a hard time these days? Changes in society, they tell us. Really? Maybe it's just the high priests of the Vatican banks and all the crooks in church circles. There, that's the point: no one has the courage to condemn individual human beings for their sins, but there's this lovely word 'society' to serve as scapegoat for everything...it's not true, we mustn't be taken in...I can't take it any more...and in any case the truth is...well...another beer, please."

The barmaid looks at you coldly. "Perhaps it's time you two went home," she says. Then she turns and goes back to the other end of the bar. You pretend nothing has happened and automatically face the entrance. Just then, four bottles of Ceres come in, held in the hands of four young men shorn like identical poodles. They stop in a circle to discuss something, then one of them emerges from the group and heads for you. He looks around diffidently, then says, "Any chance you guys know where I can find some, like, pills?" looking hopefully at you.

Milo is his normal lucid self again in an instant; he looks him up and down, glances at his friends—all three with their eyes fixed on you—then gets down from his stool and says to the young man, "Follow me," as he heads to the exit.

You stay on your stool. You're half drunk, the smoke is creating an unbearable fug, the music is deafening, it's so hot your clothes are clinging to your body, and two idiots ordering something at the bar keep jabbing you in the only back you have. In short: you feel great.

Suddenly, a red plastic starfish falls off the ceiling, bounces off the bar and lands in your lap. You grab it and turn it over in your hand, amazed, while the barmaid, who saw the whole thing, comes closer. You look at her for a moment, then at the starfish; finally you hand it to her with a smile, saying, "Okay, I hereby appoint you deputy sheriff."

She takes it and smiles at you, instantly in love. She is the woman of your life, the woman you want to marry, the woman you want to bear your children, the woman you want to grow old with: for a moment you can see yourselves, ninety years old, in matching rocking chairs in front of the fire. Meanwhile, she puts the starfish down on the bar, picks it up again and then, with a swift movement, throws it in the waste paper basket behind her.

Milo comes back over.

"How did it go?" you ask quickly.

"Big success. Got rid of ten 'limbo coblatz' just like that, all I had."

"G-r-r-eat. So business is going great guns. I propose another toast, to the manufacturers, i.e. me, and the sales network, i.e. you!"

Milo shakes his head. "No, it's been a profitable evening…let's leave and go to beddy-byes."

"Have it your way," you say, getting up.

Outside, the evening is in full swing. Young men and women are coming in and out of the bars, and the doors become filters, raising and lowering the volume of the music. Groups of people are hanging around outdoors, ignoring the cold, smoking and drinking. You make your way through the maelstrom and proceed quickly towards Piazza Vittorio. Somewhere in the world an old woman is dying alone while her neighbours weep over a soap opera. More than a million Italians died in the Second World War. In Mauritania, slavery was abolished in 1980. On the planet Uranus, each night lasts forty-two years. An icy blast of wind cuts into your face, rousing you from your drunken state for a few moments.

"Watch out for polar bears," mutters Milo, who has stopped to adjust his scarf.

You walk swiftly for a couple of blocks, until you reach the blue van, which is conspicuous because it's parked in the middle of a stream of cars. Milo gets out the keys and is just about to open the door when someone appears from nowhere and piles into you. You're grabbed by the shoulders and thrown against the van, with only just enough time to put out your hands and soften the impact so your face doesn't smash into the bodywork.

"Police!" say two voices in unison behind you.

Chapter two

*In which the Big C and Uncle Grissino are
mentioned for the first time and our subjects are
policemen, fate, human nature and curry.*

A harsh voice gives the order from behind you, "Hands up against the van," while a kick on your left calf forces you to spread your legs. Two nervous hands start frisking you, and your wallet and pack of cigarettes are taken away. You start to react, but in response your arm is jerked behind your back and you feel the icy metal of handcuffs, first on your left and then on your right wrist. Your heart is beating hard; you're not drunk any more.

You turn slowly, trying to mask your fear: there are two men in plain clothes, about forty, both pretty solid. One of them—he has a small goatee beard—is checking the contents of your wallet and the cigarette pack. The other one opens the door and starts searching the cabin of the van. Four young girls go by, glancing at you quickly as they pass, and you look over at Milo beside you, likewise in handcuffs. He looks baffled: even you are almost taken in.

"There must be some mistake, officers," he says. "We haven't done anything and I don't see what the problem is." He speaks calmly, like a mother patiently explaining something to a naughty child. At that moment the policeman with the goatee finds the capsules among your cigarettes, goes up to Milo and shouts in his face, "The problem is people like you—goddamn drug pushers."

All the way back to the police station, instead of thinking about what's happening, you find yourself thinking about Cristina. As a procession of tree-lined avenues, flashing lights, unlit buildings and deserted bus stops passes in front of your eyes, a mental film is being projected inside your head.

In this film, Cristina has come home from the night school where she teaches photography. She has eaten something hurriedly, watched a bit of television and gone into the bathroom. She has brushed her teeth and carefully applied some skin cream, massaging it into her face with a circular motion so that it's thoroughly absorbed. She has noticed that her eyes are bloodshot, but she has looked at herself in the mirror and feels satisfied with her prominent cheekbones and her sly little smile. She has got undressed, she has looked at the reflection of her breasts in the mirror over the sink, first from the front and then from the side, her back arched. She has looked at her behind, for which purpose she has had to rise up on tiptoe and twist her upper body all the way round. She has found everything satisfactory, she has smiled at the mirror and put on a short, dark-red nightgown with thin shoulder straps and lace at the bust. She has stretched out on the bed and picked up a book from the bedside table, then she has put it in her lap without opening it and dropped some cigarette ash on the cover. She has got out some papers, a lighter and a lump of hash. She has made a filter. She has slowly rolled the joint and lit it. She has looked at the clock and *only now, for the first time,* asked herself, Where's Milo?

Who knows, maybe for moment she thought about you being with him. In which case, who knows exactly what she thought.

The office is bare and badly lit.

The policeman with the goatee and his partner are sitting at the desk, with you and Milo facing them: you look like a pair of customers in a fourth-rate travel agency. The second policeman, who has greasy hair and a large mole on his left cheek, has removed the handcuffs, not unkindly, and said, "You can smoke if you want."

16

On the desk there are some piles of photocopies, an old Olivetti typewriter, and a holder with various uncapped ballpoint pens. In the centre of the desk, eight transparent capsules filled with fine white powder can be seen: from where you're standing they seem to make an upside-down L. The man with the mole has spent the last twenty minutes typing a verbatim statement, hitting the keys of the typewriter with two fingers. He's quite slow.

He stops at one point. "The two suspects were found in possession of eight capsules of—"

He looks up at you. "Of what? What is this stuff? Amphetamine or ecstasy?"

You go on looking at the capsules.

"Officer," you say, "you should get these capsules analysed. They're aspirin." You speak slowly, trying to be as convincing as possible.

The man with the goatee stands up suddenly and points at you threateningly. "DO YOU TAKE US FOR FOOLS?" he yells, enraged.

You wait a few seconds, looking him calmly in the eye. "Officer, I'm not trying to make a fool of anyone. It's like I say: they're aspirin."

The man with the goatee grabs a capsule and shakes it in your face. "Look, Mr Pharmacist, explain to me what brand they are, because I've never seen them before."

You pause again. "I swear, officer, they're aspirin. We slice them up and put them in capsules, that's all…otherwise they give you heartburn. It's not a crime, is it? But they are aspirin. Get them analysed."

The man with the goatee loses patience. "DON'T TRY TO MAKE FOOLS OF US! JUST DON'T!" he yells again. Then he sits down again, agitated, shakes his head and asks again, "What do you take us for? We saw you: you sold them to some kids. I saw you with my own eyes. Aspirin my ass, they're ecstasy or amphetamine or some other shit and you know it."

The policeman with the mole, acting all paternal now, adds, "Serious drugs, guys, we're not talking a casual roll-up here. You're taking a big risk. Let's see if we can't help each other out."

Milo, whose expression has remained surprised throughout, is ready for the clincher.

"Officer," he begins in a low voice, "we didn't sell anything to those kids. One of them came up and asked if by any chance we had something for a headache. I gave him two aspirin. That's the whole story, officer: get it analysed."

The policeman with the goatee gets to his feet again, picks up the capsules one by one and then, when he's gathered them all into his clenched fist, whispers, "Right, I'm going down to someone who'll take one look at this stuff and know what it is, the hell with analysis and more analysis."

He brings his face close to yours, so you smell his breath. "You'd better pray it's not drugs," he says threateningly.

Milo looks at him wide-eyed, then smiles to himself incredulously—what an actor—and says, "Trust me, officer, it's aspirin."

"We'll see," he says, slamming the door.

The man with the mole on his cheek picks up your papers and says, "I'm going to get a cup of coffee… and check your ID's. You don't look like people who'll make trouble, but I'm going to lock you in anyway. Don't do anything stupid, or when I come back I'll bust your balls. Touch anything or make any noise, and when I come back I'll bust your balls."

"Don't worry, officer, we won't move an inch," says Milo, oozing false innocence.

The man heads towards the door, but when he reaches the threshold he turns and looks back at him. "Hey you, don't be too much of a jerk. Don't push it too far."

Then he slams the door and turns the key in the lock, twice.

You stay quiet for a bit, looking at the absolute emptiness of the room you've been locked into. You prick up your ears: in the next room you can hear thuds and moans in a language it's hard to identify. You stare at the only thing pinned to the wall, a tourist calendar of India. According to Mahatma Gandhi, the six virtues of the world are: wealth with work, pleasure with conscience, knowledge with character, commerce with morality, science with humanity, and politics with principles.

You throw yourself onto an imaginary couch made out of your own body and sigh.

"Hey, relax," says Milo. "As soon as they've done their analysis they'll have to let us go."

I know, gentle readers: there will be those among you who probably think cheating kids by peddling fake ecstasy isn't such a big deal. Maybe you're the one who—during your usual friendly kick-about yesterday evening—took a dive in the penalty area to win a non-existent penalty, the one who's just finished lying on the phone to her best friend, the one who never stops complaining about property taxes but sublets his apartment without a contract, the one who says the opposite of what he thinks, the one who's unfaithful, the specialist who complains how intolerable the tax burden is but never issues a receipt, the artist who follows his agent's suggestions instead of his own talent, the postman who occasionally throws junk mail away, the television presenter who passes off actors as real people with stories to tell, the one who does something just because it suits him, the one who, in the course of an argument, invents facts and figures to support his case, the one who's bent the truth on an insurance form, the careerist who's blamed his own mistake on a colleague, the advertising executive who's proposed misleading campaigns, the moonlighting civil servant, the one who got his job through connections, the one who's taken the praise due to someone else, the one who plays solitaire on his computer during working hours, the one who has a dodgy scale in his delicatessen, the cleaner who—though she denies it—has never really cleaned the windows, the journalist who cheats his readers by passing off press releases as his own articles, the sportsman who takes drugs to win, the guy who's managed to dodge military service, the one who claims a pension that isn't his due, the one who's falsified the results of a scientific study, slightly, in order to receive funding, the one who's powerful or skillful or shameless enough to make himself the truth he wants. In short, someone who cheats. Someone who cheats his wife, someone who cheats his fiancée, someone who cheats his friends, who cheats his colleagues, who cheats the state.

Come on, gentle readers, the world is an open pit of minor deceits, swindles, fiddles, scams and aggravated frauds. Hold up your hand if you've never in your life cheated anyone, if you've never in your life resorted to some pathetic fiddle to extract some equally pathetic advantage! Come on, do you expect me to believe you've never copied an exercise in class? Be honest, with yourselves at least, don't try to fool yourselves: we're talking about human nature, which as we know is hardly pristine.

As for me—and I offer no excuses—I couldn't tell you how I started with the scams. There just came a moment when I suddenly realized I was an adult with no proper job, no money, a useless literature degree in my pocket and my whole future in front of me. Or rather, my whole future found me in front of it. I felt like a guy in a cell being stared at longingly by a naked one-hundred-and-ten-kilo lifer. You know, sooner or later, that something unpleasant is going to happen to you.

Yes, of course I know the First Rule of Life: never stop and think for one moment. And yet there are times when you can't help but weigh things up: that's where I found myself at twenty-seven and, like Milo, I wasn't in any particular place, I hadn't chosen any particular road, I wasn't going in any particular direction. I wasn't going, period. I'd missed the starting gun, for crying out loud!

The worst thing, gentle readers, is that I realized this all of a sudden. Can you imagine? It was like when you're playing chess and suddenly your queen is taken. In one second you realize that the whole series of moves leading up to that point was wrong, but you can't go back: the match goes on, with your options reduced to practically zero.

And it's at that moment that Milo suddenly reappeared in my life after three years of rehab. I just found him next to me; like me, he was drifting, but unlike me, he had an irrepressible *joie de vivre*. It's his desire to be up to something, always and despite everything, that put me under his spell from the very beginning: his urge to come up with scheme after scheme, never completely legit, to make money; schemes that cancelled the future and put aside the questions, schemes to which he could dedicate all his thoughts, schemes that filled time and chased away fear.... It was he that got me going again, until I understood that even though you've lost the queen you can still play to the end, and your opponent—these are the rules of life—had better be careful not to make a false move: because you'll be there, waiting to cut him to pieces. Milo taught me all this: to play by my rules, to get something good out of everything, to try to laugh about it. He opened my eyes to the fact that in reality *no real misfortune* has ever touched us: we were not born into absolute poverty, we weren't set to sewing shoes or weaving carpets at the age of ten, we don't have any serious diseases, our part of town isn't full of anti-personnel mines, we don't live in the middle of a civil or religious war, it doesn't occur to us to sell a kidney to survive, we've never suffered from hunger or thirst. We're immensely fortunate and we can play the game of life by our rules. Play by our rules. Lose, but by our rules. He made me understand that living isn't a question but an answer, that you have to feel welcome in the world. He it was, gentle readers, who made me really understand how dazzling and miraculous it is, this reality ticking away from one second to the next.

Milo rouses you from your torpor by tapping your arm.

"What time is it?" you ask, stretching.

"Nearly three," he answers.

"What are you saying? Have they forgotten about us?"

Milo doesn't answer for a few seconds. You turn to face him: he's not moving, he's staring like a commuter on the bus at seven o'clock in the evening. After a while he starts to talk. "You know, Vittorio, I was thinking about our last few scams...."

Then he stops again. It's like he's waiting for the hypnotist to snap his fingers, but suddenly he starts again. "By now we're specialists in the usual three or four, always the same ones. Think about this past month: last week we did the best shops in Via Roma, with the fake cassette from the Long-Distance Adoption Association. It went well, right?"

You nod. He goes on. "Of course it did, we came out with more than a million. Then, Monday. On Monday we did a huge apartment building, the kind where it's obvious no one knows anyone else...we went up floor by floor and collected money for a memorial wreath for the non-existent Eugenio Rossi, from Block F. Poor man, madam: twenty-two years old, a tragic accident on Saturday night, everyone in the building has contributed…. And that went well too, right?"

You nod again. He goes on. "At night we go round the clubs selling aspirin to kids. Sometimes it goes well, sometimes it goes less well—like now, for example…."

Milo settles into his chair. "But Christ, Vittorio, this way we'll just half-live through years of mediocrity without doing anything really big. What happened to our Big C idea, the Big Con? Shouldn't we be saving for it? How far are we from the amount we need? The money we earn is barely enough to pay the rent and survive…. Vittorio, we're wasting too much time: we need to make a move."

He stops abruptly and looks around.

"Go on, spit it out," you say.

Milo hesitates for a moment, then goes on. "I know we said it was our thing, and that we wouldn't take on partners, I know, but time is passing and we're not getting anywhere… and the idea's a good one and we need to carry it out before we hit seventy…."

"Go on, spit it out," you say again.

"Okay…Vittorio…I'm more and more sure it's time to talk it over with this relative of mine, my uncle Grissino."

"Uncle Grissino…what kind of name is that?"

Milo brightens and continues, excited. "His real name is Franco Grasso. I've never really understood the name Grissino, I think it's a kind of nickname—the kind they give you when you're little and it follows you for the rest of your life. It doesn't really suit him. Physically he's kind of an overweight Jesus Christ—he's tall and fat, with a beard, long hair, well-groomed—in any case, nothing like a bread stick. He's got style, you'll like him, he's got a way about him, I can't think of the word—wait, I've got it—it's patrician."

You stand up and start to pace about the room.

Milo looks at you anxiously.

You shake your head, half way between surprise and irritation. "For Christ's sake, Milo, are you kidding? We're talking about the Big C! We're talking about the Big C," you repeat. You're very agitated.

22

"The best idea that's ever come into our heads. The idea we've worked on for months. The idea we've *dreamed* about for months. Down to the last detail. And...and we should share it with someone else? No, I tell you. Are you crazy?"

Milo doesn't say anything for a moment, then he gets up and starts pacing about the room too. After a while he starts to speak, calmly. "You're right, Vittorio, I'm talking about the Big C. The idea we've *dreamed* about—as you say—for months. The idea we've worked on for months. It's all true. But maybe you're forgetting one small detail: that to play it we need a whole heap of money. That's right. Maybe you're forgetting that our scam, to coin a phrase from economics, 'has high start-up costs'."

Milo sighs. Then he goes on. "And the problem is that you can't go to the bank to ask for money to organize a scam: that's *their* speciality, they don't trust anyone else, you know how it is."

You smile faintly.

Milo stops in front of you. "The truth, my dear Vittorio, is that the Big C is at a standstill. And time is passing."

Then, like an actor, he turns and sits down.

There follows a long silence, broken only by the noise you make as you sit down awkwardly in your chair.

"And what exactly does he do, this uncle Grissino of yours?" you ask after a while.

Milo brightens again. "Nothing...he's a cousin of my mother's, he's done big scams, a real master. I've told him about us, you know, he's always been fond of me, ever since I was little...."

"You've never said anything about him to me."

"Well, actually uncle Grissino's been away for a while."

You give him a searching look. "So tell me the truth, does 'he's been away' mean what I think it means?"

"A fake mutual fund...he was caught...he had to disappear for a while."

"A fake mutual fund?"

Milo takes one of your cigarettes from the pack, lights it, and goes on. "Look, that's his field, he's an expert in fake mutuals. I'll keep it simple...basically it works like this: he opens a mutual fund and begins to offer unbelievable rates of interest to people who deposit their money. Okay, so the mark comes in and says he wants to invest ten million. When he comes back two months later, his ten million have turned into twenty—not really, of course, it's just written on bits of paper—but what do you think the mark's going to do? Take his money out? Of course not: he deposits his entire savings and brings in his friends and relations too. At this point you have to wait a while; then, when the cash register's full, that's when you do a bunk with the loot. Simple, eh?"

"Unless something goes wrong…."

"Yes, well," Milo shrugs complacently, "he made a couple of mistakes and they caught him."

You shake your head. "And we should get together with him? Do you think we can trust someone like that?"

"Of course. Vittorio, he's my uncle!"

At about seven in the morning, you hear the key turn in the lock. You're a bit woozy and it takes you a while to focus on the person who comes in. It's the policeman with the goatee, and he looks really annoyed. "Wake up, you two. Out! We've wasted enough time on you. You can piss off now."

Then he looks at the capsules in the palm of his hand, lowers his voice and mutters, "They seem to be aspirin after all. I don't know how, but they really are aspirin. I don't understand this business and I don't believe it."

Milo yawns, bored. "It's about time…" and you leap to your feet like a jack-in-a-box. The man makes you sign some forms, gives you back your papers and capsules and escorts you downstairs to the main entrance, where he says goodbye, half threatening and half joking. "Remember, I've got my eye on you," he says, then closes the door.

"Hey," you realize, rather late, looking at Milo, "who's going to take us back to our van?"

Milo takes a long look at the empty street, shrugs his shoulders and gives you a hug. "Bye, Vittorio, I'm walking home. I'll pick up the van tomorrow. Cristina will be worried."

For a whole minute you watch him walking away. The wind has swept the street like a worn-out broom, and the pavement is covered with sheets of newspaper, bits of cardboard, plastic bags and cigarette ends. Two drivers are arguing. Somewhere in the world, two sixteen-year-old kids have run away together because their parents don't want them to see each other. Lured back home with the promise of a wedding, the couple are killed by their respective parents: they have broken with tradition. The eye of the ostrich is bigger than its brain (I know some people with the same problem). Whales make noises to communicate; the noises can travel thirty kilometres. You look up: a flock of swallows flies overhead, forming a boomerang shape in the sky. An old lady taking her little dog for a walk comes up to you and says, "Can you smell curry on the air too?"

You say nothing for a minute, looking at the dog, and answer her reassuringly, "Yes, ma'am, it smells of curry."

Chapter three

*In which our subjects are the beauty of a
lawn, rugby, and the Trojan horse, and we meet
someone who argues that the world is a con.*

It is an extraordinarily mild Sunday. From the sky, which is a
uniformly bright grey, occasional light sprinkles of rain fall almost
imperceptibly, like the spray on your hand when you play with the
peel of an orange.

Cristina is walking along the main avenue of the Parco del
Valentino with you and Milo. Her chestnut hair is gathered low in a
loose chignon, from which two curls escape to frame her face. Not
to stare at her requires some effort.

You walk past a long line of mopeds parked in front of the
ice-cream stand and sit down on the slightly damp grass of the long
lawn at the corner of Corso Vittorio and Corso Massimo. At the other
end of the space, where the trees start, a group of kids is sitting in a
circle, playing bongos and tambourines and passing round something
which you can't identify for certain from this distance but which,
judging by the cloud of smoke, must be a pipe or a bong. Dotted
here and there on the lawn, couples are necking, talking intently,
pushing enormous buggies around; old people are walking about

27

slowly, children are playing and laughing: no one seems bothered by this imperceptible rain.

Cristina is trying to convince you to go to the botanical gardens, over by the Exhibition Centre; she says there are amazing plants and miniature waterfalls, so well tended it feels like a Japanese garden. You answer that you don't feel like walking and Milo adds that later he's meeting up with uncle Grissino near Corso Vittorio, so it's better to stay nearby. Cristina persists for a while, but eventually she joins you on the grass.

About thirty kids are playing a version of rugby on the lawn. They run, egg each other on, abuse each other; they crash into each other, yelling like lunatics and spontaneously forming scrums which leave the participants jumbled up and out of breath, until the oval ball squirts out towards someone on the edge of the game, who launches himself at an invisible line but invariably finds himself chased down and trampled by ten fanatics from the opposing team. And when this happens, when a ball carrier is brought to the ground, the entire opposing team—and probably a few of their friends too—jumps on top of him, laughing and shouting, forming a twenty-person pyramid of flesh which, when it breaks up, leaves some kid on the ground whom you expect to find in agony. Instead, as soon as he is free of the last human burden, he bounces up as if on springs, hurls a few insults around and, laughing, immediately starts playing again.

These human pyramids appear to be the only point of this game, which is played without rules, without scoring and without referees, on a field with no obvious boundaries. You and Milo enjoy commenting on the action, noting how little violence there really is, and how much fun, and you try to work out which team is which from their appearance. This is a difficult enterprise, since they're all wearing the same clothes: trainers, baggy trousers and sweatshirts. In the middle of this maelstrom of kids there is also a medium-sized boxer dog running around, you can't tell whose, chasing the ball in a frenzy, barking continuously every time there's a scrum—even he is having the time of his life. It's a spectacle of undiluted pleasure, and you really have to ask: isn't it amazing how dazzling and miraculous it is, this reality ticking away from one second to the next?

Milo is doing a sort of humorous commentary on the match, giving the players a series of nicknames, while Cristina starts to roll a joint. You look at her eyes, then your gaze slips down to her mouth, then back to her eyes and your eyes meet and stay glued to each other for a few seconds. Then you turn away abruptly and your eye is caught by a man playing with his little daughter: they're sitting on the grass and she's laughing, sliding her fingers slowly along his cheek, like scissors. Her fingers move like caresses, and the man hugs her, and his is a full and enviable smile. The tam-tam of the bongos echoes through the air the whole time, mingling with the shouts of the young rugby players.

After a while a gent of about fifty—white shirt, tie, impeccable grey pinstripe suit—starts walking across the lawn, right through the middle of the game, paying no attention to the intense competition going on around him. He's carrying a small collapsible stepladder under his arm. Having reached a point about ten metres from the three of you, he stops and sets up the stepladder, climbs elegantly up the four steps, stands on this improvised podium and starts bawling, "LISTEN UP, YOU USELESS LOT, LISTEN TO WHAT I HAVE TO SAY TODAY!"

The rugby players turn round as one, look at him for a millisecond and then go back to chasing each other around. But the man is too close for you to ignore him and, as four or five curious passers-by approach, he starts bawling again, "TODAY, LADIES AND GENTLEMEN, I'M GOING TO TALK ABOUT THE TWO PRINCIPAL LAWS OF THE WORLD!"

Having said this, he leaves a pause like a true orator and goes on. "The two principal laws of the world, ladies and gentlemen. First: everybody cheats. Second, everybody deserves to be cheated."

You react by turning to Milo. "Fabulous: Shakespeare, *King Lear,* Act Four, Scene One."

Milo smiles craftily and whispers, "The time has come. May I present, my uncle Grissino!"

You experience a moment of doubt. You look at the man on the stepladder. Then you look at Milo.

"Are you joking?"

He looks at you very seriously. "Not at all. I'm introducing you to my uncle Grissino."

You look back at the man on the stepladder. You're stunned.

Cristina joins in. "But...um...does he do this often? I mean, is this a habit of his, or is it just in our honor?"

Milo's smile is strange. "Wait and see."

Meanwhile, the man has raised his powerful voice and is continuing. "Let us talk about the first law: everybody cheats! Well, ladies and gentlemen, the first law is under our very noses: isn't the whole world a global con and life itself a big con and God the con artist-in-chief?"

An old man in the front row yells out at the top of his lungs, "THAT'S TRUE, THAT'S SO-O-O-O-O TRUE!"

"Silence, subject, don't interrupt!" the man on the stepladder says sternly. "Well, ladies and gentlemen, I invite you to think first about something very important. Consider, first of all, the following rule: cheats are never judged harshly enough."

He pauses, satisfied that the small crowd of curious onlookers around him is growing, then goes on. "Would you like an example? Very well. Take the Trojan horse, the first documented scam. How has that tale come down to us, for crying out loud? As an act of sheer genius! Never forget it, ladies and gentlemen, an act of sheer genius. Not bad, eh?"

The old man starts yelling at the top of his lungs again, "TRUE, THAT'S TRUE TOO, SO-O-O-O-O TRUE!"

"Thank you, ladies and gentlemen," the man on the stepladder continues with a slight bow. "But let us proceed. Let us start with the great institutions...and I'm just talking about what's under our noses, for crying out loud. Though really, ladies and gentlemen, even kids know what I'm talking about: politicians are frauds on the take, changing parties whenever it's in their interest; insurance companies are swindlers who get together and agree among themselves so that we pay more than we should; banks are the centre of world usury, the pharmaceuticals are criminal organizations that lie and make money on the backs of the people..." He pauses again, takes a long look round and continues passionately, "Cheats, ladies and gentlemen, all of them utter cheats."

Christ, you think, and we're supposed to associate ourselves with this guy? With someone who wanders around parks giving rabble-rousing sermons? We're supposed to share the most brilliant idea that's ever entered our heads with him? Cristina is looking at you, her expression equally perplexed.

Meanwhile, the man continues. "Think about it: politicians who use advertisements to get us to go along with them, are they not cheats? Politicians who, starting in middle school, organize students! Indoctrinate them! For crying out loud, are they not cheats?"

The old man starts yelling at the top of his lungs again. "TRUE, VERY TRUE, SO-O-O-O-O TRUE!"

"Thank you, ladies and gentlemen, thank you. But let me proceed. You have no idea of the extent of the cons. You think man has been to the moon? Well, it's a con. Man has never been to the moon. Read Bill Kaysin or, if you don't have the time, ask yourself a simple question: How come he hasn't gone back in all these years?"

The audience responds with an intense buzz of conversation. You turn to Milo, who's hanging on every word. "What's this all about?"

He puts his finger to his lips to shut you up. "Shh, Vittorio, be patient."

You look for Cristina's support, but she's transfixed by the rugby kids, who are going on with their very energetic game behind the man. In front of him, by contrast, a small crowd is forming: some people arrive, listen for a few seconds and then leave, but others sit down and stay, and the group is getting bigger.

The man on the stepladder goes on. "I'm not even going to talk about the banks: if I suggested that you lend me money at zero point one percent interest so that I could lend it back to you at thirteen percent, I'd probably be lynched on the spot. And rightly so! Including taxes, it would mean that I'm getting from you one hundred and sixty times what I'm prepared to give you. Okay, as you've probably guessed, I've just described the normal rates of debit and credit interest on a checking account...these are our banks: worse than a con, a scandal!"

Heartfelt applause comes from the audience. You begin to enjoy yourself.

The man bows in thanks and proceeds. "But I'd like to move on to one of the biggest tricksters at the global level: advertising."

A raging scrum of rugby players breaks out three metres away from the stepladder, and the boxer dog barks furiously. The man doesn't bat an eye and raises his voice. "Advertising! Advertising, which doesn't sell the best products, just the ones with the nicest packaging! Isn't that a con? Advertising, which fakes everything! All these beautiful women, all these magnificent women on TV and in the magazines, all fake, all retouched by surgeons. Isn't that a con? And what about all these useless products sold to us as indispensable! Isn't that a con?"

Cristina whispers to Milo, "Wake up, Milo, why do you let yourself be taken in like this? This uncle of yours is just trotting out tired clichés."

And you mutter ironically, like a TV news presenter, "The unwelcome surprise in this learned catalogue is the unexpected omission of the multinationals...."

Milo shrugs. "It's all very well for you two. You went to university, you've got the critical tools...."

You and Cristina look at each other, smirking questioningly, but you are distracted by the rugby kids celebrating a try. Meanwhile the orator is having a go at sects, horoscopes and fortune-tellers.

Then he moves on to sport. "Ladies and gentlemen, the whole thing's a fake, phoney, it's all a con. All these doped-up athletes, for a start, they're cheats. Even football's bogus: doped-up champions, overpaid foreigners with fake passports—and no championship is complete without its share of suspicion and allegations of fixing and bias."

The audience explodes with fresh applause, and there are even a few chants of "Juventus! Juventus!" The man on the stepladder puts the record companies under the microscope next, carries on to the multinationals and then, just as the rugby kids are getting ready for a place kick behind him, to the accompaniment of constant barking from the boxer dog, moves on to fashion.

"And what about fashion? That's another con, good and proper. Fashion is the following of fashions. One of the subtlest cons: it makes people think that if they don't have this dress or haven't seen that film they can only be marginal members of society. Fashion's a con."

Then he yells out, "AND THAT CLAUDIA SCHIFFER? CLAUDIA SCHIFFER'S ANOTHER CON!"

Cristina looks at you, dumbfounded. "Where did this lunatic spring from?" she whispers, laughing.

The man goes on. "Claudia Schiffer—it's about time someone said it, ladies and gentlemen—is certainly not the most beautiful woman in the world: she's just the woman with the best press office!"

At this the audience breaks out in clamorous applause and the old man yells, "TRUE, TOO TRUE, SO-O-O-O-O TRUE!" and you declaim to Milo, "Shakespeare, *King Lear*, Act Four, Scene One," and the crowd of onlookers grows, the rugby kids stop playing and stretch out on the grass, exhausted, and even a few of the bongo-players come over to find out what's going on.

The man lifts his hands to the sky and yells, "The whole world is a con, that's the truth! What we're in is nothing less than a gigantic fraud machine, ladies and gentlemen, note it well, once and for all. Would you like another example? What about everyone who retires at forty: cheats! Cheats, cheats, cheats, cheats!"

This time the old man screams out like a stuck pig, "TRUE, TOO TRUE, SO-O-O-O-O TRUE!"

You take a short break and look over at the bongo-playing area. You spread the collar of your shirt and squint down, checking the state of the red mark between your shoulder and collarbone. Meanwhile the man puts journalists under the spotlight, demolishes the movie world and goes back to the drugs companies ("who put an expiration date on a jar of forty pills. You use four and, when you need another four next year, well, you find out they've expired and you have to buy another forty. Is that a scam or what?")

At this point a substantial group of young people leaves.

"What's this, gentlemen?" says the man on the stepladder, annoyed. "Don't leave, please. I was still on point one. Now I have to explain point two: which is, everybody deserves to be cheated."

And he sets off again enthusiastically. "That's the thing, gentlemen, I've almost finished and I don't want to keep you much longer, but we've reached the crux, the second law: everybody cheats because people are stupid. And they deserve to be cheated."

The small group of bongo-players turns away, a few of them arguing because they're impatient to leave. The man pauses, takes a handkerchief out of his pocket and wipes his forehead, which is dripping with perspiration. Then he goes on. "This is the real conclusion of my lecture today, ladies and gentlemen: people allow themselves to be cheated. People buy nice packaging with crappy products instead of good products with crappy packaging. People allow themselves to be cheated by banks and insurance companies, they go on electing moronic politicians. People fall in love with mediocrity: mediocre artists, mediocre films, mediocre books, mediocre newspapers…people allow themselves to be brainwashed by PR—"

One of the bongo-players suddenly interrupts him. "Aren't you going a bit far? If that's the way you see it, why don't you go and shoot these 'people' you talk about with such contempt, instead of going round speaking in public?"

The man on the stepladder doesn't say anything for a second, then goes on in a gentler tone of voice. "I don't talk about anyone with contempt. I have the greatest respect for everybody. That's the only way to tolerate life: exercise the greatest respect for everybody. But I cannot but describe the actions of men and hope that they will be enlightened and that humankind will change. But thank you for your comment, sucker…."

The young man bursts out laughing. "Fuck you too! What kind of respect is that? You've just called me a sucker!"

"But I have the greatest respect for you, sucker," smiles the man, to the accompaniment of irritating laughter from some of those present. Upon which the young man and his friends go back towards the trees, shouting abuse.

The man comes to a close, strangely hurried. "At this point I'll

34

say thank you for your attention and repeat the main points of today's lecture: the two principal laws of the world, ladies and gentlemen. First: everybody cheats. Second: everybody deserves to be cheated. And now, my presence is required elsewhere. Good afternoon, everyone, and thanks again for listening."

Having said this, he jumps down off the stepladder and folds it up. A few people clap and say nice things, others whistle and hurl abuse, then the small crowd breaks up and Milo stands up, shouting, "THAT WAS THE BEST, UNCLE, YOU WERE GREAT!"

The man waves his hand and disappears quickly, the stepladder under his arm, leaving the three of you open-mouthed.

Chapter four

In which our subject is man's desperation when confronted by innumerable misunderstandings in his 'search for the other,' in which there are traces of cocaine, red marks, and irresistible telephone calls, and in which we hear the story of a revival of rock and roll and where Vittorio and Milo were at the time.

You rest your hand on the tap and look up at the shower head. The little holes are no longer black, they are filling up with silvery droplets, the warm water engulfs you. Information crowds into your brain from the radio: bribes at hospital, attempted extortion—two gypsies under arrest, IPO, incentives for the South, fall in share prices, GDP of developing countries, smog alert, accident on the ring-road, drug traffickers, opposition criticizes government, starvation-level pensions—better off dying, illegal loans, delays at airports, hit-and-run in Casoria…the shower cabinet becomes an isolation cell where you are subjected to experiments in brainwashing by info-bombardment. Scientists report that you have a surprising capacity to adapt. You like having showers; in fact you think being able to have a shower every day is a good reason to be thankful you were born in the twentieth century. Think what you like, gentle readers, but Alexander the Great couldn't have a shower every morning; there were limits to his good fortune.

You like the order in your bathroom, the way you look after it, especially when your flatmates—two students from Palermo who turn up in Turin from time to time, just for exams—are away. You like the rectangular mirror in which, as on many other mornings, you're examining the red mark between your left shoulder and your collarbone.

You don't like what you see.

In a week, the mark has grown from a quarter of an inch across to the size of a fifty-lire piece. It's red, like meat: it's like a porthole, revealing your internal tissues, and you begin to feel fear. What the hell can it be? Once, on television, you saw a programme about degenerative skin diseases and the memory of Kaposi's sarcoma still terrifies you. So you leave the bathroom and go looking among your books for the medical dictionary. You find it and consult it. Your magico-animistic demons come to life again. You call your mother to ask for the doctor's telephone number. "Good morning, mother," you say ceremoniously.

"Good evening, more like; it's seven o'clock," says this woman, who once rolled up your sleeves to see if you had needle tracks on your arm.

"Really?"

"How are you?"

"Fine, mother. I've just confirmed that I'm a remarkable machine. Take my skin, for example: it covers four square metres of body, it's elastic, it regenerates by itself, if you cut it it grows back, it's more resistant to water and other liquids than any waterproof watch, and it regulates its own temperature. In short, my skin is extraordinary."

"Like everyone else's," mutters my mother, rolling her eyes, you imagine. You adore her.

"Yes, mother, but not everyone thinks about it. I know I'm a perfect machine. By the way, I need the doctor's telephone number...."

An hour later, on your way home after a trip to the tobacconist's, you switch on your mobile in the hope of finding a message—from Cristina, who wants to talk to you, or Milo, to tell you Grissino wants to meet you, or a friend, who has an idea for the evening—and you stop at the traffic light on Via Rossini in the middle of a swarm of people; a bus goes by, full of faces that look tired and pissed off, and you guess that you, taken as a group, standing at the traffic light, must likewise look to the people in the bus like a bunch of tired and pissed-off faces, and a moment later the mobile trills and you put it to your ear and listen to the electronic voice telling you "you have one new message," and this is always a wonderful piece of news which makes you feel alive—and fools us all into thinking someone is looking for us and needs us, or maybe they really do—and you immediately dial the number, feeling strangely apprehensive, imagining first Cristina's voice, then Milo's, then—who knows why, since it's impossible—Grissino's, and instead you hear a woman's worried voice, saying slowly, *"Antonio...estoy en Roma y el teléfono del hotel es...cero-seis-tres-cinco-dos-tres-tres...ll'mame pronto. Te quiero."*

There's something desperate and irresistible about this voice— *ll'mame pronto, te quiero*—and the desperation is accentuated by the fact that it reaches you not as the intended recipient but as a stranger. You're deeply upset, you think about this woman and immediately you imagine her to be South American, not Spanish, in a difficult situation, looking for this Antonio and perhaps this wrong number—your number—is her only hope of salvation, and maybe she doesn't have enough money for another call, and maybe the wrong number was given to her on purpose, or she got it wrong by chance and now they'll never meet up, she and Antonio, and in short you've landed in the middle of a drama you know nothing about, and you'd like to be of assistance, you'd like to know more, so you listen to the message again: *"Antonio...estoy en Roma y el teléfono del hotel es...cero-seis-tres-cinco-dos-tres-tres...ll'mame pronto. Te quiero."*

You're tempted to call the hotel in Rome and tell this woman that the number she has dialled is wrong and so Antonio doesn't know she's in Rome and is there any way you can help and so on, but you remain undecided as to what to do and, still undecided, you listen to the message one more time. *"Antonio...estoy en Roma y el teléfono del hotel es...cero-seis-tres-cinco-dos-tres-tres...ll'mame pronto. Te quiero."*

Again you sense something truly desperate in this voice— *ll'mame pronto, te quiero*—a heartbreaking feeling that throws you off balance and stirs something dormant deep inside, something you've got rid of and don't want to reawaken, something you're afraid of and thought you'd forgotten about, so you react hastily and fearfully, deleting the message and putting the mobile back in your pocket, trembling.

Ten minutes later you're going along Via Catania and, just as you're mentally tracing the curve of Cristina's lips, a man hanging about by a telephone booth unexpectedly stops you. "Excuse me, could you do me a favour?"

"Sure," you answer uncertainly, taking a step back.

"Here's the thing…I need your help: could you make a phone call for me?"

You examine him: about fifty, badly cut suit, frightened eyes; his expression is genuinely anxious.

"Okay," you say.

He thanks you, forcing his features into a sad smile; then he turns round and puts a phone card into the machine, picks up the receiver, dials a number and hands it to you. "Ask for Barbara," he tells you.

"Okay. And when they put her on the line?" you ask, putting the receiver to your ear.

"Nothing…. Tell them you made a mistake."

The telephone is ringing. You look into the man's eyes, *"Antonio, estoy en Roma"* is running through your head, suddenly you put the receiver back. The man looks at you questioningly.

"I'm sorry," you say, "but it doesn't make sense."

"Why not?"

"Simple: I call this number and ask for Barbara, right?"

"Right."

"And then, if someone answers, I'm supposed to say I made a mistake, right?"

"Right."

"That's what I thought, but if the person who answers says, 'This is Barbara,' well, I can't really say: 'Sorry, wrong number.' It doesn't make sense."

The man thinks for a moment, then says, "That's true, you're right. So let's do this: if the person who answers says, 'Speaking,' you hang up."

"Okay."

The man dials the number again and you grab the receiver. The telephone rings once, twice, three times. Then there is a mechanical sound and the answering machine clicks on.

"Answering machine," you tell the man.

"So hang up, hurry up," he say.

You look at him, dismayed. He recovers his card from the machine and stands beside the booth looking serious, then he takes both your hands and presses them hard.

"Thank you. Thank you with all my heart," he says.

His eyes are miserable, and in them in one second you read unhappiness on a cosmic scale, in one second you read about misguided relationships with people who seek out others who don't wish to be sought; you read about quarrelsome relationships with people who complain that where there's too much excitement there's no harmony and placid relationships with people who complain that where there's too much harmony there's no excitement; you read about mismatched relationships with people who think they love other people but don't want to believe they're fooling themselves; you read about corroded relationships with people who fool other people who don't want to believe they're being fooled. Isn't it amazing how harsh and ruthless it is, this reality ticking away from one second to the next?

You watch the man disappear into the crowd and you realize you're suddenly alone, you realize that in a few minutes two love stories have blended with your life and that one glimpse was enough to recognize and understand them; two love stories with something tragic about them have spilled over you and your imagination, leaving you suddenly discouraged and depressed, and you feel an urgent need to combine them with your story and you decide you have to hear Cristina's voice, so you get out the mobile and dial Milo's home number, but as you might have expected, he's the one who answers.

You change mood rapidly. "So, any word from Grissino?" you

ask in a cheerful tone of voice, almost surprising yourself with your hypocrisy.

"I talked to him yesterday. He's going to be away for a few days, but we'll get together as soon as he gets back."

At this point you don't know what else to say, and your faith in your acting ability is dissipating fast. You come out with a classic: "What are you up to?"

From the time it takes him to answer, Milo doesn't seem to know what to say either.

"I don't know," he answers without much conviction, "I heard there was a concert on somewhere...."

As a sort of check, to see whether everything is in order mentally, you and Milo move from the bar to the room where the music's playing. Cristina didn't come, she had a class at her night school. The drums are set up on the stage, along with the microphone stands and a confused mass of wires, loudspeakers and electronic equipment; a young man is checking all the connections, moving from one component to the next, slowly inspecting everything.

People are gathering idly in the room. A yard away from you, some kind of Conan wearing a fake fur waistcoat over his naked torso is directing a sort of braying "A-a-a-ah—how's that?" at another ferocious-looking Conan with ears like wing mirrors. You go back to the bar and Milo quickly zooms in on each of the five girls in the room. One of them is sitting at a table. Her clothes are very tight. Everything's on the verge of falling out: she looks like she's about to overflow, and there's something vacant about her expression.

You go up to the bar and order drinks. Milo looks over your shoulder and murmurs, "Look out, here comes Paolo. He'll be after money as usual...."

The next moment, Paolo appears, stinking of rum like a pirate. "Hey, good to see you, how are you guys?" he asks with exaggerated courtesy.

Milo looks at him firmly. "Save your breath, Paolo: the answer's no."

Paolo stops for a moment, taken aback, then turns to you. "Hey, what's with him? Has he been smoking weed?"

You shrug and he orders a straight rum.

The wait is tedious. The concert's supposed to start at nine-thirty, but nothing happens until eleven. During the wait, you have a sort of private Oktoberfest.

When they finally start to play, there are about a hundred people in the club. Among them, a couple of young American roadies, wearing checked shirts and selling T-shirts, stand out. You look down: high incidence of work boots, one pair of horrible beige moccasins, some cowboy boots, and two weird items of footwear: one Captain Nemo-style, one three musketeers. Paolo is telling you the life story of tonight's featured artist, he really knows his stuff, he could be in the running for official biographer. It gives you food for thought, though, to think that seven or eight years ago the guy torturing his guitar in front of you was the lead guitarist of the most popular group on American campuses, he played gigs in front of forty thousand paying spectators and he was going with a famous beauty. You wonder how he feels here today, in front of maybe a hundred people in the heart of Chocolate City?

You know when a film is a good film. When a book is a good book. When a concert is a good concert. You know, you all know, gentle readers, it's simple: there comes a moment when you suddenly feel a long tremor at the top of your spine, right between your shoulder blades and your neck—like when your hair gets under your collar—you feel this long, powerful, warm shiver and you're happy because you feel all the little bits of your self properly connected to each other, you feel you're alive, your magico-animistic demons hold hands and dance round in circles and reality is something dazzling and miraculous; you feel the warmth of the world and for an instant you can even believe that perhaps there's something more than flesh and blood beneath your skin.

Well, in that sense today's concert is nothing special; the most interesting thing is the drummer, who is introduced as Johnny Heart

43

or something like that: he has a typical white Anglo-Saxon Protestant face, twenty or so, square jaw, dark glasses, punk hair, bleached and outrageous. He's beating a strange bass drum on wheels with a stick taped to two other sticks, which in their turn are stuck to a sort of cowbell. It makes an incredible din. Every now and then he flings one arm up in the air and holds it, like a druid waiting for a divine signal. Behind the dark glasses his eyes are probably closed. In the finale he appears in a bizarre jam session with the guitarist. It makes you want to run away, but then even the guitarist leaves the stage and our friend is on his own. So he gets up, hangs the drum around his neck and walks menacingly over to the microphone. The front row retreats a step, the people standing close to the speakers retreats a couple of yards. Johnny Heart starts hitting the drum like he's punching someone he's hated for decades, he produces terrifying rhythms, appalling broadsides, the audience retreats again before such power, but suddenly he stops and stands still: he half-opens his lips, leans down over the microphone stand and is about to say, do, maybe even sing, and anything might emerge from that mouth, but what does emerge is surprising. Johnny Heart, his tuning on the button, explodes into

> "Got a black magic woman,
> got a black magic woman,
> I've got a black magic woman,
> got me so blind I can't see...."

And then you feel the long tremor at the top of your spine. It's incredible. It means that that frenzied drum session was a Santana cover. Fantastic, unexpected: it's as if someone played the dustbins for three minutes and then sang, with conviction, "*Volare ooh ooh ooh ooh.*" Christ, if they lined up the whole world and put all the madmen at the front, this guy would be in the first ten thousand. Milo is speechless, he's shaking his head and laughing, fifteen years of militant attendance at every concert in northern Italy and he's never seen anything like it.

44

While the crowd is still buzzing, you go back to the bar. Paolo has disappeared, but Milo is in high spirits and wants another couple of beers. At the bar he's beginning to make a fool of himself with one of the two barmaids: he gives her a mammogram with his eyes, starts up a conversation, introduces himself, introduces you, goes over the top with the compliments. The girl, whose name is Sabrina—very blonde hair, wide face with prominent cheekbones, like a couple of eggs—seems pleased at the attention and responds willingly. When Milo jokingly tells her there's too much foam on his beer, she removes a swirl with her index finger, carries it to her lips and licks it off slowly, looking him in the eye the whole time. From that moment you know it will be impossible to drag him away from here.

In the end you have to be present during every phase leading up to the closing of the club: you spend a bit of time hanging around by the stage, and you're amazed how quickly the guys in the checked shirts manage to dismantle the equipment and instruments. Then you go back to the bar, where the second barmaid and the bouncer are making a great show of work, carefully cleaning the bar, wiping glasses, sorting bottles and finally putting the chairs up on the tables. Milo shows no sign of moving, he's chatting away agreeably, but then the second barmaid turns to you for help as she starts sweeping the pavement outside. "Look, Sabrina's supposed to lend us a hand and so far she hasn't done a thing. Is there any way to get rid of your friend?"

You glance at Milo, who is now beyond controlling, and shake your head.

"Got any sharpened stakes?" you answer with a smile.

You end up dragging Sabrina to Raul's. You met him and his girlfriend in the last bar in the city centre to close. He's a nice enough cretin whose father set him up as managing director of one of the family businesses, but he's got about as much brains as a cardboard box.

So why are we here? Simple, he has a nice comfortable place and we can always pilfer a couple of excellent CDs and drink up half the cellar—and we're talking top-quality bottles. And then, Raul *is* the most hospitable person in the world. Gentle readers, you mustn't examine it too closely: you have to accept the good in everyone.

Raul lives in this beautiful apartment in Piazza C.L.N., with a view over the fountains, minimalist furnishings, a hydro-massage bathtub and all those cold white things you see in interior design magazines. The place is usually filled with a mob of pseudo-artists with very artistic clothes and green and blue hair—the type whose creativity begins and ends with their clothes and hair—but tonight, fortunately, there's nobody else.

You watch a western in black and white, while Raul says a string of unimaginably stupid things: half-baked ideas about high finance, the Galassia Nord project, Agnelli, Cuccia and Romiti, Americans, Germans, Fiat; a bunch of moronic comments from which the only clear conclusion is that he doesn't understand a thing, and suddenly it dawns on you that Milo is paying serious attention to Sabrina, he's kissing her on the sofa, and you're horrified and wonder how he can even think of doing such a thing when he has Cristina waiting for him at home.

Meanwhile Raul talks and talks, and his new fiancée is there too. She's exquisite, dressed unusually—like the voodoo version of a model, no pins in her clothes but pierced everywhere else—with two beautiful grape-green eyes. She must be French, because she adds amusing accents at the ends of words: "Any*one* want some kiw*i* fruit?" she asks at one point. She never stops talking either, and every time she opens her mouth she rolls her eyes up to heaven, waves her arms about, bites her tongue, rolls her eyes again, touches her hair—in short, she's one of those people who thinks a conversation with someone has to be something of a performance.

Finally Raul starts talking about his company and how important he is in it and comes out with something truly special. He says, "Just so you understand: last week I didn't go to work for three days, and everything started to go so badly wrong that the staff went out on strike. Honest, guys, two hundred workers out on strike!"

It's one of the stupidest things you've ever heard. It's insulting. Sabrina and the voodoo model pretend nothing's happened and line up some coke in a figure-eight ("one *cercle* each," laughs the French girl), and you take the opportunity to go to the bathroom, a mas-terpiece in steel and cherry wood which must have cost as much as a small airliner. Milo promptly joins you, and while you're rinsing your noses under the tap he says, "He's entirely too stupid. He has to be made to pay somehow," then makes to leave, but you grab his arm and ask, "What about Cristina?"

He looks at you, pretending not to understand what you're talking about, so you insist. "What if she did something like that to you? Put yourself in her shoes."

He shrugs and turns to me before leaving. "Put myself in her shoes? What for?"

You stand in front of the mirror for a while, unbutton your shirt and have a quick look at the red mark: the situation seems stable; you swallow hard. You think how this is the first time you've seen Milo behave like this, he's always been very faithful to Cristina; you think maybe things aren't going too well between them any more, you think this with a sort of foolish glee and your mood darkens. Somewhere in the world a woman is looking for an Antonio. Somewhere in the world a man is looking for a Barbara.

When you reappear in the living room, Raul is still talking sublime nonsense and Milo goes on the offensive. "You know what I'd like to do? I'd like to go to a club and fuck three or four whores at the same time."

Sabrina stares at him incredulously, but she doesn't inter-rupt—curiosity gets the better of her: what the hell is he saying? Raul, however, rises to the bait and, cocksure as ever, asks, "So why don't you?"

"Because I've only got my cheque book on me and they only take cash."

It stinks to high heaven, but Raul doesn't notice (he has no sense of smell) and says grandly, "No problem. I'll cash a cheque for you."

Milo carefully pays out a bit more line. "I don't think you've got enough cash. For what I have in mind I'll need at least a couple of million...."

"No problem," says Raul even more grandly. "I'll cash it."

The voodoo doll smiles proudly, does a nice thick circle, then gathers up the remnants with her finger and rubs it into her gums.

"You're a pal, Raul," says Milo, getting out his cheque book.

You sit there, stunned: it's so blatant, so clear and obvious. How could anyone fall for it? Even Sabrina seems to have understood as she calmly sips a scotch on the rocks.

The hours trickle by and the night goes on, with Raul getting more and more hyped up and talking more and more nonsense—stiff jaw, enormous pupils and, despite all the coke, a vacuous, bovine expression in his eyes—and you all go on saying silly things and laughing and talking about subjects like crypto-zoology and fantastic inventions and life on other planets, the usual stuff.

When Raul and the voodoo doll finally show signs of wanting to be alone, Milo cashes his cheque and you and Sabrina leave with him. Raul claps him on the shoulder and says, "Give them one for me!"

You say goodbye, kiss each other on the cheek, say *ciao*, love you, call me, then you get in the elevator and start going down and you don't say anything and Milo gets out his wallet and puts a wad of hundred-thousand notes in your hand.

You look at him questioningly.

"Your share of the plunder," he explains.

"For what?" says Sabrina irritably.

"For his work. Tolerating idiocy is work. And it should be rewarded, don't you think?"

She smiles mischievously. "And what reward do I get?" she asks, rubbing herself against him.

Milo places himself a centimetre away from her, says, "What do you think?" and slaps her on the backside, and she kisses him and whispers, "If you catch something it's your problem; don't come running to me…" and fortunately the doors open and in your head you're hearing *"Antonio, estoy en Roma, ll'mame pronto, te quiero."*

Chapter five

In which the exemplary story of James Addison Reavis,
Baron de Arizonac and Caballero de los Colorados,
is told, also a dream entitled "Quadripedante
putrem sonitu quatit ungula campum."

Y ou see, subjects, you did right to come to me. This thing of
yours with the fake ecstasy, that's all very clever...and the insurance
thing, that's clever too...but how much does it bring in? And above
all, how long can it last?"

The nickname Grissino really doesn't match the man who
bears it and who's standing before you now. The man with the salt
and pepper beard who left the park in a hurry, now that you see him
up close, has pleasing features and does in fact remind you of a fifty-
year-old, slightly overweight Jesus Christ. Grissino's speaking style is
condescending yet courteous, his expression shrewd but benevolent;
his pale bright eyes communicate a sort of instinctive sympathy.

You have come to his house after an entire hour of argument.
Cristina wanted nothing to do with it, she said you shouldn't have
brought him in, that the Big C was your idea and he had no part in
it and besides, after the scene in the park she didn't think he was the
ideal partner. But in the end Milo prevailed, cutting all discussion
short by playing the most convincing card in the deck: you've had

49

the idea of the Big C for years and you haven't managed to put it into practice; Grissino has experience and he's family, so he's a useful and reliable partner. How can you argue with that?

Grissino lives in an apartment in an old building in Via Barbaroux. The rooms are big, the ceilings very high, and the whole place is strangely untidy. Spread out on the carpet is an unbelievable quantity of books ripped in half, torn-up newspapers and magazines, broken CD and video cases; the whole thing looks like the result of a zoological experiment carried out with the aid of LSD and bears.

Right now you're sitting on a big white sofa in the living room. The only other furniture in the room is a futuristic television set and a card table with four chairs.

Grissino goes on. "Take insurance: your accident scams are penny-ante stuff. In this field there are people like Martin Frankel, an American from Ohio, who's hiding out somewhere in the world after a hit worth a billion dollars."

"A billion dollars?" asks Milo.

"In other words, more than two billion lire?" you add.

"Precisely, subjects, all through a fake religious foundation which he used to buy up insurance companies. After which he emptied the cash registers and disappeared, naturally. Frankel is one of the world's most wanted men. But that's not all. There are even more interesting men: not even Frankel compares with the great James Addison Reavis."

"Who?" you ask.

"James Addison Reavis," says Grissino again.

"And who's he?" asks Milo.

Grissino rolls his eyes. "That's my point, you see, you lack culture...or even a bit of cinema. There's an interesting film from the fifties about him, with Vincent Price."

Cristina gives you a puzzled look and you shrug; meanwhile, Grissino carries on forcefully. "James Addison Reavis is the greatest there has ever been: a beacon eclipsing everyone who came before and lighting up everyone who came after."

"A kind of prophet..." you say sarcastically.

Grissino's rebuke is swift. "Silence, subject: there's plenty to say about them too."

Milo interrupts. "So when are we going to talk about the Big C?"

Grissino stands up abruptly and walks out of the room.

"There, now you've pissed him off..." whispers Cristina teasingly.

Grissino comes back a minute later and places a ream of printed papers, a box of envelopes and a stick of glue on the card table.

"A favour, since your hands are free: help me fold these pieces of paper and stuff them in the envelopes," he says.

You get up and take your places around the table, just as if you were going to play a game.

"What is this stuff?" asks Cristina.

"Nothing much, just a little job I have to finish," Grissino answers evasively.

You fold the first sheet of paper and glimpse the letterhead: "Editorial Services International." You ask yourself what on earth it might be, but your curiosity has only hung in the air for a second before it's distracted by Cristina's question to Grissino: "Okay, so what kind of scam did this James whatsisname do?"

Grissino stands up again and disappears.

"You see, now it's you that's pissing him off," jokes Milo, who's facing Cristina but not looking at her. Your curiosity swerves back to the sheet of paper: you examine it carefully but you don't learn much. It's a letter of introduction from this Editorial Services International; it asks the recipient to send product samples, promising that they will be forwarded to the editors of certain women's magazines in order to get free editorial coverage. You take a couple of envelopes and read the address labels—two well-known cosmetics firms—and now you begin to get an idea of the scheme.

Grissino comes back carrying a tray with a bottle of port and four small glasses. He puts it down on the table, among the letters and envelopes, and ceremoniously fills the glasses. Then he raises his glass and says, "James Addison Reavis—let's drink to him—carried out a unique, magnificent, breathtaking scam. Something extraordinary, something that has entered the annals of history."

You raise your glasses in a toast and, curious, prepare to listen.

"Ah," sighs Grissino, sipping his port and leaning back in his chair. "It's a mind-boggling tale. Listen and learn: it all starts in about 1883."

"Ah, old stuff," Milo remarks.

"Silence. Don't interrupt, please. As I was saying, it all starts in about 1883, in Tucson, Arizona. Well, subjects, what happens in that year? What happens is that the mayor of that city finally has an audience with a man with an aristocratic manner—it's our friend James Addison Reavis—who introduces himself with the grand-sounding title of Baron de Arizonac and Caballero de los Colorados. Please note: he has been asking for an audience for months, to discuss a matter which he says is extremely important."

"Get on with it, uncle," says Milo.

"Don't interrupt, subject. This is an extraordinary story in every detail. And educational. Where was I?"

"An extremely important matter," says Cristina.

"That's right. So, as I was saying: here's our friend, appearing before the Tucson authorities to discuss an extremely important matter. To cut a long story short, with his aristocratic manners and considerable style, James Addison Reavis shows the mayor a whole series of documents—various papers, notarized statements and so on. And these papers demonstrate, on the basis of a very complicated sequence of descendants, heredity and successions which I don't wish to go into here…well, they demonstrate without a shadow of a doubt that he, James Addison Reavis, Baron de etcetera etcetera, is the legitimate owner of practically the whole of Arizona."

"Really? Arizona? And it's a scam?" you ask.

"Don't keep interrupting me, please, and don't sit there with your arms crossed: there's work to be done. As I was saying, the legitimate owner of the whole of Arizona, just like that. I won't go into the historical details, but it was something to do with the treaty by which the United States bought Arizona from Spain…. According to this agreement, all Spanish real-estate contracts before a certain date were considered valid."

You and Milo are intrigued by the story and are stuffing envelopes reluctantly, but Cristina has discovered a super-quick method: she's opening the envelopes and folding the sheets of paper five at a time. You watch her as her hands move gracefully but frenetically, and you notice that Grissino, too, looks at her more than anyone else. "In conclusion," he goes on, "our friend, papers in hand, proves it's all his: a few million acres of territory and everything in it: mountains, rivers, deserts, fields, farms, mines, railways, and so on and so forth; all his, including cities the size of Tucson and Phoenix."

"Unbelievable!" you say, almost slicing yourself with a piece of paper.

"Precisely, subject, unbelievable. So, what happens at this point? What happens is that the Tucson authorities don't know what to do: they stall, and eventually they decide to ask the federal government for advice. But Reavis starts claiming his rights immediately. He puts up thousands of posters all over the area, informing the populace that the land concessions granted to colonists by the American government are worthless because it's all his. All his, do you follow me?"

"So what do they do?" you ask.

"Well, they do the only thing they can to regularize their position: they buy their land back."

Milo interrupts. "They just pay up, without going into it any further?"

"Calm down, nephew, have a little patience. Okay: obviously the best lawyers in the land are called in, plus a lot of historians, policemen and all kinds of investigators. This whole bunch of brainboxes seizes Reavis's papers, analyses them carefully for months and, in the end, concludes that things really are as described: James Addison Reavis is the legitimate owner and his demands are completely legal."

"Unbelievable. So they pay up?" asks Cristina.

"Of course. To begin with it's the ones with money who pay up: mines, banks, landowners, railways…. Then, a few at a time, ordinary citizens start to pay, assisted by the platoons of collectors recruited by Reavis and let loose around the country. Within a few months,

Reavis is one of the richest men in America—just think: his house was one of the first in the world to have running water."

"Unbelievable," you say.

"Precisely: unbelievable," Grissino continues. "But now our friend makes his first mistake: he becomes greedy. He becomes greedy and increases his demands, he hits the citizens hard. And you know how these things go: they start to hate him. More important, they start to look into him a bit more closely. So there's a new examination of the papers, more thorough this time, and a few inconsistencies come out. People take their cue and stop paying: the game seems to be up for Reavis."

"What does he do?" you ask.

"He wastes no time, no time at all. He gives a plausible explanation for the inconsistencies in the documents, after which he marries a gorgeous fifteen-year-old Mexican girl and decides the time has come to go on a European tour. He gets in a boat and goes off to Spain. And there he receives a hero's welcome as the Baron de Arizonac and Caballero de los Colorados, he gets invited to parties by all the royals and nobles in Madrid and makes a lot of friends and contacts."

By now your brain is far away from the envelopes. You're having visions of farms and cowboys, stagecoach-loads of lawyers in derbies with Colts in their holsters, Spanish palaces, steamships.... Oh, gentle readers, one of the loveliest things in life is being told a story, it really is, and Grissino's a wonderful storyteller, gesturing like an actor, pausing for effect, taking a sip of port, keeping you on tenterhooks.

"And then?" asks Milo.

"Then Reavis goes on to London, and his welcome is even more heroic. He's a guest of the queen, and they say Rothschild, the banker, and the Prince of Wales both fell madly in love with his Mexican bride at a party."

"How come you know all these details?" Cristina asks diffidently.

Grissino ignores her and goes on. "Finally, Reavis goes back to America. And, since he's used up just about all his money in Europe, he makes his second wrong move. He asks the American government for an inconceivably large amount of compensation—ten million dollars at the time—for what we would call 'lost earnings' today."

"And the government pays up?" you ask.

"Of course not, subject. A government? Pay up? You must be joking! The American government has had enough and decides finally to get to the bottom of the affair, so it organizes a new investigation into Reavis' papers. By now there's too much money at stake, so they do it properly: the best available researchers are chosen and immediately sent out around the world. The old world and the new world. They take ships, check archives, ride on horseback and in carriages throughout half of America and half of Europe. They visit dozens and dozens of churches and monasteries, looking for baptismal records. For months it looks as if everything is in order, but finally it emerges that one of Reavis' documents is a forgery: and then, in a domino effect, they find that almost all of the documents he has presented are forgeries."

"Ah, I thought so…" comments Cristina.

"Yes, good forgeries, but forgeries. Reavis is up against it. In the end, all his documents are declared forgeries: they decide to try him in court. Then the most surprising thing comes out: these documents are the result of more than fifteen years' work…."

"Unbelievable," you say.

"Precisely: unbelievable. Fifteen years to put together a scam. And even the trip to Europe had only one purpose—to nose about in the Spanish archives and try to organize things to his advantage. A great man. Someone who has earned his place in history. And a magnificent scam: a scam prepared over fifteen years, during which Reavis substituted or invented names, titles, signatures. A scam in which he showed talent and a detailed knowledge of many subjects. Just think about it for a moment: history, genealogy, heraldry…also languages and law…restoration, the chemistry of papers and inks. A true genius, in short."

"What happened to him in the end?"

"Ah," sighs Grissino, "he died a pauper's death. He was convicted and ended up in jail. With the final satisfaction of knowing he never returned a single dollar to the people he'd cheated: he'd squandered it all. When he came out he was a hopeless case, a bum who spent his time in the public library, reading about the days when he hung around with kings and queens and was one of the most important men in America."

"That's an amazing story," says Milo.

"The most important thing is that it teaches three things," Grissino continues. Then he pauses, for the umpteenth time.

"First: the preparation of a scam is the most important part. It has to be meticulous, nothing must be left to chance. You need intuition and intelligence but also discipline. Second: never get too greedy. Once he'd reached a certain sum, Reavis should have disappeared. It's like gambling: the winner is the one who leaves the roulette table at the right moment."

At this point Grissino gets up, gathers up the empty glasses and the bottle of port and disappears, so you take the opportunity to get up and look for the bathroom. You find it straight away, right at the beginning of the corridor: you go through the half-open door into a fairly large room, finished in sea-green tiles and packed full of stuff: whole cases of perfumes, shampoo, bubble bath and canisters of shaving foam. It's like a perfume counter, and you don't need to be a rocket scientist to work out that all this plenty has something to do with the mailing you're assembling.

You go up to the mirror over the sink and open your shirt, just enough to have a look at the mark on your left shoulder. You nearly have a heart attack. You run to lock the door and then take off your shirt. The whole of your upper body and back, all the way up to your neck and shoulders, is covered with little red pustules. You look at yourself in the mirror again and again, part frightened and part horrified. At first you try to convince yourself that it can't be serious, it looks like one of those childhood illnesses like chicken pox or measles, but shit, you've already had both of them and you know you can't get them again. Then full-blown terror grips you as you realize that all these little pustules could become like the big mark on your shoulder. You imagine your whole body as a single blood-red sore—like the drawing of the muscular system in your schoolbook, the drawing of a man with no skin, and you can see the red of the tissues and the groups of muscles—and you're tempted to call your mother, or else an ambulance. Then, slowly, you start telling yourself again and again, like a mantra, that tomorrow you have an appointment with the doctor, and at last you regain your self-control.

When you get back to the card table, white as a sheet, Milo is just finishing his explanation of the Big C idea. Grissino is lighting a cigar and inhaling a couple of mouthfuls. He looks pleased, but you don't know whether it's due to the cigar, the Big C or even the apprehension you can read in Milo's face. Finally, he says the idea sounds really good, but he wants to think it over.

Then he adds, "Now do me a favour: help me finish the envelopes."

There are three famous cowboys on white horses in the streets of the old city centre; they're riding majestically across a deserted Turin, holding long rifles in their hands, wearing straw-coloured capes to protect themselves from the light rain. They have piercing eyes and leathery faces. Their huge horses are galloping on the cobbles, a frightening sight, the clattering of hooves filling Via Pietro Micca, echoing among the arcades.

They're following you.

They're following you, and you escape on a blue Vespa which bears the logo of a courier company on its body.

Suddenly you turn, smelling the odour of the horses, and now their enormous heads are very close and you're gripped by panic. Your front wheel gets caught in a tram track, the Vespa skids off to one side and you fall to the ground, rolling over and over. The horses go by without trampling you—a whirl of iron hammer blows brushing against you without touching you—and disappear in the mist; for a few seconds you can hear the echo of their hooves and then nothing, silence.

You get up slowly, frightened, feeling your aching ribs: a long ragged tear through both jacket and shirt reveals the mark between your shoulder and collarbone: it looks like a bullet hole. You're studying the wound, dismayed, and picking at it with your finger, when out of the mist appears an Indian, naked. He looks a bit like Grissino and he's holding something in his hand. Having made his way to you, the Indian kneels and holds out a wooden box. On it is written: The Third Teaching of the Baron of Arizona.

You try to open it, but it won't open, so you dash it to the ground and it breaks open, revealing a photograph of a woman with Cristina's face. And then you wake up.

Chapter six

*In which our subjects are doctors, vans, farmers and horses,
and the unpredictable duel between Man and Destiny.*

At the fifth unanswered ring you turn to Cristina.

"No answer, maybe he's gone out…" you mutter, disappointed.
You're about to put the receiver down when you hear the click of
the answering machine followed by a recorded voice. "Hello. This is
Grissino. I'm not at home. I've gone out to beat up a few policemen,
get a fix of heroin and pick up some thirteen-year-old girls."

You smile to yourself, and when you hear the tone you say, "Hi,
it's Vittorio, I'm here at Milo's, he told me to call you to—"

A dry click interrupts you, then you hear Grissino's voice.
"Greetings, subject."

"Uh…hi…how's it going?"

Pause.

"Well," he answers.

"And…what are you doing?"

Pause.

"I'm talking to you."

"…yes, so you are."

You look over at Cristina and go on. "Listen…we got your

message. We just wanted to tell you it's okay, we'll see you there this afternoon…all right?"

Pause.

"All right."

"Okay, bye."

Pause.

"Goodbye to you, subjects."

You're in the van, on your way to the racetrack. Cristina's sitting in the middle, between you and Milo in every sense. Meteorologically speaking, the weather's glorious and sunny; mentally speaking, the weather's changeable, calm with occasional showers, some heavy and thundery. Milo, in the driving seat, has spent the time repeating I-know-where-I'm-going-don't-worry-I-know-where-I'm-going until you're lost in the countryside miles away from Vinovo. On the radio someone is saying that if you yawn during the act of sex it increases potency; something to do with hormones (a voice explains): chimpanzees do it, as do some species of ape. Milo yawns and giggles, says "Ooh, Ooh," scratches his armpit and looks at Cristina, but she ignores him.

You're looking at the Rolex Andrea brought back from Thailand. It's a top-class fake, because the mechanism is actually automatic; the second-hand doesn't move in increments, like a quartz watch, but smoothly: an unstoppable progress, non-rhythmic, stress-inducing; you spend entire minutes staring at the second-hand and thinking how far it might go if it could retain its energy without being fixed to the centre, like a donkey to a millstone; you imagine the second-hand free to float in the air, like a pine needle on the wind, but with its own energy and a definite direction, and you can't explain it but in this watch you properly *recognise* time.

You remember the day you had yesterday, the doctor, the crowded waiting room, the anxiety growing inside you each minute. You remember when your turn came, how you lay down on the bed, the sense of security that flowed over you. You remember your doctor's well-fed, convivial face, what a fuss he made over seeing you again, how envious you feel every time you see in his face how tired yet contented his job makes him. He told you to get undressed, examined the marks for a long while, unhurriedly, then shook his head. He picked up a magnifying glass and examined them again, muttering something to himself, and finally spread his arms in disappointment and confessed. "I've never seen anything like this."

Then, seeing your horrified expression, he went on. "Not to worry, I don't think it's anything serious. You need to see a specialist, a dermatologist."

The appointment with the dermatologist is set for Tuesday, and you know these three days are going to be torture, but right now you try not to think about it, to concentrate instead on Milo and his talent for dissembling.

"You'll see, guys," he's saying right now. "My uncle will accept our idea, he'll find a way to get it going, and within a year we'll be stinking rich, living on some Caribbean island." As if to emphasize his point, Milo takes a corner wide, slows down and stops at the entrance to a dirt track.

"Shit, look at that," he says, pointing at a warning light on the dashboard. Cristina leans over at the same time as you and your heads nearly clash.

"It's the temperature gauge," you say. "Either we're overheating or there's no water in the radiator."

Milo switches off the engine and you sit there in silence for a few seconds. Not a soul goes by and all around you is a hot and dusty landscape and the humming of insects, and your eye is caught by a phrase spray-painted in huge letters on a half-overgrown wall: CHIARA I'LL LOVE YOU FOREVER, but time has started to fade the FOREVER.

Cristina breaks the silence. "Well, what's half a mile more or less? Start the engine and we'll look for a petrol station."

Milo shakes his head. "I'm not moving an inch. I don't want to risk screwing everything up," he says. Then he releases the catch under the steering wheel, gets out of the van and opens the hood. You and Cristina get out and look too.

The engine is a boiling hot mass of metal and dust. You look at it for a while, undecided as to what to do, until you notice that the coolant reservoir is completely empty.

"Okay, I'll take care of it," you say, pointing to a farm building at the end of the track. "I'll go see if they'll give us some water."

After a few hundred metres under the murderous sun, you see an old farmer sitting in the shade of a tree by the side of the road and go up to him. He seems to be asleep.

You try "good morning" first.

His eyes become faint slits.

"Good day," he says after a while.

You look at him in silence as a couple of flies crawl across the deep lines of his face. You can't guess how old he is; in fact he's not old, he's ancient, prehistoric. Cicadas buzz in concert around you.

"Don't those flies on your face bother you?" you ask, for some reason.

The farmer opens his eyes a little and examines you for a long time. Then, unruffled, he says, "You have to let them be flies. Swatting them is just a waste of time. But if you ignore them, they go away of their own accord."

He looks away from you, towards the countryside, and adds, "Like your worries."

Christ, you've hooked up with Diogenes!

"Look, I wonder if you could do me a favour: our van has broken down over there, we're out of water."

He opens his eyes a little more and examines you again. Then he says, "Cars are always breaking down. Out of fuel, out of oil…. Out of water is less common."

Then he gets up suddenly, his speed so unexpected in a man of his age that you jump.

"Come," he says, "follow me," and starts walking slowly, beneath the sun, towards the building.

You follow him in silence as far as the yard, where perhaps ten chickens are scratching about. A dog on a chain is barking; there's a smell of stables, rotten apples, dry grass and rosemary; something indefinable hangs in the air, something peaceful and sad, you can't bear it.

The farmer opens a rough wooden door and shows you into a sort of tool shed, as if to shelter you from the sun. "Stay right here," he orders as he leaves without turning round.

There are a couple of tables loaded with clamps, a small circular saw, screwdrivers and pincers and hammers and wood shavings everywhere. A fat bumblebee is trying ponderously to get through the glass of the window, buzzing and charging persistently, and if it would just move a foot or so to the right it would find the other pane open, but it doesn't, and it reminds you of you. There's a small radio on a shelf, playing a song in the background, and on the air there's this gorgeous, gravelly, tragic voice saying, "I'm pushing an elephant up the stairs," which is rather what you're thinking, like the bee, and in fact, when you stop and consider the surface of things, you see that everything is connected.

The old man reappears after a minute with a huge tin watering can and puts it on the ground in front of you.

"Be sure to bring it back," he says.

Finally you're at the entrance to the racetrack at Vinovo, and Milo, as soon as he sees the enormous queues in front of the ticket offices, starts complaining. "I wouldn't stand in a queue like that, not even to see Jim Morrison come back to life."

Then he looks at you and Cristina, smiling mischievously. "Maybe for Hendrix. For Hendrix I might do it."

Then he starts explaining that he hates horses, they're stupid creatures, really stupid, that nobody could make an intelligent animal run races—"Have you ever seen a cat race? Of course not, they're obviously intelligent animals." He's enjoying himself and goes on. "But you can bet, that's the good part. At least there's proper racing today—I can't stand trotting."

Cristina gives you an odd, long-suffering look, you give her the expected smile back, then offer to stand in the queue.

You haven't been to the races for years. Your father used to take you all the time when you were a child, he was mad about betting, especially the complicated stuff: he never placed bets to win or place unless it was over two or three consecutive races; he always placed combination bets: forecasts, tri-casts, trebles, and in all this he followed a specific doctrine concerning Man and Destiny. You remember a phrase of his: "Betting isn't a game, it's a duel between Man and

Destiny." Now it sounds grandiose. You want to add: Of course, Shakespeare, *King Lear,* Act Four, Scene One, but when you analyse it you realize there's a whole lifetime in this phrase. You remember your father's habit of shouting "Well done!" to the winner at the end of every race, even when, especially when, he had bet on another horse. He used to say, "We all need somebody to say well done to us: it's one of the few truths in life. Everyone, even the greatest among us, needs to have somebody say well done: employees need their bosses, bosses need their bosses, top politicians need voters, great actors need directors, great directors need reviewers, famous reviewers need readers…everyone, everyone, everyone."

Even this you've only understood with time: we all need somebody to say well done. Even God needs someone to say well done. Take a sunset, for example, gentle readers: what else do you think it was invented for?

When you go in, Milo is as excited as a child. He drags you straight to the newsstand and buys a couple of sports papers and a copy of *Trotting Sportsman.*

"Shouldn't we be looking for your uncle?" asks Cristina.

"And where are we supposed to look for him?" he answers irritably. "Can't you see the chaos around you? Anyway, we'll come across him sooner or later…or else he'll find us, who gives a shit."

Then he goes on, happy again. "Playing the horses is easy," he explains. "You take three or four papers and check their tips for each race against the programme they gave us at the door. It's easy. You can't lose."

So you each take a newspaper and go and sit in the grandstand. You study them for a good quarter of an hour, in which time you manage to establish that the favourites for the first race are Jailbird and Uncertain Smile.

"Perfect, let's go have a look at these horses," you say, standing up.

And that's what you like about the races: the routine, the ritualistic to-and-fro of all the bettors at each race. They look up the favourites in the programme and the newspapers, they check the odds on the monitor, they go over to the track and have a look at the numbers displayed on the bookies' stalls, and then it's over to the paddock to watch the horses on parade. They check physique and nerves, admiring the well-groomed ones with the glistening hides, go back to the monitors to check how the tote's doing and what the latest odds are, then finally place their bets, take their positions along the rail beside the track or in the grandstand and watch the race, they cheer, they yell, the losers tear everything up, filling the air with curses, the winners wait by the tote to see when winnings are being paid out and then cash in. After which they open the papers again to look up the favourites for the next race and the cycle starts over, and there's something comforting, almost humdrum about this routine that immediately makes you feel good.

So you go to the paddock to watch the parade of horses for the first race. Everybody's here, glued to the rail, vociferous, cheerful, alive, as the grooms lead the enormous saddled horses round and round in a circle like a merry-go-round. You find a space next to a man with hairs coming out of his ears and try to spot the favourites. Jailbird is a magnificent bay mare with a white mark on her face; Uncertain Smile is a carbon copy of Jailbird, but with a narrower face and no marks. Cristina says they're fine strong horses and bound to win, so you go and place your bets together in good spirits: win, place and paired. Then you go back to the central stand and look for a place high up, where you can be a bit apart from the crowd. Milo points out Grissino a few rows above; making your way through the spectators, you join him.

"Good day, subjects," he says as you take up your places around him; he has a small pair of binoculars around his neck and is unhurriedly consulting a copy of *Trotting Sportsman*. From here you can see the whole race.

"We've plumped for Jailbird and Uncertain Smile," Milo announces happily.

There is no visible reaction from Grissino. In front of you, on the other side of the track, the horses are being pushed into the starting gate. There's a tremendous amount of shouting and people crowd onto the terraces and along the home straight, so thickly you can't see their feet. Grissino folds up his newspaper with great care. "Dear me, the three of you are so frighteningly, incurably young," he sighs. "Only suckers bet on the first race."

Then he adds, "Anyway, number four is going to win."

Having said this, he turns away, the crafty devil, holds the binoculars up to his eyes and, after a long sweep over the track, comes to rest on the starting gate.

"Number four, "he says again. "Sunday Morning, the jockey in the green blouse with white sleeves."

A moment later the siren goes off and the horses leap out of the gates as if they were loaded on rubber bands. The whole crowd is instantly on its feet.

"Come on, Jailbird!" a group of men in front of you bawl at the top of their voices.

"Knock 'em dead, Tango Atlantico, knock 'em dead!" is the cry from your left.

You can't distinguish the horses very well, but the distorted voice on the loudspeakers comes to your aid. "And it's Jailbird in the lead from the start, then Tango Atlantico..." but suddenly you can't hear anything any more: the speakers are crackling, the crowd is shouting and screaming and cheering and waving betting slips. Jailbird stays ahead up to the curve, but another horse appears very quickly from behind, catching up fast, and the only thing you can see, dammit, is that the jockey is a green and white blur.

At the beginning of the final straight the horses are still bunched together: a homogenous, indistinct yell of encouragement rises and fills the air with energy as the crowd lining the track appears to move in waves, like the sea. And now they're on the home stretch: the horses are almost directly in front of you and you can hear the thundering of hooves at full gallop and the crowd is yelling and there's chaos on the terraces and you almost have to jump in the air to see that blasted number four speed over the finishing line, followed, some distance behind, by Jailbird in second place.

Around you a few people are celebrating, hugging each other happily. "He did it! He did it!" but within a few seconds the shouts of the crowd die down and all that's left is a few curses here and there and the noise of feet going down to the cashiers.

Grissino doesn't bat an eye. He sits down gracefully and opens up his newspaper again.

After a few moments' hesitation, Milo cheers, "We won, we won!" and hugs Cristina, who, like you, doesn't understand. So he searches his pockets and takes out the three receipts. "No, not this one...or this one...here it is: number five, Jailbird, to place. He came in second, so let's go collect," and he hugs Cristina. She backs away but he pulls her by the hand and they disappear. You stay behind, reflecting that you've won perhaps three or four thousand lire and lost more than twenty, then you go and sit down beside Grissino as the last spectators leave the stand, which is carpeted with hundreds of losing slips.

"You see, Vittorio," says Grissino, closing his newspaper, "Milo is my favourite nephew. He's one of those people with happiness deep inside: someone like that has been kissed by God."

Then he stands up. "I'm going to play me some horses," he says. "Let's see: Mambo Sun, Yeke Yeke and Blue Monday in the second. I'm not betting on the third. In the fourth: Emi, Stay Free and Time. In the fifth I can't make up my mind between Sister Golden Hair and October for second place, but I'm betting on Next to You to win. In the sixth, everybody's favourite is Gone Daddy Gone, but I'm betting on Small-Town Boy and Charlotte Sometimes, paired. But I'll see you back here in a while."

It's amazing: he says this whole list of names from memory, then makes to leave. But he's called you Vittorio instead of the usual "subject," which is encouraging, and you get up and ask him point blank, "Weren't we going to talk about our plan, the Big C?"

Grissino looks at you coolly, then comes closer, puts his hand on your shoulder and, looking you in the eye, says, "Yes, that. I've been giving it a good deal of thought."

Then he pauses.

"I've been giving it a good deal of thought, and I must admit it's a good idea and it'll certainly work, no doubt about it. All that remains now is to get busy and put it into practice."

You're about to explode with happiness. "You mean you accept?"

"Of course, just try and stop me."

You almost hug him.

"I'd like to ask you something, Vittorio," he says instead.

"I'm all ears."

"Do you think I'll win all my bets today?"

You shake your head. "Hard to believe."

He looks at you and sighs. "Well, as for that, it's even harder to believe that we're standing on a boulder covered with earth and water that's moving at nearly six thousand kilometres a second."

You're queuing for the toilets at the track, which are packed, and next to you there are a couple of guys dressed like the Beagle Boys: the only thing missing is 167-761 on their sweatshirts. One of them is gripping his betting slips like they're really precious and staring at the tote in the distance, as if it holds his results in an important exam. Under the tote, Milo and Cristina are having an animated argument and she slaps him, but then they suddenly vanish from sight. Somewhere in the world, in Italy, a man has calculated that the probability of getting six numbers in the Mega Lottery is one in seven hundred and thirty-eight million. Somewhere in the world, near Eastbourne, a titled lady is writing a book containing the golden rules on "how to lay the table." Somewhere in the world, near Islamabad, a village court has condemned a thirty-four-year-old widow and her lover, a married man, to death. The execution of the two adulterers will be carried out by stoning.

Here's the thing, gentle readers: I don't know whether you share my sense of constant disorientation. What I mean is this: on an ordinary day like today, I woke up and listened to the news on the radio while I was in the shower, then went to a bar and had breakfast, had a glance at the papers and listened to a few comments from around the place, then went home and watched a couple of news broadcasts on TV, and the result of all this is that an enormous amount of information has entered my head that maybe I don't need. Just today I've learned, among other things, that somewhere in the world, somewhere in the United States of America, the latest craze is a selective diet whose purpose is to change the flavour of the vagina and make oral sex more attractive to men. Eliminating dairy products and brassicas—cauliflower and the like—has the effect, according to some people, of changing the taste of vaginal secretions and making them sweeter. I have learned that there are more than thirty-six thousand metres between the dish we put on our balcony and the satellite the dish needs to "see." I have learned that as many as eleven million drops of ink exit the head of an ink-jet printer per second. I have learned that five hundred rangers were killed on Omaha Beach in the first minute after they disembarked. I have learned that a hundred and twenty thousand people died from conventional bombs in one night at Dresden. I have learned that if you yawn during the act of sex it increases potency: chimpanzees do it, along with many species of ape.

What do you say, gentle readers, does the same thing happen to you? And, if so, how do you 'select'? Because that's my problem: everything comes into my head at once: I'm in a queue for the toilets at the racetrack and feeling fine, I'm not thinking about the red marks, Milo or Cristina, and I feel relieved, and I want to celebrate the fact that Grissino is joining up with us, I'm full of energy and I'm finally hopeful that we'll carry out our plan, I'm happy and the world is huge and there are plenty of things to do and see and you never know what life has in store for you. But instead it occurs to me that somewhere in the world something has happened, something that shouldn't matter to me at all. Isn't it surprising how inexhaustible and superabundant it is, this reality ticking away from one second to the next?

Suddenly, Grissino bursts into the toilets.

"Ah, what a lot of ugly people!" he says very loudly as he comes in. Then he goes up to 167-761 with a cigar in his hand and says, "Have you got a light?"

167-761 looks askance at him and answers, "No. I don't smoke."

Grissino nods. "You're right. That stuff'll kill you."

You go into the toilet and as you undo your trousers you're left open-mouthed by a phrase written on the wall in felt pen and signed

CB, "I love horse racing because it makes me understand where I am strong and where I am weak, it tells me how I feel this day and how we change and everything changes, all the time, and how little we know about it all."

Chapter seven

In which our subjects are codes of honour, horoscopes, a supergarage and moral ambiguity, how we human beings are a mass of contradictory elements and why no one ever tells the whole truth about himself.

*H*oroscope of the day. Taurus. *The turning point you have been expecting for some time is approaching: it will have a positive effect on your future. Maintain your mental fitness and use your time thinking of yourself a bit more. Write to an old friend who currently resides in prison.*

Taurus. Like everyone born under this sign, you enjoy masturbation more than real sex. You are enthusiastic and optimistic, but you are conceited and take pleasure in farting. You have an undeniable tendency to trust to luck, given that you have no talent. Your chances of a job and making money are non-existent. You worry a lot about other people's problems, which makes you a fool, but you expect a lot in return for very little, which makes you a greedy sonofabitch. Everyone in jail is a Taurus! You are an idiot.

The voice on the TV is unbearably shrill. The Famous Singer whose voice it is, having uttered a list of platitudes and primary-school banalities about war and racism, smiles radiantly at the interviewer and closes with a wonderful "…but I have great faith in mankind."

"Thanks for your faith, you magnificent tart," Grissino comments.

Milo, sitting beside you on the sofa, changes the channel and the Famous Singer Who Has Great Faith in Mankind disappears, to be replaced by a quiz show.

Grissino is sitting in the armchair on your right, with a pack of cards in his lap; he's casually flicking them, one by one, at a black fedora upturned on the carpet next to the television, and he's scoring a basket nearly every time. Cristina is sitting apart, at the poker table, even more beautiful than usual, intent on solving a crossword.

"Indispensable element for life on earth, six letters," she says.

There's a moment's silence as four people rack their brains, then Milo giggles. "Salary!"

You take control of the remote and stop on MTV, where four huge black guys, covered in gold, are singing something in English, gesticulating and glaring at you accusingly. Grissino immediately seizes the opportunity. "Brilliant, well done, you've lost no time in finding some more crap. And what are these four morons trying to tell me? Yes, I see, they're very pissed off…brrr, I'm quaking in my boots, so much rebellion…. And what are they going to do? Set fire to the whites' houses and take back America, in alliance with the Hispanics? The hell they are…. As far as I can tell they just want to show off that they drive around in big black Benzes, surrounded by lots of nice pussy…. And these guys are pissed off with the world? I wonder what the porter who carries their bags up to their suite thinks, I wonder what he thinks about their being pissed off with the world…. Let them go fuck themselves, fuck off out of here for the rest of eternity."

Milo sniggers; he takes back the remote and, after a very quick survey, stops on an advertisement.

"This ad is so stupid," Cristina comments unexpectedly, without looking up from the crossword. Grissino's last card, the ace of hearts, teeters on the brim of the fedora, then falls onto the carpet. He gets up to fetch it and starts grumbling. "It's time you started to turn the

6666

relationship between cause and effect around, subjects. For example: it's not the advertisement that's stupid. Advertising just adjusts to the stupidity of the people who watch it: people are stupid, and advertisements adjust. People like them and follow them and buy the products, so it works: advertising isn't stupid at all."

Cristina snorts and quickly tries to break his stride. "Capital of Gabon, ten letters."

"Libreville," answer Grissino immediately, then glances complacently at Cristina and starts up again, looking at you and Milo. "Take television, for example. Television's first goal is to make as many people as possible watch it. And it pursues this goal conscientiously. If television offers mostly trash, it's because most people watch trash, wallow in trash, are trash themselves...."

"Banal fascist snobbery," says Cristina from behind him.

"Oh right," he says. "God forbid anyone should make a blanket criticism. But of course, all men are equal and God forbid you should say anything against them. Ah, you're young and that's what they tell you, but I'm old: I've known plenty of men who weren't human beings. I've known plenty of men who weren't even mammals: they were reptiles, arachnids...."

"Banal fascist snobbery," says Cristina again.

This time Grissino doesn't react, but turns again to you and Milo. "Anyway, the blame for trashy programmes doesn't lie with the people who make them. The blame lies with the millions of morons who could shut down any programme in a few days, simply by pressing a button: just long enough for the people in charge to look at the ratings and decide to cancel the programme."

"That's not what TV's trying to do," you protest. "TV has to lead, not follow."

"That's what I'm saying, subject. TV is leading, not following. It knows that people will switch off in half a second, so what does it do? It defends itself. By only offering things that are safe, made to be watched by the majority: in other words, crap. And people watch crap for the simple reason that they're morons."

"Oh, cut it out, Grissino, we heard all this at the Valentino... give us a break," says Cristina, shaking her head.

Grissino sits down again, picks up the king of clubs between two fingers and flicks it sidelong into the fedora. "I'm not going to cut it out at all, on the contrary.... I don't think most people even watch the television, they just stare at it, hypnotized...."

Cristina interrupts him again.

"Maybe people are just tired, they want to sit down for a minute to have a rest and have their family nearby...and they don't give a damn what's on...in fact, maybe they spend their whole time laughing and saying: Look at this crap! Just like you...."

"Would that it were so," sighs Grissino.

"Of course, silly us: only the chosen few shall be saved," she replies, rolling her eyes. Grissino, apparently bored, throws the whole pack at the hat, scattering the cards on the carpet. Then he directs a self-satisfied look at Cristina. "That's right: only the chosen few shall be saved."

"Meaning you?" she asks, coolly.

"Well," he answers, "I'm a fool too. But I understand that there are people who are more foolish than I am and I protect them."

Cristina explodes with scornful laughter. "Do me a favour! And how would you protect them? Let's hear it."

Milo changes the channel, trying to distract Grissino and lighten the atmosphere, but he goes on. "Very simple, my dear young lady. For a while now I haven't been cheating everyone. It's my code of honour: you don't cheat the stupid, you don't cheat the handicapped, you don't cheat the old, the poor, pensioners, the weak, the sick, etcetera. The truth is, everyone's cheating them anyway. So I leave them alone. I cheat those who cheat us—public administration, insurance, banks, corporations, and whenever possible all of them at the same time, as we're about to do!"

You take the opportunity to intervene. "It's true, the Big C sits perfectly with your code of honour."

"Yes," says Milo, but without conviction, as if it's just something to say. "What I like is that we're going to rip off the fat cats, the ones who rip us off as a matter of course. We're almost heroes."

Just then the intercom buzzes. Grissino stands up quickly,

rubbing his hands. "Ah, at last: the people who want to buy my delightful little apartment."

Milo looks at him, puzzled. "But aren't you renting?" he asks.

"That's the beauty of it, nephew, that's the beauty of it!"

At the door is a couple in their sixties, oozing health and well-being: both are very chic in their pastel-coloured outfits, both very blonde, both very tanned. Barbie's grandparents, if such things are made.

Grissino introduces you as a group of students whom he is coaching in history of art, at which Barbie's grandmother gasps, "O-o-o-h, A-a-a-rt!" Then the pair is guided around the rooms by Grissino and swamped with words which you can't help listening to from the living room. "Look at this, madam…a kitchen which wouldn't look out of place in a restaurant…the bathroom is brand new…and then it's so convenient to live right in the centre…a steal at this price…you don't like the carpet? We'll take it up: there's a fabulous parquet floor underneath, they don't make them like that any more, all inlaid, unbelievable…a very quiet apartment, madam…surrounded by the most delightful boutiques, charming…I'm leaving in six months and then I'll vacate it for you, but I need to close right away…."

Then the pair goes down to the basement, accompanied by Grissino. As soon as they're out of sight, Cristina comments, "His manner's too false, they'll never fall for it."

"We'll see," answers Milo immediately, as if challenging her.

Five minutes later, you hear Grissino's voice again, this time from the courtyard, and you watch from the window as he displays the myriad virtues of the garage to the two unfortunates; in fact, as an amused Milo explains, the garage probably belongs to an unsuspecting tenant. "A fantastic garage. Look at the size of it. It's not like those garages they build just for runabouts, where if you park a BMW it takes five minutes to get out because the gap between the wall and the gate is tiny: you're looking at a 'supergarage'…and take a look at the gate…fully automatic, no unnecessary effort, no throwing your back out…."

By the time Barbie's grandparents get back to the apartment they're completely dazed, so Grissino fires his closing broadsides. "This is an unmissable opportunity. I wouldn't let go of this apartment for just anyone, I'm too fond of it, it's been in my family for generations. You know, I've seen dozens of potential buyers, but I didn't feel I could trust them, it's like handing over a child.... I need to be able to rest easy. And who better than you? And you, madam? With your elegance and refinement I'm sure you'll turn this place into a gem...."

In the end he succeeds in getting a cheque for four million out of them. He's right: it is a derisory down payment.

"Well, subjects: I've been thinking. To get our idea started we'll need about a hundred million," Grissino announces without beating about the bush.

Cristina looks at him, stunned. "We thought thirtyish. What do we need a hundred million for?"

Grissino gets out a piece of paper densely covered with writing and sits down at the poker table. "Come here, subjects," he says, inviting you to sit down. "Here's the shopping list."

You are the first to look the piece of paper over. It's a comprehensive list detailing absolutely everything: office and computer rental, photocopier, telephones, fax, phone lines, down payments on furnishings, purchase of clothes appropriate for prosperous people, fees for a notary and all the paperwork necessary to register a company, payments to a complaisant bonehead in whose name it will be registered, deposit to the advertising agency and towards the cost of posters. The list is endless and goes into details you would never have thought of, from the coffee machine to the office stationery.

The sheet goes on to Milo and Cristina, who examine it gravely.

Finally Milo speaks up. "Okay, uncle, it's all perfectly correct. But where are we going to get a hundred million?"

Grissino stares at the wall opposite for a few seconds, then sighs. "Ladies and gentlemen, we live in an age of swindles, where everything's a big or a small con. The important thing is to recognize this and take appropriate action."

Cristina rolls her eyes.

"Great," says Milo again, "but where are we going to get a hundred million?"

"Simple," says Grissino. "We must rely on the first law of entrepreneurship." At this point he pauses and looks at you with his usual know-it-all expression.

"Go ahead, shoot," you say encouragingly, and you stop trying to sneak a look at the marks under your shirt.

"Okay. The first law of entrepreneurship, subjects, is the one that goes: 'Who can I copy?'"

"Meaning?" says Milo, puzzled.

"Meaning, subjects, that the problem is simple: we need a hundred million and we haven't got it. How do we intend to get it? The only way we know how, which is to say by means of a con. A small con to prepare for the Big Con. So let's think what we can do: let's bring to mind some kind of 'copyable' scam."

Milo shakes his head. "You're the expert, uncle. If I knew how to put together a scam worth a hundred million I wouldn't be here."

"No, let's all give it some thought together," says Grissino. "Pity we're not a banking or insurance group, the masters of the field. But their inventions are the hardest to copy: like those of the state, the other great master, they start from a solid and impregnable basis—"

"God, off he goes again," snorts Cristina, resting her head in her hands.

"You're right, my dear young lady, let's not stray off the subject. So: first of all we need to think what the fraudsters have been doing lately, and what's been working for them. Let's bring some ideas to mind and analyse them until we find a decent one we can work with."

You have a shrewd suspicion that Grissino has already thought it through and has the solution in his head, but wants to create a bit of drama. Nevertheless, you decide to play along. "Well, weeping madonnas are very fashionable at the moment."

Grissino nods. "True. But ideally you live in some village in the country, and you own a hotel or an inn...or a restaurant...or at least a bar...or else how do you make any money? Besides, madonnas only start weeping in out-of-way places, in front of virgin shepherdesses, never in front of pushers of fake ecstasy...."

You and Milo exchange a smile as Cristina comments, "It's amazing how people keep letting themselves be taken in."

"Banal fascist snobbery," says Grissino swiftly.

"Well," Milo chips in, "we could set up one of those really expensive training courses that guarantees you a job but are just a scam."

Grissino shakes his head. "No, the preparation is very complicated. You need lots of time and the risks are quite high. Not to mention that people are beginning to be suspicious. It's like the fake lotteries: now *there's* a field in which people have really gone too far."

"Or else," you suggest, "we could come up with a work-from-home scheme, with the wrinkle that you have to pay a joining fee. You cash in and ship out."

Grissino winces disapprovingly. "Hmm, I don't know: the preparation is complicated there too. And it takes a long time to earn anything. We need something in which we don't expose ourselves, risk very little and cash in quickly."

"A fake franchise?" suggests Milo.

"Don't make jokes, nephew. It's extremely lucrative but too complicated to organize. Besides, it's very difficult to get anyone to bite in a short time."

"Well," says Cristina, playing with a lock of her hair, "along the same lines as what you've just been doing, we could look for a house that's under construction and demand the deposit on the purchase."

"Too risky," answers Grissino. "You risk a bad beating if you get caught: I've had it happen to me."

"I could be a wizard," says Milo. "I could look into the future, lift curses, that kind of thing...."

"True, nephew, I know what you're talking about. But to earn a hundred million you need to build a following—which takes at least a year."

And now Grissino lights up. "Maybe I've got it. I'll be back in a minute. Stay tuned," he says, getting up and disappearing in the direction of the bathroom. You're more sure than ever that he knows exactly what to do.

About twenty minutes later, Grissino reappears, all excited. "We're in business," he says, collapsing into the armchair.

"Spit it out, uncle."

Grissino looks at Milo, then Cristina and then you. "How many of you regularly go to a newsstand?" he asks.

You shake your heads.

"Wrong, wrong. It's essential to go to newsstands. The first people to understand the mysteries of life, before the doctors and physicists, are the newsagents."

"What about the philosophers?" says Cristina.

"Don't be flippant, my dear young lady, and don't interrupt. So: since you're such poor frequenters of newsstands, I assume none of you know what *Zodiac 3000* is."

"No, I only read *Nathan Never* and *Brendon*," says Milo.

"Wrong, subjects, you're not doing well. You should read more. It comes in handy. It adds ideas to life's standard issue…. Anyway, *Zodiac 3000* is the most popular astrology weekly in Italy."

"Astrology? Why should we read that stuff?" says Milo.

"Ah, the young of today…." Grissino shakes his head. "Even the young of today aren't what they used to be. Pay attention, subjects: some issues of *Zodiac 3000*, December for example, with the predictions for the coming year, have as many as two million readers."

"You're joking," says Cristina, surprised.

"Certainly not," he answers seriously.

"That can't be," you remark. "I've never believed in horoscopes. When I read: 'Taurus: your partner is making you madly jealous,' I think about my grandmother, whose birthday is the twenty-sixth of April, Taurus in other words, who's ninety years old and has been a widow for the last sixteen. If she read it it wouldn't make sense. So this horoscope stuff is a load of rubbish."

"Up to a point, subject. Some horoscopes are pure nonsense and others are very serious. The ballistics of life are very complex, and sometimes the calculation of trajectories is influenced by a series of factors that can be predicted.... It all depends who's doing the horoscope.... In any case, people have an absolute need for this calculation of trajectories, we all need it.... But this isn't the time to talk about that."

"Right," says Milo, losing his patience. "Let's get back to the hundred million. It was fun talking about horoscopes, but now, spit out your idea."

Grissino strokes his beard. "Okay. The first step is very simple: we take out a full-page advertisement in *Zodiac 3000*."

"How much does that cost?" Cristina asks immediately.

"It doesn't matter," answers Grissino. "Besides, it's free."

Then, seeing your astonishment, he explains. "In the sense that if we play our cards right we can get ninety-day payment terms. Ninety days is three months, and in three months we'll have completely erased our tracks."

"Fine," you interrupt, "but I don't understand what we're going to put in this ad."

Grissino beams: "Simple, we put in a good photograph of a lovely lucky charm, along with a nice account number, and then we're in business. We promise our customers the following: order our lucky charm by filling in the coupon and sending us your money, and as soon as your payment has cleared we'll send the lucky charm direct to your home."

There is a moment's silence, then Cristina comments. "Is that it? Seems like bullshit to me."

Grissino gets up from the armchair and leaves the living room.

"See? Now you're the one that's pissed him off," jokes Milo.

"You bet," she retorts irritably. "Does it look like a hundred-million-lire idea to you? To me it looks like bullshit."

Grissino comes back in with a well-known women's magazine in his hand. He comes up to you and, still standing, starts reading. "Amazing enzyme discovered in Austria: consumes sixteen hundred times its own weight in fat."

Then he tosses the magazine onto the poker table and leaves again.

Cristina picks it up and you and Milo pull your chairs up closer to see better. Graphically, it's a perfect advertisement, much like one for a pharmaceutical product, complete with coupon, endorsements from satisfied customers and an interview with an unlikely-looking medical expert on diets. The close is a real gem: "Our enzyme pills are made with natural ingredients, so they cannot be stored in a warehouse for very long. This is why our stocks are limited. To be sure of receiving your supply without delay, send in your order today, using the coupon below." The special enzyme costs an amazing two hundred and thirty-nine thousand lire.

"Unbelievable," says Milo, then he gets up and calls Grissino, who comes back in triumphantly. Cristina, stunned, says apologetically, "Okay, I didn't know cons that big still existed."

Grissino pays no attention. He looks shrewdly at you. "What do you think?"

You equivocate. "Well, I think this shows the idea is valid. But will it work in our specific situation?"

Grissino shakes his head. "God, subjects, it's uphill all the way with you. Are you joking? Are you saying that out of the two million readers of *Zodiac 3000* we won't find two hundred suckers who'll send us half a million each?"

"Half a million for a lucky charm?" Milo breaks in, astonished. "But that's silly money. No one will pay that much."

Grissino drops back into the armchair. "Oh, subjects, how incurably young you are…you just don't get it." He starts again, patiently. "We sell a charm that guarantees love and success: if you want these things you're not going to pay what you pay for a pipe of tobacco. You have to spend a pile of money. Don't forget the first rule of commerce, subjects: you get what you pay for. Consumers automatically link high prices with quality: it's one of the big cons people already have in their minds, and it's up to us to exploit it."

Then he adds, "Do you remember those ladybird magnets for mobile phones? The ones to protect against electro-magnetism?

Well, those ladybirds did practically nothing and yet they sold thirty thousand in Italy alone. Thirty thousand, subjects, *three-zero thousand*. And they went for sixty thousand lire each, not three thousand, otherwise everyone would have seen it was a con."

None of you say anything for a whole minute. Milo is busy re-reading the article about the Austrian enzyme, while Cristina is looking at you so intently you feel uncomfortable, you think she's seen the marks under your collar and you react by doing up the top button of your shirt.

Then Milo breaks the silence. "Okay, uncle, you're right, your idea could work. To sum up: we put an ad in *Zodiac 3000* which says, essentially: the talisman of good fortune, etcetera. Send five hundred thousand lire to the following account, etcetera. Within a few days, as soon as your payment has cleared, it will come direct to your home and you will live happily ever after, like in the fairy tales."

"Precisely, subjects. Any more objections?"

Cristina looks up at him defiantly and says, "Yes."

Grissino is imperturbable. "Let's hear it, my dear young lady."

Cristina looks like she's gathering her thoughts for a moment, then she starts speaking. "Okay, well…Christ, Grissino, this way we're cheating people! How do we square it with what you were saying a while ago? How do we square it with your code of honour?"

Grissino nods gravely and gets up from the armchair again. "It's true, you're right. But people's stupidity is in their DNA. I mean, anyone who, in the year 2000, buys a lucky charm, has the IQ of a lump of rock. He doesn't deserve any respect."

Cristina interrupts him. "Right, but before you were saying the exact opposite, that it's precisely people like that that need protecting."

Grissino loses patience. "Enough. You can't always be doing good. Take the old story of St Martin, who meets a poor man, cuts his cloak in half with his sword and gives half to the poor man. What if he'd met another poor man around the next corner, and another half an hour later? He'd have frozen to death, wouldn't he? They're all fairy tales. Give a man a fish and he'll eat for a day; teach him to fish and he'll eat for a lifetime. Fine, but teach everybody to fish and there'll be no more fish and you'll be the one looking for someone to feed you."

"But that's not true, and anyway what's it got to do with anything?" you say.

Grissino drops back into the armchair and spreads his arms. "Okay, I'm full of contradictions. So what?"

Then his tone softens. "All right, subjects, I'll admit it: I'm just making it up as I go along. It's true: our con will affect the weak, who should be protected against exploitation. That's exactly why I've never put it into practice. It didn't seem right. Do you think it only entered my head just now? Really? Surely you're not that stupid? I certainly don't need your help to set up a little scheme like that. But I do need accomplices who are, so to speak, 'moral.' I need someone to share the responsibility with me."

Grissino stops for a moment, sighs and thumps the arm of the chair with his fist. "And besides, I like the idea of the Big C: sometimes the end has to justify the means...."

He gets to his feet and concludes. "So now you know exactly where we stand. I don't have any other ideas at the moment. So I'll leave it up to you whether we go ahead or pack the whole thing in."

Chapter eight

In which our subjects are dermatologists,
trains, Easter cake, mother-of-pearl caskets and
man getting to grips with technology.

Marketing proverb: Beauty isn't beautiful, what sells is beautiful.

The dermatologist's waiting room exudes bleak sterility: three brown leatherette benches cluster around a small glass table covered with old magazines. Sitting in front of you is a dried-up matron in a warm-up suit. She is holding the hand of a twelve- or thirteen-year-old girl with a face horribly ravaged by acne and an air of long-suffering which ought to attract maximum tact.

Somewhere in the world, a group of men has calculated infant mortality rates between zero and five years; in Italy the rate is six dead for every thousand born, in Zambia it is one hundred and two. Zambia is one of the ten most indebted nations in the world and has the highest percentage of children orphaned by AIDS. In Zambia, the average life expectancy for a human being is forty-one years. In Italy, life expectancy is seventy-eight years. You close the magazine and toss it onto the table as your eyes fall on the only picture, a black and white print of Augusta Taurinorum, then fasten on the dirty white wall.

Just then, a girl in a white blouse comes into the waiting room and murmurs a surname—Cortazza—bringing you back to reality: the mother and the girl with the acne stand up and disappear.

You pick up another magazine, this time about art, and leaf through it slowly until you stop at a caption: "His latest work, *A Man Called Ernesta*, attempts to reaffirm a more secret measure of its inevitability: it no longer covers the paradigmatic argument of its predecessor, *A Man Called Teresa*, but paradoxically displaces the vital act from the symbology of internal friction towards the circle of disquiet, betraying the consequentiality of all possible theoretical propositions."

"Shakespeare, *King Lear*, Act Four, Scene One," you murmur, yawning, then toss the magazine onto the table. You support yourself on the arms of the seat and move the weight from your left buttock to your right. You look wearily at the print of Augusta Taurinorum, then stare into nothingness again.

"Pityriasis rosea," says the dermatologist after a while, switching off the lamp directed at your upper body. Then, pointing at the large red mark between your shoulder and collarbone, he continues in a scientific tone of voice. "This one here, that's the primary lesion, the so-called mother spot. It forms first and grows gradually bigger. In the second phase—as in your case—so-called daughter spots appear: these little spots, normally spread centripetally about the trunk area. On the back, however, the lesions are distributed radially about the spinal column, creating the characteristic Christmas-tree shape."

He is an elderly man with dyed-black hair, glossy as a crow's plumage. He's wearing a huge pair of tortoise-shell glasses. The worrying thing is that he hasn't touched you since you came in; even now, when you're lying on the couch, he continues to keep a certain distance. What's more, his voice betrays no emotion of any kind: it's like listening to a series of voice messages generated by a computer.

You pluck up the courage to ask, "And…is it serious, doctor?"

He purses his lips and goes and sits at the desk. He leans down, slowly opens a drawer and pulls out a prescription pad; then, in slow motion, he removes the cap from a fat fountain pen. Finally, his flat voice answers, "*Pityriasis rosea* Gibert is a dermatosis. Characterized by scaly lesions."

He replaces the cap on the fountain pen and pauses. "In truth, not much is known about it," he sighs.

You sit on the couch, legs dangling, and give the dermatologist a glance of hatred blended with fear. "Yes, I understand, doctor," you say, trying not to show your unease, "but is it serious?"

He emits another series of voice messages. "It can appear at any age, but it is most common in the young. Some attempts to isolate the infective agent have led to the hypothesis that the causal factor is viral. Others classify it among the psychosomatic dermatoses, though it is called a pityriasis because of its resemblance to the true pityriases, which are fungal conditions. In truth, even today the causes are not known."

Another pause.

"Yes, I understand, doctor," you say, losing patience, "but is it serious?"

At that moment the telephone rings and he picks up the receiver placidly. "Yes, dear…no…yes…I've got a patient with me… Yes, dear, of course…. Eight o'clock is fine…. Yes, dear, of course…. No need to worry…. Bye, yes, bye…. Yes, dear, of course…. Bye, yes, bye."

The moment he hangs up you almost shout, "So, doctor, is it serious?"

He looks at you complacently. "The condition will run its course without intervention."

"AND WHAT THE HELL DOES THAT MEAN?" you yell, enraged, getting up from the couch and stepping up to the desk. He pushes his chair back hastily, opens his eyes wide and looks at you severely, shocked by your tone. "The condition will run its course without intervention, which is to say that *pityriasis rosea*, after a period of spreading, tends to cure itself spontaneously. Generally within four to five weeks, without needing treatment."

You look at him incredulously. "You mean it's harmless?"

"That's right," he agrees. "It's not irritating, it doesn't give rise to itching, it isn't contagious. It doesn't leave marks or scars, unless you expose it to sunlight—by the way, don't."

"In short, it doesn't do anything?" you ask happily.

"That's right," he answers. "It will go away just as it came."

Then, starting to write, he goes on. "I'll just prescribe an ointment to use instead of soap. You'll see, in a matter of weeks there'll be no sign of it."

Oh for goodness' sake, now you'd really like to hug and kiss this fleshly robot, you'd like to kiss his dyed hair, throw him in the air shouting hip hip hooray, you'd like to share a bottle with him at the bar downstairs and celebrate all night long, you'd even like to pay him with a good cheque instead of the one you're about to give him.

The Turin–Milan intercity is rattling along the tracks, and meadows and towns and rice fields and roads and houses appear and disappear in the window. Stretches of open countryside alternate with stretches where the vegetation becomes denser, completely blocking your view until the single track you're travelling along is suddenly flanked by a second, then a third, and suddenly the vegetation disappears and the train is flying towards a little station, passing it, and then, with a loud bang, it's back in the middle of the countryside, on a single track, and in the distance you can see pylons and street lights and groups of houses surmounted by the bell towers of churches and the cranes of construction sites.

Milo is dozing as the train comes alongside a siding and passes a long column of red goods wagons, sitting there as if they have been forgotten for years. You think about the events of the last week, which you have spent setting Operation Zodiac 3000 in motion. You remember how meticulously Grissino worked out the steps that needed to be taken, the speed with which he handed out roles and allocated tasks to everyone. You revisit yourself sitting at the poker table at Grissino's place in the middle of the night, checking out the competition with Milo and Cristina by leafing through an entire year's worth of astrology magazines, page by page. You remember your unease as you realized how thoroughly the idea of a lucky charm had been exploited, and then you see your enthusiasm at Grissino's suggestion that you create a magic powder instead. You remember Cristina standing up and ecstatically embracing Grissino and then Milo and then, with a euphoria that seems excessive, you. You see yourselves arguing excitedly, ballpoint pens in hand and pads of paper on the table, copying ideas from the magazines and writing notes and reminders: Milo inventing the "Pizzonic Rite" and the character of the "Wizard Rembrandt," Grissino getting exasperated with each idea, you and Cristina inventing the magical properties to be attributed to a powder and reading them out loud, happy as children in a cake shop. "A pinch may be sprinkled on your most precious possessions, or on your beloved's clothing; it may be poured into a goblet to read the future, passed through the fingers to restore your serenity, or carried about the person in a magic pouch..." and you laugh and Grissino and Milo clap and there's enthusiasm and complicity and you feel good, and happy, and it really is amazing how dazzling and miraculous it is, this reality ticking away from one second to the next.

Among the tasks that have fallen to you and Milo is that of finding a container in which to place the lucky powder, so that Cristina can take care of photographing the whole thing. Milo immediately thinks of a small wooden casket he's seen a thousand times at his grandmother's home in Novara, covered in dust on a side table in the living room, and since the van is at the mechanic's to check out another radiator leak, here you are on the Turin–Milan intercity in a six-person compartment.

You're facing the front of the train, you by the window and Milo in the centre seat; opposite you is a kind-looking old dear staring calmly out of the window, while the other three places are occupied by a coloured man, opposite Milo, and two women. The fact that the women are dressed very scantily, even at two o'clock in the afternoon, and that the man is wearing a brand new shell suit, a gold watch and designer glasses makes you think, reflexively, that he is their pimp.

When the train goes past a long row of industrial warehouses you decide to get up and go into the corridor to smoke a cigarette. You pass a lady sitting on her suitcase and reading a romance novel by Liala which might be called *The Red Bridle*—it's hard to tell, because her hand is over part of the cover—then reach the end of the carriage and light a cigarette as you lean against the door of the toilet. Beside you, a man in his forties, his face tense, is gesticulating with his mobile phone to his ear. "...No, dear, I'm sorry," you hear him say, "I've already told you: I'm running late and I still have another appointment. I won't be home before eleven tonight, maybe midnight.... Yes.... I'm sorry too. Say hello to the kids. Bye.... Yes.... Bye.... Yes.... Bye.... Bye."

He closes the lid, then opens it again and dials another number. His expression relaxes. "Hi, honey, I've got a couple of hours free, we could have dinner in this nice little place...."

Just then, three identical young guys in black heavy-metal tee-shirts and backpacks emerge through the connecting door, and one of them asks you in a low voice whether the ticket inspector has gone through and you nod yes, even though it's not true, then you put out your cigarette and go back to the compartment. As you take your seat, you happen to look at one of the women's thighs (she's quite fat), just as she starts talking to the other one in an unfamiliar language, almost shouting; the man in the shell suit gestures to them to lower their voices and they both obey instantly. Then he gets out a mobile phone, starts punching buttons and waits, but in the end he seems dissatisfied and pulls an electronic organizer out of a pocket in his suit. With his right hand he opens the organizer and starts using his thumb to search, while dialling a number on the mobile with his left, and you are very impressed and do several rounds on your mental exercise bike: this man, who grew up—you guess—in some Nigerian shanty town, arrives in Europe somehow, finds a way to survive, but above all else he masters technology, he consumes electronics with more ease than educated people, and so you think "up with technology," which will bring to the world a universal fellowship regardless of race, creed or colour.

Just then, one of the women stands up and gets a blue plastic shopping bag down from the luggage rack. Then she sits back down on the edge of her seat, so as to get as close as possible to the two opposite, who do the same, sliding their backsides as far forwards as possible. The woman places the plastic bag on her knees and rolls down the sides to open it: a big tangle of spaghetti with tomato sauce appears, overcooked and greasy-looking, and the three of them, having taken out paper handkerchiefs, start eating with their hands, straight out of the plastic bag. The old dear sitting opposite you smiles, half amused and half embarrassed.

Just then, Milo wakes up. He glances at the three and is almost unable to tear his eyes away from them, then puts his head close to yours and whispers, "What's going on? Are we on 'Candid Camera: Bingo Bongo on the Train'—or have manners gone out of fashion recently?" and sniggers.

You'd like to tell him about the electronic organizer and all that: you're a bit disappointed and pretend to be uninterested, at least until one of the women gets out a phone card and uses the edge to pick her incisors, leaving you open-mouthed and thinking that if you were one of those journalists with a daily column, well, tomorrow's piece would be all wrapped up.

"How sweet of you to come and see me." Milo's grandmother smiles happily at you, having shown you into a sunny living room in which every piece of furniture is covered with ornaments. Her hair is grey and fine, held close to her head with two hairgrips; she's wearing a light cotton dress with a printed blue and white pattern.

"Sit here at the table and give me a minute," she continues. "I'll bring you some dessert: I'm sure you're hungry."

Milo spreads his arms and winks as if to say, "What did I tell you?" then his expression changes and he whispers, "I forgot to say: whatever you do, don't mention Uncle Grissino's name."

You shrug and just then Milo's grandmother comes back in, a little unsteadily, balancing in her hands a pewter tray with what's left of a dove-shaped Easter cake. "There, Milo," she says in her high-pitched voice. "This morning, after you called to say you were coming to see me, I went out and bought a nice cake, specially for you."

Then, noticing your puzzled expressions—there's not much

more than the head of the dove on the dish—she adds, "Well, I tried a bit. Just to be sure it was good."

"Help yourselves," she says, putting the tray down on the table. "I'll get some wine."

She hasn't brought plates or a knife, but Milo doesn't seem surprised: he breaks the head in two with his hands and starts biting into his part as he offers you the other half.

"What is this?" you ask, accepting it. "Are we on 'Candid Camera: Bingo Bongo' at Grandma's?"

Milo smiles as his grandmother comes back in with another pewter tray, this time with a bottle of Bonarda and three small glasses. She places the tray on the table and looks at it as if she made it herself, uncorks the bottle in a practiced manner and pours the wine, filling her glass to the rim and yours half full. She raises her glass and, eyes shining with happiness, says, "Cheers!"

You drink a toast and chat for a while, exhausting the topics of friends and relations, after which Milo changes the subject to the attractiveness of the house and ornaments, until he asks point blank, "What about the casket, granny? Whatever became of that little wood and mother-of-pearl casket, the one you got on your Egyptian cruise? I don't see it anywhere."

She smiles secretively, refills her glass and puts the bottle as far away from you as possible. "Go easy on the wine," she says. "Drink as little as possible, because if I have to go without, it ruins my digestion."

Then she shuffles in her seat. "The casket, eh? The one I bought in 1981, with granddad, during our Egyptian cruise?"

"That's the one," confirms Milo.

"Ah, what a wonderful holiday that was," she says, lifting the glass to her lips.

This is the cue for some two hours of illuminating and detailed anecdotes about the cruise—from the cabin furnishings to the sailors' uniforms, including descriptions of every single fellow traveller. Your frustration is made worse by the fact that Milo's grandmother doesn't let you smoke and finishes the whole bottle of wine without offering you a single glass. Torture. Which is rewarded eventually, however, when the grandmother fetches a tissue-wrapped package from a drawer and unwraps it on the table, revealing a gorgeous wooden casket, the inside lined with red velvet and the lid inlaid with tiny pieces of mother-of-pearl.

Two days later you're standing at the window of the launderette below Grissino's apartment, thinking about Cristina. You move aside to let in a man with a huge green cuddly crocodile. Sitting inside is a magnificent Slav girl, her expression simultaneously proud, sad and distant. Standing in front of the dryer which is spinning your clothes, a very short man with glasses is talking to a girl whose arms are much shorter than they ought to be. Opposite you, right on the kerb, a young girl in a mini skirt is talking to a young man straddling a scooter. He's saying, "I'll give you a lift on my scooter if you like" and then, "Shall I take you?" and then, "Come on, get on, I'll give you a lift." She is answering, "No thanks" and then, "No" and then, "No, really." He leaves, just missing an enormous Japanese four-wheel-drive with the spare tyre attached to the rear door. On the wheel cover it says, "APPALOOSAS: RIDE WITH PRIDE." On the wall someone has written "WE'RE THE SHARKS, YOU'RE THE PIGS" with a marker pen, along with the initials N.A.D.S. An old lady with mad-looking eyes goes by. She stops in front of you, bares her lipstick-stained teeth, says, "You should really behave a bit better," and goes away. A dark-skinned little girl with a pouting lower lip and budding breasts under her sweater goes by, alone. A woman in her sixties goes by, wearing a black T-shirt with a picture of Roberto Baggio's face printed on it. An old man goes by. He spits on the ground, then pulls a crumpled wad of ten-thousand-lire notes out of his pocket, extracts a filthy handkerchief from among them and blows his nose with it. A woman goes by in a burgundy track suit and high-heeled shoes. A sheep wanders by; on second glance it turns out to be a dog. Two drivers are arguing furiously, shouting at each other. A man is taking pictures of the sky. Why do we exist?

Milo opens the door to Grissino's apartment. He's white as a sheet and has a big bruise under his left cheekbone.

"How did it happen?" you ask as you go in.

"The banana conga," he says laconically, shutting the door behind you.

"What do you mean?"

Milo points at Cristina, who's sitting on the white sofa munching potato chips from a paper bag, then rubs his cheek. "I mean: struck full in the face by a hardcover copy of Corto Maltese's *Banana Conga*, that's what."

Cristina turns and looks at him witheringly.

"Hi, Vittorio," she says, more seriously.

"Hi," you reply. "Where's Grissino?"

"In the kitchen," says Milo. "He's made an inhaler for his sinusitis."

You cross the living room and stop on the threshold of the kitchen. Grissino is sitting at the table, with a pink towel completely covering his head and his face over a steaming pan. The scent of eucalyptus fills the air. You try saying hello, but he doesn't answer: you can hear him breathing deeply in and out. So you go back into the living room; Cristina has switched on the TV and Milo is sitting at the poker table.

"How are we doing for joints?" you ask, sitting down next to him.

"I was supposed to see my dealer today," he says, rubbing his eyes, "but when I called him he said he couldn't. His aunt died."

"So what do we do?"

Milo shrugs. "I'll call him later and see if they've buried her."

"Ah."

You automatically turn to the TV. Cristina is frantically changing channels, unable to stay on one programme for more than a few seconds.

"She's in a bad mood," murmurs Milo. "The Filipinos who live over her place woke her up at six o'clock this morning with music at top volume. And not just any music either, Neapolitan songs remixed and sung in Filipino."

"Ah," you say again.

Just then the doorbell rings and you feel something like anxiety as Milo gets up and calmly opens the door without even asking who it is. The carrier for some courier company appears with a big package in his hands.

"Editorial Services International?" he asks Milo, peering inside in puzzlement.

"Yes, of course," he answers. "Where do I sign?"

The carrier offers Milo a pen and points to a space at the bottom of a form, then hands him the package and disappears. Milo shuts the door and puts the package in the corner, along with two or three other smaller parcels you haven't noticed before.

"What's that stuff?" you ask.

Milo rejoins you at the table.

"You remember those envelopes we stuffed the first time we came here? Well, what's happened, as far as I can make out, is that Grissino sent them to a bunch of cosmetics companies, asking for samples. To advertise them in women's magazines for free. To take pictures and put them on those pages packed with products with captions like 'new this spring,' stuff like that."

"And they fall for it, like mugs? No one ever calls to check up?"

"I don't know," says Milo, "but that's the third courier today."

Grissino comes into the living room with the pink towel rolled up over his shoulder and his usual self-satisfied smile. "It's not always like that, unfortunately," he says. "It's just that right now it's 'new hair and body products month,'" and he stresses "new hair and body" ironically. He bends down to pick up the most recent package and puts it on the poker table as Cristina gets up and comes over, curious to see what's in it. Grissino opens the package and takes out a letter, which he ignores, and then puts five or six items of shampoo, soap and bath foam on the table. He puts them back in the box in no particular order and puts it back on the ground.

"Well," he says as Cristina sits down, "it's time to review the situation."

He rests his palms on the table and pauses. "I'll start...and I'll be very brief. The part we have called 'bureaucratic' is in place. We have bought a page of advertising in *Zodiac 3000* and we have an account number."

"All in whose name?" asks Cristina diffidently.

"In the name of a helpful individual with no criminal record, who is lucky enough to have a VAT number and who will be hard to reach in the immediate future," answers Grissino imperturbably.

"And who's that?" she insists.

"That need not concern us at all, my dear young lady," he answers, in a tone that brooks no discussion. "What I want to know from you, though, is this: are we on schedule? How are we doing with the powder and the casket?"

"Casket acquired, sir," you answer facetiously. "Sparkling powder also acquired: half a kilo of iron filings sprayed with metallic blue varnish, sir. Used: one canister automobile retouching spray."

"Good result, captain?" he asks.

"Excellent result, sir, but nothing compared with the photograph of the casket full of powder. Cristina's work, needless to say."

At this point Cristina unfolds a colour proof showing the photograph of the casket and the text, laid out. Grissino checks it unhurriedly, reading and re-reading every single word; after a few minutes passed in devout silence, he asks, "Who did this layout?"

"A highly prestigious nineteen-year-old graphic artist, sir," you answer, "acquired by me and Milo by means of an advertisement on the notice board at the Design Institute. And induced to work with the promise of lucrative jobs in the future, sir."

Grissino smiles, satisfied. "My compliments. You've done well. Really. And are we ready with the artwork too?"

"No," says Cristina. "We just needed the official account number, but now we've got it we're in business. Tomorrow we can send everything to *Zodiac 3000*. We're a bit late, but we should be able to release our advertisement in the mid-March issue."

"Good," says Grissino, satisfied. "The plan is, by early April, exactly two weeks after it appears at the newsagents', we disappear with the money we've received, regardless of how much we've collected by then."

"What?" protests Milo. "That way we risk losing all the money that might come in afterwards."

"Remember James Addison Reavis, nephew, and the first rule

of the gambler: don't be greedy, and disappear as soon as you've filled the tank. Besides, if the people who come after us find some money in the account, they'll think we're going to turn up again to claim it—and that'll give us months. Make sense?"

You and Milo indicate that it doesn't, while Cristina says to Grissino, "I still have one small question about the processing of the pictures. Could we talk in private?"

"Of course," he answers. "Will everyone please not listen?"

Chapter nine

*In which our subjects are an alchemist, the
contradictions of existence, induced alcoholic
states, camels, pelicans and advertisements.*

Somewhere in the world, gentle readers, a man has done some
sums: if we reduced the entire population of the world to a village
with a hundred inhabitants, keeping the proportions intact, the result
would be, more or less, as follows:

The village would have:

8 Africans.

14 Americans.

21 Europeans.

57 Asians.

Of these:

48 would be male.

52 would be female.

Of these:

30 would be white.

70 would not be white.

Of these:

30 would be Christians.

70 would not be Christians.

Of these:

89 would be heterosexual.

11 would be homosexual.

Of these:

6 would own 59 percent of the entire wealth of the village.

80 would live in hovels.

70 would be totally illiterate.

50 would be malnourished.

1 would be near death.

1 would be near birth.

10 would be experiencing war or prison or torture.

25 would have food in the refrigerator, a toilet and a bed.

8 would have savings in the bank.

1 would have a higher education. Just one, gentle readers.

"Take Faust, for example: it doesn't make sense. The moment you sell your soul, you know it's immortal, so what do you care about earthly life? You'd tell Mephistopheles to get lost, and thank him for finally giving you some certainty."

Cristina strokes your cheek with her hand and says, "Vittorio, you're all mixed up," and smiles at you kindly.

You're reaching the end of your dinner at Gaspare's, behind the central market. Milo got up half an hour ago and—having checked that you have two crash helmets as usual—asked you to take Cristina home. You agreed and he gave her a quick kiss on the cheek, said mysteriously that he had stuff to do, and vanished.

Gaspare is preparing another of his liver-destroying alchemical concoctions: limoncello plus "Gaspare blue" plus "Prussian fury." He brings to the table two vodka glasses in which the liqueurs have settled in layers without mixing: yellow at the bottom, red in the middle, then blue. You're sure that somewhere—probably in the cellar—Gaspare has a secret laboratory, full of alembics, where he studies the Philosopher's Stone, the one that turns base metals into gold, and the Ultimate Potion, the one that makes you fall into a trance at the first sip.

You empty the glass in one gulp, and after a few seconds your lips, mouth, throat and stomach simultaneously catch fire. You grimace with pain and start talking again. "Take Adam and Eve and the business with the apple and original sin. The story doesn't hold water. What original sin? No legal system makes you pay for other people's crimes. Sorry, in some countries parents have to pay for the crimes of under-age children. I mean, if anyone's to blame for the apple business it's God himself. You see, even that story doesn't hold water, it leaks like a sieve."

"I don't know about such things, I never was much good in catechism," says Cristina jokingly.

You smile at her. "But they're important. Take hell, for example, eternal damnation. Come off it: if I were God I wouldn't even be able to imagine hell, seems to me only a bastard could. Does that mean I'm better than God?"

Cristina drains her glass in one gulp, winces, goes red and looks at you. Her eyes are bright as buttons.

You go on. "The truth is, Cristina, all these stories contradict each other and don't hold water. Actually, the whole world was designed so that everything would contradict everything and nothing would hold water...and not just that...it was designed so that life itself would teach everyone different things, often contradictory, and all of them somehow valid."

Cristina shakes her head. "You've lost me, Vittorio."

"Me too, come to that," you answer. "I'm talking gibberish. It's all thanks to Gaspare's potions."

Cristina nods.

"Do you want to go home?" you ask her.

She shakes her head. "What for? God knows when Milo will get back. No, I'd like to cruise around for a while, what do you say?"

"Okay," you answer. "Fine by me."

You look into each other's eyes for a few seconds, without looking away, until you look down at your plate. You'd like to ask her how things are with Milo, how come they're always arguing, and for a moment you even flirt with the idea of asking her if she knows he's cheated on her, but you decide not to play such a rotten trick: Cristina is so lovely, and she's here with you, so just enjoy it, you tell yourself, try to play it a bit straighter this time round. So you look up again. "You know, I'd like to see a play in which the characters talk to each other about the author who created them...."

"What's that got to do with anything?" Cristina interrupts, smiling. "It's amazing how you always manage to come up with something completely unconnected."

"No," you say seriously. "What I say is always connected: basically, while we're tying ourselves up in knots trying to understand whether we're on earth for no reason or whether we were created by some superior being, I want to be sure that, well, it seems only right that that fucking superior being should tie itself into knots about what created *it,* no?"

An hour later you're jammed into a bar on the banks of the Po, floating in the grey area between religious transcendence and alcohol poisoning. Your brain has begun to show clear signs of imbalance, the most obvious of which is that you keep thinking you're a protagonist in a video game called *PlayTorino2000.*

This bar is at the third level of the game, in which the goal is to find Cristina and go home. But first you have to find your way through the Harmless Monsters and reach the Moustachioed Monster sitting at the cash register. You have to give him ten thousand lire and get a receipt in return; armed with this you make your way to the Circle of the Damned and, once you've caught the eye of the Wizard Barman, you request some Vital Fluid, which is worth two lives. At this level you have to be careful not to make mistakes that might have you ejected from the game, such as giving counterfeit money to the Moustachioed Monster or bumping too hard into someone in the Circle of the Damned. If this happens, two Gorilla Warriors appear instantly and, in the best case, you go back to the previous level; in the worst, you end up in another scenario, a white one with a red cross.

Once you've managed to obtain some Vital Fluid, you lean up against the wall behind the Circle of the Damned, and a Monster of Tedium promptly appears. The most skilful players usually avoid this with a "Hi, how's it going?" and a swift retreat in the other direction, but you're not quick enough, so you furiously click *Select* + *Esc*, yet the Monster of Tedium doesn't go away. You have to be careful: you're in *PlayTorino2000*, and even in expert mode it proves to be a game with plenty of nasty surprises.

You attempt flight, zig-zagging suddenly through the Circle of the Damned, trying not to spill any Vital Fluid, and go upstairs to the next level. Usually there's a Gorilla Warrior at the bottom of the stairs saying nothing but "Private, Private," but this time you're lucky and the stairs are empty. At the top, though, there's a surprise (you should have expected it), and you end up trapped in the quicksands of the Swamp of the Stoned. You play a desperate card: you swallow all of the Vital Fluid and, with a single bound (*Select* + *w*), you make it to the emergency stairs. From there, if you've been paying attention—or, as in your case, if you've checked the right websites for the cheats—you reach a secret door and fall directly into the fourth scenario, in which a High Priest of Music is holding a multitude of Flailing Monsters under a spell.

Every time you reach' this level of the game you think you're meant to tear the High Priest of Music to pieces, but your task is actually to join the Flailing Monsters, smile and pretend you're madly in love with the music. But this time you can't remember which keys to press. You try *Select* + *z* and *Control* + *k* in vain; nothing doing, so you click *Select* + *Quit* simultaneously, but you still can't escape the situation. Besides, you've been distracted and a Monster of Tedium comes up and offers you an insidious Bonus Fluid. You manage to turn it down—it might be a Non-Alcoholic Poison—but he holds you back for at least a minute before you can escape, so you lose three lives: you can feel yourself becoming faint. The moment you notice this, you run breathlessly back the way you came, all the way back to the Moustachioed Monster, and obtain more Vital Fluid.

The Wizard Barmen do the right thing almost immediately— the trick is to wave the receipt practically under their noses—so you drink all the liquid in a few gulps. Strangely, you don't feel your powers returning; on the contrary, you feel their absence even more strongly. So you light a cigarette, click *Select* + *Pause* simultaneously and stop everything. Your head's spinning and you need to be very careful: you know that *PlayTorino2000*'s response to vomiting is unbending: back five levels.

But suddenly you meet Cristina, who kisses you very close to your mouth and whispers "take me home," opening up a whole new level that holds no nasty surprises in store, the one in which you walk quickly between the Indifferent and the Sedated, you reach the Two-Wheeled Vehicle, you put on the Combat Helmets, you leave and you have to stay upright on the Two-Wheeled Vehicle while respecting the rule of the road which says: green light = proceed; yellow light = proceed; red light = proceed with care. And as you arrive at another scenario, below Milo's place, Cristina strokes your cheek and you forget the video game for a moment and remember what Milo has to say on this subject: he says if a woman strokes your cheek it means she wants to fuck you. A strange theory; in any case you swiftly press *Select + Save* to save this last scenario before you quit, to save it for tomorrow, to take up the game *exactly where you left off.*

Now, gentle readers, in my present condition—even though at this precise moment I feel like a Brazilian striker: unstoppable—it doesn't occur to me for one moment not to go home, as suggested by Cristina before she disappears inside her front door. What I'm dreaming of, I swear, is my bed; and thirteen hours of sleep. But fate often keeps unexpected tricks up its sleeve for us human beings, and we human beings often help fate in various ways, for example by putting off refuelling a near-empty Vespa for days.

When the fuel runs out you're on a side street off Via Po, almost at Piazza Vittorio. You hurl a few choice terms of abuse at yourself, then you resign yourself to leaving the thing there and proceed on foot towards the Murazzi. As you walk you see a young street vendor about twenty metres away, with the usual arsenal of lighters, Brazilian bracelets and paper handkerchiefs. He looks slightly familiar, but strangely, instead of approaching you to try to sell you something he looks at you anxiously and crosses to the other side of the street. It takes you a while to get his face in focus: but of course, it's Rachid, a young

Moroccan with a conjurer's skill in playing with coins, especially good at making five hundreds and thousands disappear into his pockets.

"How's it going, Rachid? Haven't seen you for months," you slur in party mood, standing in his way. "I even asked Mohammed and his brother about you, but they said you'd gone back to Morocco."

Rachid tries to remember who you are, among the thousand faces of his customers, then sighs, "Yes, I go back to Morocco, but I not succeed."

You look at him in surprise. "What do you mean, 'not succeed'?"

He shakes his head. "I been in Italy one year and two months. Everybody's friend, good business. After, I go back to Morocco and buy six camels, but I not succeed."

You laugh. "What's this rubbish you're telling me? Camels? You're pulling my leg."

"No," he says, all seriousness. "I not pull your leg. I buy six camels with all I earn in Italy. But they cheat me: camels weak. For six months no rain in Morocco, so camels tired and thin and I sell. Sell for half I paid. I not succeed. I come back to Italy."

You look at him suspiciously. "Are you joking? You bought some camels? Is that how it works: a guy comes to Italy, spends fourteen hours a day selling lighters to make a few lire, then goes back to Morocco and buys some camels? What is this, some kind of Moroccan joke? Are you making fun of me?"

"No," he repeats, eyes wide open. "I not make fun. I buy six camels and they cheat me: camels weak. For six months no rain in Morocco. No rain. So I sell camels for half I paid. I not succeed. I come back to Italy."

You look at him like you expect him to burst out laughing any moment, but he doesn't bat an eye, so you take out a five-thousand-lire note and give it to him. He puts it in his pocket and gives you four lighters.

"Thank you, my friend," he says.

"Bye, Rachid," you say uncertainly, and you look hard at him again, wondering whether what you've just heard is a massive wind-up or a tragedy. Maybe he notices, because he shrugs and adds, "Crazy animals, camels." Then he disappears into the darkness.

From Piazza Vittorio, of course, you descend to the Murazzi, looking for someone to give you a lift home. You bump into Giuly, magical Giuly, whose eyes gleam wolfishly as he tells you about a drunken Japanese who screwed a pelican, the symbol of the island, in the port of Mykonos; then you meet Eugenia, magical Eugenia, whose eyes gleam wolfishly as she tells you she's furious because her fiancé says he's finally "found his way in life," decided be a squatter and gone to live in Hamburg. She went to join him in Germany and they had an argument. "Christ, Vittorio, the place was filthy, disgusting. I can get used to anything, but how disgusting is a place where you can't even take a shower? So in the end I left. I don't get it: two thirds of the world will do anything to escape from their shanty towns and I have to be engaged to someone who wants to go live in one."

Immediately afterwards you come across someone who's certainly got wheels, viz. Antonio, but he's with his fiancée Angela, who—far from being angelic—is notorious for her obnoxious personality. Your mental state, however, and above all the fact that you're on foot, means you can't be choosy, so you explain that your Vespa has run out of fuel—that's what you always say: it ran out of fuel, but wasn't it you, you idiot, who forgot to fill it up? No, *it ran out*, the silly thing—and Antonio says, "No problem, we'll give you a lift, but let's have another drink first."

So you have another drink and you talk only to Antonio, leaving Angela out of it, and that's your first mistake and you're aware of it but you don't think it's important, and she starts looking at you with hatred and looking daggers at Antonio, while he, half drunk, is whispering admiring comments about the barmaid into your ear (she has breasts like a yacht's fenders), and that's your second serious mistake and Angela notices. She raises her clenched fists. She's furious and she wants to leave and says so, and says it again, and since you pretend to ignore her she finally grabs Antonio by the hair and pulls it and gives the order "we're leaving," and he hits her, gently, and you say "Sure, let's go, it's getting late" (you jerk, since you ought really to call a cab or look for someone else). So you go back up towards Piazza Vittorio and Angela's abusing him, "you lousy piece of shit, shove it up your ass," and he's shrugging it off and saying "Leave me alone, leave me alone" like a mantra, and she blows up and kicks him in the backside, so he turns round and hits her again, this time hard, and she starts flailing her arms and legs and somehow or other she makes contact and you try to calm them down, saying "Take it easy, take it easy," like it's going to do any good, and you pull Antonio out of the way and try to get between them.

Suddenly, and fortunately, she changes her tune completely: she bursts into tears, so you try to comfort her while asking yourself what you've done to deserve this, for Christ's sake. You comfort Angela and gradually you start walking again, and by the time you reach Antonio's Panda, which is parked near Bar Flora, she's calmed down, or so it seems, and she's not crying any more, she just looks furious. Antonio opens the door and makes another mistake: he orders her peremptorily to "Get in!" and she, just because of his tone, reacts and starts screaming, "I'm not going home with you, you filthy bastardshitsonofabitch!" and you raise your eyes to heaven and start thinking it might be better to leave, but Antonio takes Angela by the waist and tries to throw her into the car by force, and she goes berserk and starts punching and kicking and, most of all, screaming like a stuck pig "FUCK OFF! FUCK OFF YOU LOUSY PIECE OF SHIT!" and you don't know what to do, whether to go home or help him get her into the car, but you're too drunk to make a decision and they're still screaming at each other "YOU WHORE! GET IN, BITCH!" "GET YOUR HANDS OFF ME, YOU SONOFABITCH! LEAVE ME ALONE!" and you're looking around, worried, when she starts screaming at the top of her voice, "HELP! THEY'RE RAPING ME!" and your eyes open wide and you say to yourself, "What does she mean, they're raping me? He's raping me, maybe. What the fuck have I got to do with it?" and you try to cover her mouth and she bites you and starts screaming again, even louder, "HELP! RAPE! RAPE!" and people start running over, the usual group of four idiots who tell you to "Leave the girl alone" in policeman-like tones, so you say "By all means, feel free to take her home yourselves," and they begin to understand and smile and now you use all your eloquence to explain the situation and by now she's calmed down, she apologizes, she didn't mean to make such a fuss, and soon it's all been cleared up and the four disappear in their fake leather bomber jackets—hope they rot in hell too.

At last you're in the Panda and you're on the way home, with Angela sitting quietly in the back and Antonio driving like nothing has happened, and just when you think it's all over you feel a draught by your left ear and you see Angela's leg stretched out in a great kick which smashes the rear-view mirror, at which point Antonio stops the car in the middle of the road, puts on the handbrake, turns round and starts raining blows on her face and she fights back with kicks and scratches and bites and more top-volume screams, "HELP! RAPE! RAPE!" and you hastily open the door, get out and run away as fast as your legs can carry you, wondering at the kind of people allowed out on the streets.

The days trickle away fast, with Cristina in Milan visiting her parents and you and Milo given over to your usual solitary night-time partying, until this fine afternoon with its warm sun and its fresh, sparkling mountain air.

You and Milo have spent the last few hours sitting on a stone bench by the Po, on the deserted Murazzi, betting on the times of the canoeists gliding rapidly across the still water. The round of betting, with stakes never higher than fifty lire, has ended with a net loss to Milo of twenty lire, which shows that our luck was pretty well balanced.

After a while you get bored and Milo, unusually for him, starts talking about Cristina, saying she's changed recently, she's become intolerant of everything and they're always arguing and their relationship is getting difficult. You don't really know how to take this, and in fact your expression is quite unnatural as you say, "It's normal, Milo, men and women can only understand each other fleetingly."

He smiles in agreement and looks over at one of the infrequent passers by, a woman in her thirties, pretty, wearing a lightweight lemon-yellow dress.

"Hey, but you must be a mirage," he says to her as she goes by. "Where did you spring from? Has someone forgotten to seal the book of fairy tales and let you escape?"

The woman speeds up, ignoring you, as you look disapprovingly at Milo. He looks down at the ground—the area around the bench is covered with pistachio shells—then asks out of the blue, "Do you know why there's no male equivalent for the word nymphomaniac?"

"Why?"

"Simple. Actually there is a word: male nymphomania is called satyriasis. But it's not used much because a hundred per cent of men suffer from it. Sexually, we're all basically clinical cases."

"I see where you're heading. You're going to tell me a man can cheat on a woman because it's a natural urge for him, whereas if a woman cheats on a man she's a whore."

"No," he replies. "I'm only saying the first part: monogamy is hard work for men."

Just then a man in a checked shirt goes past your bench, on his way to the riverbank. On one side he's holding a blond child by the hand, on the other an enormous baker's sack.

"Help me out here," you say. "If you mean that men always want to fuck, that's no big news. A few evenings back, someone was telling me that last summer in Mykonos some half-drunk Japanese guy went and screwed one of the pelicans in the port..."

"But that's disgusting," he breaks in. "A pelican? How's it possible?"

"I don't know. I don't think the pelican enjoyed it. It died."

Milo is silent and thoughtful. Then he says: "Strange things sure do happen in this world."

"And how," you agree. "This morning I read that Salvador Dalí used to work at Disney when he was young."

"And?"

"Well, I can't really imagine him drawing Gus Goose and Grandma Duck."

Milo smiles and looks at the blond boy.

"Are you sure that's not just made up?" he asks.

"It's in today's paper, with a bunch of photographs."

"You're certainly well informed," he says ironically.

"Oh, you'd be surprised how much I know. I keep abreast of everything."

The man with the checked shirt puts down the sack and, crouching down, opens it, pulls out whole loaves of stale bread and puts them down on the pavement. He gets up again and breaks one up, crushing it several times under the heel of his shoe, then gathers up the pieces and throws them into the water near a large young goose. In less than a minute there's a flock of around twenty birds by the bank—geese, ducks and gulls—filling the air with their strident calls. The man with the checked shirt goes through a whole routine, and the little boy copies him, but he isn't strong enough to break the loaves up with his feet: having jumped up and down on them, he collects them up and throws them into the water practically whole, great huge crusts of bread which occasionally hit a goose or a duck with enough force to make it fly into the air in fright.

You and Milo watch the scene in silence until, after ten minutes or so, the man and the boy run out of bread and leave.

"Any word from Grissino?" you ask then.

Milo watches a gull fly up into the air and completely changes the subject. "You know, the other day I met a guy who told me that each of us has three guardian angels."

Your magico-animistic demons promptly take up their posts on the stone bench.

"I don't see what that's got to do with anything," you answer, unmoved. "Anyway, I've known it for ages. What can you tell me about your three?"

"I don't know," says Milo. "I haven't given my hypothetical three angels much thought. But a few things have occurred to me."

"Such as?

"Well, in a football match, can you imagine the chaos caused by sixty-six angels from two teams? Add in the referee's three and you get precisely sixty-nine angels. Sixty-nine: an honest-to-goodness orgy of angels."

You shake your head. "Oh, but you're obsessed. Either you're not getting any from Cristina or you're using some kind of aphrodisiac instead of your usual drugs."

You stare at him in the hope of unsettling him.

"By the way," he replies hurriedly instead. "I have to leave you soon. I need to do some business with the bearded one."

"Oh," you say, disappointed. "And who might that be? Another dealer?"

"Naah, Vittorio," says Milo, flapping at the air in front of his face as if swatting a fly. "Dealer is a word I don't like. It sounds so negative. Let's say he does business, in a spirit of equality and solidarity, with Colombia, his speciality being its regional products. As they say: God will provide...and weigh accurately."

You smile and look at the pistachios on the ground: "Can we get back to serious business? Any word from Grissino?"

Anyone looking through a copy of *Zodiac 3000* at a newsstand a few days later would have found a page showing a photograph of a gorgeous inlaid wooden casket, overflowing with sparkling blue powder, accompanied by a long text:

"Here is the secret behind anyone who is successful in show business and sport: the Wizard Rembrandt's Magic Powder, which guarantees success, love, good luck, prosperity and well-being. It is exceptionally powerful against negative energy, keeps bad luck at bay, preserves the love of your partner, combats relationship problems and sex-related stress. It is indispensable during journeys and [this was a little addition of Grissino's] legal proceedings.

"Order the Magic Powder within seven days of the cover date and the Wizard Rembrandt will send you your own personalized four-page horoscope, in which he will reveal the secret laws of the supernatural and their hidden occult powers. In particular, it will contain a piece of essential information which will help you transform your life."

After this text came a space for the order form, another with instructions for use ("A pinch may be sprinkled on your most precious possessions, or on your beloved's clothing; it may be poured into a goblet to read the future, passed through the fingers to regain serenity, or carried about the person in a magic pouch…") and a sidebar a few lines long, giving more details about the Wizard Rembrandt's life: "The remarkable Wizard Rembrandt has featured in 360 television programmes and 1,603 radio broadcasts since he was eleven years old, amazing everyone with his extraordinary mental powers and converting the most stubborn sceptics into enthusiastic believers. Every month, the Wizard Rembrandt predicts the front-page headlines of the next month's newspapers. His Magic Powder can help you utterly transform your life. The Wizard Rembrandt is the only master of the Pizzonic Rite in the world and the only practitioner of the Way of Saytmandu."

This article was followed by details of the offer, in small print: "The Wizard Rembrandt's Magic Powder is packed with Benevolent Magnetic Energy: it assists you in your career and your studies; it enhances love and affection; it gives the gift of physical and sexual energy; it brings success, good luck and long life; it attracts wealth, money and gambling success; it combats depression and stress; it keeps lack of confidence, weakness and all the Distresses of Life at bay; it keeps away all unpleasantness, love problems and issues at work; it protects against envy, the evil eye and other maledictions; it banishes poverty and want; it neutralizes all forms of negativity and finds solutions to all of Life's Problems, enfolding you in a permanent happiness which no one can destroy. Its magical protection is unique, and no magician in the world can vanquish it, not with spells or the evil eye."

Okay, gentle readers: on re-reading it I have to admit it's a little over the top. On the other hand, it was just a collage of texts dug out of genuine advertisements by various wizards and soothsayers. You're right, on re-reading it *is* a little over the top: but obviously it didn't seem so to the one hundred and eighty-four adult Italians who sent us half a million each over the next two weeks. Furthermore, as was predictable, four of these ordered two caskets each, with the result that we had a hundred and eighty-eight deposits of half a million each, adding up to the substantial sum of ninety-four million lire. This came as a big surprise to me, gentle readers, I don't mind telling you, but finally we were ready to get started with the Big C.

Part Two

Chapter ten

In which we reflect on money and life and note how conventional most people's ambitions on both are.

W hat about you? When we've pulled off the Big C, what are you going to do with your share of the money?"

Cristina, who's sipping a Campari (shaken), looks up to answer Milo. "Well... I'll try to be independent of anyone else for a while...just stop and spend a bit of time on myself."

He looks at her ironically and says, "Isn't that what you always do anyway?"

Cristina snorts. "I don't know, Milo, I don't have the faintest idea. To tell the truth, I don't even know how much my share will be."

Milo looks down and starts drumming his fingertips on the tabletop. "Well, my uncle says we're talking two or three hundred million a head in the worst-case scenario, but it seems a rather optimistic evaluation to me."

"A rather optimistic evaluation?" you remark, aping Milo. "Hey, what are you now, a financial analyst?"

"Oh, cut it out, Vittorio. This is important. Let's say we get three hundred million each: what are you going to do with your share?"

You look into Cristina's eyes for a moment, then spread your arms. "Well, I think I'll be happy to get it in my pocket; then I'll give the matter some thought."

Milo thumps harder on the tabletop. "No, that's not good enough. You have to answer immediately. Without thinking."

You think about it for a few seconds, then smile angelically at Milo. "I think I'd buy Bacardi, Inc. Then two or three South American kids. In case I need some organ transplants in the future. I mean, they're already showing signs of wear and tear...."

Milo looks at you with irritation.

"All right, all right. I don't know...." You look over into the empty bar. "The truth is, I haven't given it much thought yet. Not that I have no imagination when it comes to spending money. But my brain hasn't yet—how should I put it?—*absorbed* the idea of having a lot of it. So I don't know exactly what I'll do.... I might go and live in the Caribbean. With that amount I could buy a quiet little hut in Cuba and live off the income for the rest of my life, surrounded by young girls wandering naked around the pool."

"Come off it," says Cristina, annoyed. "Three hundred million doesn't go very far. Forget about living off the income for the rest of your life, and forget about the pool."

"And forget all about the young girls," laughs Milo.

You smile. "Never mind. Anyway, I'd get bored after a few months of that life."

Cristina studies you to see whether you're serious or joking, and you wink at her. She finishes her Campari and asks, "What about Grissino? What will he do?"

Milo takes a cigarette from the pack on the table, lights it and takes a couple of puffs. "Grissino? Does anyone understand him? One time he told me he wanted to set up some kind of commune...something to do with a guy called Fourier, or something like that. A while later though, I asked him who this Fourier was and he said he'd never heard of him. Does anyone understand that guy?"

"A commune? With three hundred million? Sure!" you say sceptically.

Cristina smiles. "You know what, I've thought of something

I'd do right away; a lovely round-the-world cruise. Yup—travel, travel, travel."

Milo looks at her smugly. "You're both so conventional! One of you wants to go to Cuba and the other wants a cruise. Great, I can just imagine it: a beautiful ship packed with ninety-year-old millionaire assholes. What a drag."

"There you go," she replies. "That's the story rich people peddle all the time: being rich is so bloody boring. I don't believe it—"

"You know," you interrupt, "I once read some statistics in the newspaper: some research they did in Las Vegas into people who'd won more than a million dollars on the slots. There were about sixty of them. Well, it was really sad; three or four had committed suicide, about fifty had blown the whole lot in a few years and only five or six had managed to take full advantage of their stroke of luck."

"I'd forgotten that this man is stuffed with news like no one else in the world," mutters Milo.

"Is that really true?" asks Cristina.

"Of course, people are easily ruined by money," you say in a jocular tone.

"That's true," agrees Milo. "Money's like sex—if you don't have it you can't think about anything else and if you can get it easily you don't give a damn."

"Seems a strange thing to say. Who said it?" asks Cristina.

And immediately it's you and Milo, in unison: "Shakespeare, *King Lear,* Act Four, Scene One."

"Silly boys," she says.

You catch the waiter's eye. He comes over and you and Milo order two more beers.

"I don't know. I have a feeling that being rich really is boring," you reflect after a while.

Milo stubs out his cigarette in the ashtray. "No, don't you see, we're approaching this from the wrong angle. You have to imagine everything as one long holiday. If you do that you'll never be bored."

As you finish your sentence the waiter arrives and places two brimming glasses on the table, along with the umpteenth bill.

You raise your glass and take a long drink. Then you wipe off the foam with the back of your hand. "I'm not so sure. My cousin had a diving club in the Maldives, years ago. Every time I asked if I could go and work there, she said I wouldn't be able to stick it. She said most Europeans find it impossible over there because they tropicalize within a month or two."

"Tropicawhat?" asks Cristina.

"Tropicalize—it's just a word she used. She meant you think you're on one long holiday and before long you're just a corpse attached to a bottle."

Cristina loses patience: "Listen, that's the least of my worries. Let's just start with getting the money. Then we'll see. I'm sure I'll find a way to be happy."

Just then the bar door opens and Grissino comes in. All three of you turn round and watch him walking over to your table with a self-satisfied air. He's wearing a dark suit which hangs perfectly, and his hair and beard are well groomed: a fine figure of a man, the kind you notice. Cristina watches him carefully as he takes a seat at the table next to yours.

The waiter arrives immediately, showing the attention reserved for special customers. Grissino gives him a big smile and orders a glass of port, then lights a cigar, smiles again smugly and says, "Operation magic powder is over, subjects. I've made the bank transfers and our money is safe: no one can connect us with the affair any more."

Milo rejoices. "Brilliant, uncle, this calls for a toast!"

The waiter returns immediately and places the glass of port on the table—you notice he doesn't leave a bill. Milo pours some beer into Cristina's empty glass.

"To our enemies," you say, raising your glass.

"To our enemies," the other three repeat.

After a while, Grissino looks at Cristina and says, "Penny for your thoughts?"

"Nothing special," she answers. "We were imagining what we would do with the money from the Big C."

"Ah, subjects, you're getting ahead of yourselves: we haven't even started and you're already thinking about what to do with the money. There's no guarantee it will all work out, you know—"

Milo breaks in excitedly. "Of course we've started, uncle, we've got the money to get the whole thing going, haven't we? Besides, it's an interesting subject. And we do have doubts. Go on, it's your turn now—what will you do with your share?"

Grissino pauses for effect, as usual, puts his cigar down on the ashtray and clears his throat, then murmurs, "Me, I'd like to find a woman who loves me and make children and be happy."

Milo stares at him, amazed. "You don't need money for that, uncle, all you need is bloody good luck."

"Goodness gracious me, do you mean to tell me money can't buy happiness?" Grissino asks ironically.

Then he continues, "Subjects, Ugo Tognazzi—or was it John Belushi, I don't remember, I always mix them up—used to say, 'it's better to have an idea in your head than money in your pocket.' You're right to have doubts: all this money won't change your lives. Your brain can change your life, but not your wallet."

You and Milo look at each other for a moment and immediately declaim, "Shakespeare, *King Lear,* Act Four, Scene One."

Grissino smiles at you, retrieving his cigar from the ashtray and taking a puff. "You're right, we've entered the realm of utter banalities. So I'll give you another, to wit, that the biggest con of all is the one we all acquiesce in; that money will give us whatever it is that we lack. Whereas in fact it can only remove a few worries, it can only give us a few extra comforts...but nothing that will give us happiness."

And he adds, "Besides, we're talking a few hundred million. That's soon frittered away."

"That's exactly what we were saying too," agrees Milo. "The truth is, we don't really know what to do with the money. We're afraid of getting bored."

"That's right," you reflect. "At the end of the day, we're taking no end of risks for something which—bottom line—won't make us happy."

Grissino smiles to himself. "Have you all gone mad? Money buys things, material possessions. And we tie ourselves to material things because material things provide us with emotions; the rustling of a silk petticoat falling to the ground, a soak in a Jacuzzi, a good bottle of wine, a meal in a nice restaurant and then a good film, a drive in the countryside...all these things cost money but give you positive sensations, emotions. Stuff that more than repays the expense."

"Now you're contradicting yourself, uncle," comments Milo.

"Of course I'm contradicting myself. That's the way of the world," replies Grissino. He takes a long pull on his cigar and starts up again. "Money is indispensable—and how, subjects. And right now humankind is in its best period for the enjoyment of it. Do you really want to know what I'll do? I'm overflowing with ideas. I'll go to the races every day...sign up for a course in *haute cuisine*, rent a big house with a garden and grow flowers and vegetables. I'll buy dogs and cats, write my memoirs, go for walks...and...and...let me think.... Got it, I'll go on long trips, take up woodwork and metalwork...play tennis every morning...take a water-colours course...and a tailoring course and a course in restoration.... I'll read lots of books, see every film that comes out...learn French, bake my own bread...I'll go to every concert there is, to the theatre, to festivals in the country.... I'll buy a thousand CDs...or maybe I'll run a wine shop...or a guest house in Amsterdam...or I'll buy a huge house in Madagascar and rent out three rooms...or I'll buy a yacht and sail around the world...or I'll set up a hippy commune...open a pizzeria...."

Chapter eleven

In which we learn one of the many ways to penetrate the fortress of the great Western economy, preparations for the Big C are made, and our subjects are beginnings, information and coloured balls.

Hello. This is Grissino. I'm not at home. I've gone out to beat up a few policemen, get a fix of heroin and pick up some thirteen-year-old girls."

You wait a few seconds and when you hear the answering machine's tone you start. "Grissino, it's Vittorio.... Damn it, I'm here at your place, bang on time, and the intercom's not working. I'm calling you on my mobile...why don't you get one too, that way I'd be able to find you whenever I want?"

A dry click interrupts you and you hear Grissino's voice. "Your question is your answer, subject."

Then, "Okay, it's open. Come on up."

You hear the mechanical click of the lock, you open the door and walk over to the elevator, which is waiting on the ground floor. You go in, press the button for the fourth floor and grimace at your face reflected in the mirror. As you do every time, you read the writing all over the walls. It's not the usual "Go Torino" and "Down With Juventus," but strange phrases like "Down With All the Teams and their Fucked-Up Players" "For Sale Due to Bankruptcy: Italy" "Death to Scrooge McDuck" "You're All Fools, Including Me." One stands out at the bottom, written in huge letters: "I HAVE NOTHING TO SAY."

Grissino's door is ajar, and when you go in you find him busily wrapping his futuristic television up in a clear plastic bag. After which he fits it into the polystyrene packaging and shoves it into the original box. Before closing up the box he rests an envelope containing the instructions and the guarantee on top.

"What's the matter, doesn't it work?" you ask without thinking, as you close the door.

Grissino seals the flaps with adhesive tape and stands up, looking pleased with himself. "On the contrary, it works very well. But I need a hand: I have to take it back to the shop where I bought it, a couple of blocks away."

You look at him, puzzled, so he clears his throat. "Look, subject," he says. "The great Western economy has a protective net around it, but the holes are very big and it can be penetrated if you use a little imagination."

You make a mocking face. "Of course: Shakespeare, *King Lear*, Act Four, Scene One."

Grissino smiles, steps back a bit and collapses onto the white sofa. You look at the cardboard box, take out a cigarette and light it. "Well? What have you dreamed up?"

He stretches his legs and arms in his usual smug way and answers, "It's simple. You see, a few months ago I needed a good TV, so I went out and bought one. Today I'm taking it back and I'm going to get them to give me my money back."

You still don't understand. "But I thought you said it worked very well?"

"Sure, but all the white goods companies have the same wonderful rule: satisfied or your money back. You can keep stuff like this for sixty days, at which point you can return it without having to give a reason. No questions asked. I return my television: they check the receipt, the packaging and the condition of the item... and when they see that everything's as it should be, they give me my money back. On the spot and without a fuss."

"But how's it possible?"

"Simple, subject: this is a drop in the ocean for them. They'll have sold it again by tomorrow. As for me, I'm just taking advantage of the machinery of competition: all I have to do is go from one shop to the next to have a new television every two months. I pay only the delivery charge and a tip to the delivery man; then, just before the two months are up, I return it, get my money back and go to another shop."

"Damn," you say. "Do you come up with these things yourself, or is there a manual on resistance to consumerism somewhere?"

Then, without waiting for an answer, you glance at the clock. "When are Milo and Cristina getting here?"

"Oh, we've got at least half an hour. Come on, give me a hand carrying everything downstairs. Just let me give them a call to warn them first."

Having said this, Grissino picks up the receiver and dials a number. "Yes, hello? Okay, my name is Dario Sparbule and today I'm bringing back the following item…. Yes, Sparbule…. No, young lady, not P. S…. Look, I'll spell it out letter by letter. Sparbule: S as in Steppenwolf, P as in Pink Floyd, A as in Aerosmith, R as in Rolling Stones, B as in Beach Boys, U as in Uriah Heep…. What? Who are Uriah Heep? … What on earth kind of music do you listen to down there? Rita Pavone?"

As many of you have probably noticed, gentle readers, one proof of the existence of God is that life lays down an infinitely large number of minutely particular rules but only very few really fundamental ones, the kind that apply universally to everyone in every period of history and in every latitude. One—and if you examine it in depth it's another proof of the existence of God—is that, as any student of ethics will confirm, there is no such thing as a free lunch. This statement could lead us down entire trains of thought (such as struggle is the lot of everyone, the world owes you nothing, how sad are the idle, how bored the spoiled, etcetera), but they don't help me tell you this story so I'll put them off for another day as I concentrate instead on another fundamental rule, to wit, there is nothing more wonderful in life than *starting* something. Try to remember what it's

like—starting a love affair, starting a journey, starting a project, start-
ing a friendship, starting a book, starting a search, starting to live with
someone, starting to furnish a home, starting an art course, starting to
make a model sailboat, starting anything. Starting something new, and
feeling the joy of the *new*—adrenalin and hope and exhilaration—but
feeling at the same time a kind of anxiety, wondering whether things
will go as we expect, whether it will all go well, whether it might not
live up to our expectations, whether the boy/girl is Mr/Miss Right,
the journey will be safe, the project will succeed, the book will be
good, the model will be simple to make.

And it is with precisely this inner joy tinged with anxiety that
Cristina, Milo and I followed Grissino up to the third floor of a very
elegant building in Piazza Solferino, where he took out the key and
opened the door to show us the two hundred and twenty square
metres of office space belonging to our new company, the newly born
TMCE, Turin Motorized Courier Express Limited.

I can still clearly feel this sense of electric euphoria, as if we
were all floating twenty centimetres off the ground, as we toured the
empty, sunlit rooms, looking at the perfection of the inlaid parquet
floor, the freshly painted white walls. I was almost speechless with
happiness; I saw but didn't look at Cristina, saw but didn't look at
Milo, heard but didn't listen to Grissino, who was saying: "We'll
make this the conference room," "This is your office," "We'll put the
secretary here." I heard but didn't listen to Grissino saying that the
furniture would arrive in a couple of days—then the computers, the
fax, the photocopier—I heard but didn't listen to Grissino explaining that he'd put down proper down payments for everything and
saying, "Never leave any room for suspicion, subjects, when you're
planning something big."

"No, no, no," says Grissino, facing Milo. "You still don't get it. Your
graphic designer was fine for the magic powder, but we can't go back
to him now. It would be madness. In the first place because we haven't
paid him. In the second place because we're not going to pay anyone
so there's no limit to how much we can spend, right?"

Milo looks at you, spreading his arms—as if to say: can't argue with that—and Grissino goes on. "In the third place: maybe our amateur designer is more available than a big advertising agency. Maybe so. But wouldn't you like the satisfaction of not paying one of these giants with their billions of lire of turnover? One of the companies whose express intention it is to brainwash us and persuade us that we need a bunch of useless things in order to be happy?"

Cristina shakes her head. "Please, Grissino, don't let's start on that again."

He spreads his arms out on the windowsill and looks out of the window onto Piazza Solferino for a moment. Then he starts again. "Let's be clear about something, guys. We're not putting together just any old con here. We're putting together The Con, capital T, capital C. And from now on it needs to follow a very particular ethical line; swindling the big guys, the giants, swindling the swindlers—that has to be our con. So we'll take three or four of the biggest advertising agencies in town, choose one at random and hire that one."

You're stunned by what Grissino is saying. Apart from the fact that this must be the first time he's called you guys and not subjects, what strikes you once again is this business of swindling having ethics: it's such a remarkable contradiction, yet it sounds true when he says it. In fact, it's at this point that you become aware of another side of him that fascinates you: the way he makes a convincing case for cheats needing moral stature, the way he aims for an illegality that is somehow legal, for honesty in dishonesty. From all this you gain a sort of satisfying justification for what you're doing, a justification that doesn't really have a basis, when you get right down to it (but justification enough, since you have no intention of getting right down to anything).

Milo is sitting on the floor, leaning on the wall of your future conference room and fooling around with a lock of Cristina's hair; she's curled up on the parquet with her back against his legs.

"Okay, uncle," he sighs, "let's put it to a vote. All those in favour of going to the big agency, raise your hand."

All four of you raise your hands.

"And all those in favour of going to the amateur designer…" Grissino goes on, jokingly.

You, he and Cristina raise your hands again.

"Good," Milo concludes, smiling, "four votes to three. That's decided, then. We might as well decide which of us is going to go to the agency, make the first contact and manage the work."

"Okay, let's make a choice," suggests Grissino. Then, without waiting for a response, he starts pointing his forefinger at you all in rotation and chanting: "Eenie, meenie, miney, mo, catch a tiger by the toe, if he hollers let him go, eenie, meenie, miney, mo."

His finger ends up pointing at Cristina, who immediately protests: "Grissino, you cheated! Eenie-meenie's a con: if you know what you're doing you can always pick someone else, we did it when were kids...."

To which: "Of course, my dear, of course."

"I don't think it's right that he chose the office and the furniture and everything else. He behaves like he's the boss all the time, it pisses me off. It was our idea."

Milo puts the triangle of plastic down on a chair and picks up a cue. "You're right, Vittorio," he says, "but at the end of the day he's the one with the most experience. Let's leave him to it. He is good, isn't he?"

"I'm not saying he's not good, I'm just saying he could ask our opinion every now and again.... He takes a decision and goes ahead, never consults us or asks our advice...."

Milo rests his left wrist on the green baize and slides the tip of his cue back and forth between his thumb and index finger three or four times, then suddenly gives it a sharp jab and the cue ball takes off and strikes the apex of the triangle formed by the fifteen coloured balls, which then explodes. The balls go off in all directions, they rebound off cushions, their trajectories cross, they hit each other; but then, one by one, they gradually lose speed until they stop, none of them having dropped into a pocket.

You chalk the rubber tip of your cue, calmly consider the position of all the balls and then prepare an easy shot: you strike the cue ball just hard enough for it to touch the three-ball, which is right beside the middle cushion, and sink it.

"Okay, you're on solids," murmurs Milo.

You examine the position of the balls again, go half-way round the table and decide to try for the five: you study the shot for nearly a minute, but then you hit it too hard and the ball bounces violently between the two corners of the pocket without dropping.

"My turn, my turn," says Milo impatiently.

You light a cigarette and look around. You're in a windowless, completely dark room, lit only by the greenish glow of the lamp over the playing surface. It's nine o'clock in the morning, and there's no one in the room but the two of you: just the three billiard tables, one behind the other, and then the one you're playing on, the smallest one, the pool table—except here they call it eight-ball. Somewhere in the world a woman has been beaten to death, in the name of God, by a group of men enraged by her accidental display of a naked arm. Somewhere in the world someone is negotiating to buy a box of cigars for fifteen thousand dollars. Some researchers have described the sequence of digits for the number showing how many possible combinations and interconnections there are within the human brain; the number one followed by nine and a half million kilometres of zeroes as typed on a normal typewriter. The fly buzzing around the room is the most remarkable of all flying machines: it can change course in a thirty-thousandth of a second and can even fly backwards.

"Look, Vittorio," says Milo smugly after the eleven-ball drops into the pocket with a muffled thud, "you need to relax. Leave it to those who know what they're doing and enjoy these last few days of preparation. Monday's the start of some hellish weeks, and we won't have a moment's peace. Relax, as much as you can."

Having said this, he goes round the table and prepares his next shot. He chalks his cue and goes on. "What are you so worried about, anyway? Are you suddenly pessimistic about Grissino?"

"Oh no," you answer. "On the contrary. I'm optimistic about Grissino, you and the Big C. In fact, I'm generally optimistic about everything, about life in general. And with good reason."

Milo bangs the fourteen into a pocket with an expert shot, waits for the cue ball to come to rest and then looks up. "With good reason?" he asks. "What good reason?"

"Well," you explain, "this is something I think about often. I can give you at least three good reasons: I was born a human being, in Italy and in 1970."

Milo chalks his cue again. "So what?"

"Well, for a start, imagine being born a fish."

"Great," he replies immediately, passing his cue from one hand to the other. "Hours and hours of peaceful swimming about in the warmth of the sea, and no need to earn a salary every month."

"But, you see, when I'm eating in a restaurant, there's no steel hook hidden in a mouthful of food, waiting to dig into my palate and yank me up to the ceiling and make me disappear into nothingness as soon as I move...."

Milo hits hard and sinks the nine, but the cue ball rebounds off a cushion and ends up in a pocket too.

"Free shot," you say immediately.

He grimaces. "That's because you're distracting me with your rubbish: the restaurant, the hook. When you say it like that it sounds horrible, but fish have tiny brains. And they don't have nerve endings; they can't suffer."

"That's not true. The great misfortune of fish is that they can't scream," you reply as you take the cue ball out of the pocket and replace it on the table.

"Oh," he says ironically, "but that's Shakespeare, *King Lear,* Act Four, Scene One."

Then he asks: "But let's go back a bit; what's 1970 got to do with it?"

You tear your eyes away from the table and rest the base of your cue on the floor, holding it with both hands like a lancer. "Think about it, Milo: if I showed you an illustrated catalogue, like the ones travel agents have, with every period in the history of the world and all the possible places, and I said, you can choose when you would like to live from this catalogue. What would you choose?"

"Simple. I'd like to be the Sun King, in France."

"Oh no," you protest. "In my catalogue you can't choose who you'd like to be, only where and when to live; from the North Pole to New Zealand, from the Jurassic to now. So, what would you choose?"

"Simple. The reign of the Sun King, in France."

"Fine, but your chances of being a servant were five thousand times greater then than they are today. Not to mention that they lived like serfs: by the age of twenty their teeth were rotten and their breath stank and by thirty they were dead."

"That's true," Milo concedes.

"The best time is now, Milo," you say, standing beside him, "and now in the West: there's nothing to compare with it. It's now that we can do anything; travel fast, work a few hours a week instead of all of them, not be chained to a shovel or a loom...not be one of the five hundred thousand slaves of a single prince.... It's now that we can see everything and have a load of information at first hand. It's now that we can best understand the complexity of the world. I read an estimate that more information has been produced in the last ten years than in the previous five thousand...apparently one copy of the *New York Times* contains more information than a farmer in the nineteenth century could come to know in a lifetime."

Milo steps back. "Isn't that nice.... Hurry up, play your shot. Anyway, the bit about the farmer strikes me as a load of rubbish."

"Maybe," you say, approaching the table, "but you only have to think about the TV and the radio and all the knowledge they pass on to you."

You try to sink the seven, but your shot lacks conviction and the ball rebounds limply off the cushion, two centimetres from the pocket. Milo picks up his cue and starts lining up his shot. Then, suddenly, he raises his head. "Okay, let me get today's piece of drivel straight: because we have so much information, you think this is the best period in history to live?"

"Well, that's not what I meant," you say, confused. "It's just that a big chunk of the world, including us, is in good shape. The history books will remember this period in Europe as the golden age."

Milo sinks the ten, rather luckily.

"Actually, there are some troublesome aspects," you add in a different tone. "For example, we're not ready for all this information."

Milo glances at you distractedly, then concentrates on the table and sinks the thirteen.

"That's the real problem," you continue. "We're not up to managing all this information. I mean, I find it difficult not to think of the four-fifths of the world who are living in poverty, surrounded by anti-personnel mines and filth."

Milo gets his shot wrong, missing the twelve, but the cue ball bounces back hard, cannons into the fifteen and sends it speeding into the pocket.

"That's true, Vittorio," he says, chalking his cue again, "but hasn't it always been this way? No, two centuries ago it was even worse; five fifths of the world were living in poverty."

"But in the old days nobody knew it: they only knew what happened in their own village."

Milo rests his left wrist on the baize and slides the tip of his cue back and forth between his thumb and index finger, two centimetres away from the cue ball, then raises his cue indecisively. "Well, do what I do, then," he says. "Don't think about the rest of the world. It's easy."

"But it isn't, Milo, it's difficult. It takes a superhuman effort for me to use my selfish side. I'd like it if the things that entered my brain against my will were better catalogued, in fact I'd like many of them to be discarded immediately. But too much information stays in my head: refugee camps, people mutilated, wars over oil and diamonds, children who work eleven hours a day in return for a meal and cup of sweet tea…. It all stays in my mind—not in the unused parts of my brain either, it's all vivid and in the forefront, it insinuates itself when I'm doing something else, it's hard to explain…."

By the end, Milo is yawning. "Come on, pull yourself together," he encourages you. "I only need the twelve to go for the eight-ball. Get on with it."

Then he lights a cigarette and sighs. "This is just your problem. I think about myself and things are fine: I'm starting up a large-scale con, I'm in perfect health and things are going better with Cristina. What more could I ask?"

Things are going better with Cristina?

Chapter twelve

In which our subjects are radiant smiles, boxing,
how people feel close to each other at certain
moments, the struggle between instinct and
conscience, policemen, misunderstandings and sex.

The first person to appear in the meeting room is a man of middle age, short and thickset, with thinning blond hair and a face made almost fluorescent by a UV lamp. He's wearing an impeccably white shirt, fastened at the wrists with a pair of gold cufflinks, and trousers so tight it looks like he's been sewn into them. He introduces himself to Cristina very elaborately and can't take his eyes off her even when he's shaking hands with you.

"Pleased to meet you, and thank you for thinking of us," he says as he sits down. "My name is Riccardo Scarro (please call me Riccardo), and I'll be your account manager. I'll be the contact between you and our creative team."

You introduce yourself and Cristina as Dr Manfredi and Dr Manicucci, of the newly formed TMCE Limited, Turin Motorized Courier Express. You apologize for not having any business cards, "But, as I warned you on the phone, that's what we're here for: we need everything. We need an enticing name and logo for our new service…we need designs for business cards, a letterhead, receipts, invoices, etcetera…and above all, we need a poster campaign to launch our new service."

Scarro beams, and two rows of perfectly white teeth stand out against the brown of his face. "If I understood you correctly on the telephone, your service is express deliveries within the city, motorcycle couriers, that sort of thing?"

"Precisely," says Cristina convincingly.

He looks at her, infatuated. "Good. Do you have a 'brief'?"

You look at him, askance. He smiles instantly. "What I mean is, a communications strategy, an outline of who you are and what you propose to do."

"As I've just explained," you say rather brusquely. "We do express deliveries, we need a name and a logo and a poster campaign—"

"You see, Mr Scarro," Cristina interrupts, "we don't have anything written down because we hope to develop the details here and now, with you."

He smiles. "Just call me Riccardo. Okay, that's fine: we can develop the communications plan together. It's not a problem."

He gets out an enormous black fountain pen, the size of a frankfurter, ceremoniously removes the cap, and writes at the head of a blank sheet of paper: "Client: TMCE Limited, Turin Motorized Courier Express."

Then he looks up at Cristina and says, "So: what is your 'vision' and what is your 'mission'?"

An hour later you're still sitting around the table in the meeting room. Scarro has been bombarding you with a long list of obvious questions, to which you and Cristina have been giving the simplest and most logical replies.

"Good. We're nearly there," he concludes. "What is your 'target'?"

"Easy," you snort. "Everyone who needs fast deliveries, during the day, within the city limits…."

Cristina intervenes again to temper your impatience. "In other words, Mr Scarro, various businesses and companies, all kinds of offices…and, who knows, banks, insurance companies and so on."

"Just call me Riccardo," he repeats for the thirtieth time, gathering up the three or four sheets of paper he has covered with notes. "Anyway, that's good. Very good. Would you excuse me, please? I'll be back in a minute with one of our creatives."

Upon which he stands up and disappears.

Cristina settles back down in her chair and touches your hand. "Try to be nicer to him. You're too intolerant. After all, he's only trying to do his job as best he can."

You look her in the eye and say nothing. She strokes your cheek.

"You're right," you say. "I'm behaving like an idiot."

After five minutes, Scarro comes back in. He is accompanied by a man of about thirty-five with a well-tended moustache. His clothes are restrained—neither particularly stylish nor particularly eccentric—and he introduces himself as Luca Martini, creative director. You've always instinctively disliked people who describe themselves as "creative" or "artistic," but you're forced to admit you like this guy a lot. During your whole conversation his eyes remain curious, his questions are brief and to the point, and in less than ten minutes he shows that he's understood all your needs. Finally, he asks in a confident tone, "But what's your competitive advantage, basically? I mean, why should a customer come to you as opposed to any of the various other courier companies already operating in the city?"

You look at him calmly. "This is a crucial point. The fact is, we're offering the same service at rates fifteen per cent lower than the competition."

Martini writes a short note in a small notebook.

"Forgive my curiosity, but how will you make a profit?" he asks, looking at Cristina.

"Well, you see, our operating margins are very high," you explain. "Our aim is to have as many customers as possible in as short a time as possible, so as to amortize our fixed costs."

He scribbles something in his notebook and gets to his feet. "Okay, we'll start work on the name and the logo right away. That's certainly the most important thing. If we come up with something good we can obviously use it for the posters. By the way, who's going to take care of buying the space?"

"You are," says Cristina. "As we explained to Mr Scarro, we want to take your full-service package."

"Good," notes Martini, while the disconsolate Scarro whispers, "Just call me Riccardo."

"And for how long, roughly?"

"Well," you say, "we'd like to start with our delivery service in September, starting to sell it from the first of July, so I guess the campaign will have to start on the first of June and continue the whole month."

"Hmm," says Martini quietly. "There's not much time, but we should be able to do it. And what's your budget?"

"We're thinking roughly two hundred million," you say.

At the end, Cristina asks when we can see a first sketch of their work, and Scarro, who has been silently fiddling with his huge pen for most of the time, joins in again: "Given the timing, we'll work as quickly as we can. Let's say that our 'need' is for ten days."

The days pass quickly, one after another; you move on to setting up your new offices, while Grissino recruits a secretary and you, Milo and Cristina scour the telephone books and enter data on thousands of possible customers into the computer.

One evening Cristina calls and says she has to see you: she's anxious and afraid and Milo is no help and she wants to go out and she can't stand being cooped up in the house every night any longer. She says she'll have a shower and then pick you up. "So, is that okay, Vittorio? I'll be at your place at half past seven."

"Fine, I'll be waiting," you answer, beaming. "Oh, seeing as you're about to have a shower, I'd like to tell you something that might calm you down."

"What's that?"

"Okay, so…after a hot shower, if you go up to the bathroom mirror and blow gently on it…well, your breath makes clouds on the glass and forms cute little animals. That's all. I discovered this and thought you might like to know."

"Oh," she says ironically, "that's amazing. I'll try it and let you know."

"Okay, see you at eight. Ciao."

"Seven thirty. Ciao."

You hang up and drop into a chair. You take a pull from a bottle of Moretti, reach out—almost stretch—your arms and grab cigarettes and lighter. They say a large part of the pleasure of cigarettes lies in lighting them; it seems that in the course of making those few automatic gestures—picking up the pack, taking out a cigarette, placing it on your lip, raising the lighter to light it and taking the first puff—during that handful of seconds, your brain detaches itself from everything else and stops thinking. You, on the other hand, have the clear impression that a bell has rung during that handful of seconds, releasing Conscience and Instinct into the ring.

Ladies and gentlemen, this is your very own Jack Balance, live from Caesar's Palace, Las Vegas (applause), bringing you tonight's fight between Mike "Fire" Instinct and John "Brain" Conscience, for the Mental Heavyweights Belt in the "Scruples" category (applause). The contestants are already in the ring and now the referee's starting the fight.... Instinct and Conscience are eyeing each other up without throwing any punches, it's their seventeenth meeting this year.... Conscience has the initiative, but so far he's not making much of an impact: he's punching thin air a lot of the time.... Instinct is trying to use all his defensive skill, he's using the ropes well but not landing many punches and his pattern of single punches is predictable...and Instinct is down suddenly, after a feint to the left ("Cristina's frighteningly attractive"), and Conscience, after a moment's hesitation, drops his guard and takes a terrible blow ("I want her"), he staggers to the far side of the ring, the referee goes over to count, but he raises his guard again and the fight goes on; now it's Instinct on the attack, but Conscience parries his right well and hits him full in the face with a fabulous hook ("But she's your best friend's woman"), Instinct takes a couple of steps back and Conscience is all over him, he's got him cornered and now he's working him over on both flanks ("She's your best friend's woman, she's your best friend's woman"), but Instinct suddenly lands another terrific hook ("Who gives a shit!")

135

and Conscience drops onto the canvas, unconscious, and the referee stops the fight: it's a knockout, Ladies and Gentlemen! Instinct wins before the bell for the end of round one!

You're downstairs in the warm air of this May evening, watching two drivers arguing, when Cristina arrives. Instead of Milo's van, which you were expecting, she turns up in front of your place in an old metallic-brown BMW with German number plates. You get in and immediately notice that the steering wheel and seats have pea-green velour covers.

"Where did this car spring from?" you ask right away. "Did you steal it from one of the Muppets?"

"It belongs to Thomas," she replies, "our neighbour. He's German, studying at the Polytechnic...at least I think he is, I don't know for sure, he's always stoned.... He was playing Playstation with Milo and let me have the keys.... I think it's an omen, this car, you know?"

Upon which Cristina engages first gear and the BMW sets off, making a hellish din, and you immediately fall silent, as if suspicious of each other, so she switches on the radio. Somewhere in the world, in the name of God, a court has condemned a woman to death for adultery. Immediately afterwards, the same court sentenced a man to be flogged (sixty strokes) and jailed for four days for stoning his wife to death. Somewhere in the world, a man has paid a million dollars for a collection of bottles of cognac. The virulent 'Spanish' influenza that swept the world in three successive waves at the end of the First World War left almost twenty-two million dead. An Australian writer named Jasmuheen is plugging her new book *Feed Yourself with Light*. It's based on her own experience: she has practiced meditation for more than twenty-five years, and for the last five she has not touched any food; she nourishes herself with air and light. It seems that her followers around the world, the 'breatharians,' number about five thousand. Isn't it surprising how incomprehensible and illogical it is, this reality ticking away from one second to the next?

After going round in circles several times, Cristina finally finds a parking space in Piazza Vittorio. You get out of the car and walk over to the outdoor part of a bar which Milo once described as "the kind of place that's always packed, overflowing with the beautiful people, who spend all their time complaining that the place is always packed, overflowing with the beautiful people." In fact, the real problem with this place is that everyone seems to be drinking and talking at their tables until the two of you arrive, at which point they all turn round and look at you, so you begin to suspect that in fact nobody's doing what they seem to be doing—having a quiet drink, talking with their friends, sharing a joke with their boy/girlfriend—but just pretending to do these things while secretly waiting for someone to arrive so they can suddenly turn round, all of them at the same time, and stare at the newcomers.

You get two beers and go and sit on one of the benches in the piazza. The same faces are endlessly recycled around you, gold-plated blondes with geometrically precise make-up and slack bodies, a whole gallery of still-lives-with-gin-and-tonic. You don't say anything for a while, savouring the light breeze that's beginning to freshen the air, the blue sky just before dusk, the swallows flitting playfully about high in the air.

"How are things, Cristina? Are you feeling better?" you ask eventually.

She looks down. "I'm trying."

You wince, unseen. "What's going on?"

Cristina draws her legs up onto the bench and takes up the lotus position. "You know, Vittorio, once I was only afraid of two things, only two things frightened me when I imagined them."

"What were they?"

"One, opening the door and finding my fiancé in bed with my best friend. Two, being left high and dry at the altar on my wedding day, in front of a crowded church."

Her face is sad, but there is laughter in her eyes, you'd like to hug her.

"And now?" you ask.

She rests her head on your shoulder. "Now I'm afraid of every-thing, Vittorio," she murmurs. "I'm afraid of everything."

She goes on. "I'm afraid something will go wrong, I'm afraid I'll spend three or four years inside.... On the other hand, I'm afraid Milo

137

will become even more of a dickhead with money in his pocket.... I'm afraid everything will end badly and in a few years we won't be able to sit here on this bench with these pleasant feelings. I'm afraid of everything, Vittorio, everything."

One of my great personal problems, gentle readers, is my complete and utter inability to comfort and reassure other people. I'm not cut out for it. I stand there with nothing to say, every time. Faced with someone who's worried and looking for support, I never know what to say; because their anxiety, their worry, instantly create a massive void in me: it's as if a sick person instantly transferred his sickness to me while expecting me to cure it. It's just that life's signalling system, as is well known, is difficult to interpret. When it shows me a red light I see it as a sign saying stop dead: it destroys me, I can't get going again. Someone else's doubt, once transferred to me, is like a plant transplanted into extremely fertile ground and inundated with the most powerful fertilizers. The fact is that I'm already convinced that life is one long *via dolorosa*: I have no illusions, so I rejoice in every day I feel things are going pretty much okay and I don't moan much during the bad times, because I know that bad times are really the norm. The trouble is that my silence is always taken to mean I don't give a shit; so I know only one solution—flight.

"Look, Cristina, I'll just go in and get some change, then we'll buy some cigarettes from the machine."

Cristina looks at you crossly. "You see? You're just like Milo... you just don't understand, do you? I need reassurance, not cigarettes."

You look at her, embarrassed. "I don't know why, Cristina, I'm just not cut out for this stuff. Only people who have complete certainty can reassure other people. But I don't have much in the way of certainty. I'm better off when it comes to doubting: if there were a doubting championship I wouldn't hesitate to put myself in the UEFA class."

Cristina begins to smile and you go on. "In the certainty competition, on the other hand, I'd come last."

You look up and add, "Maybe."

She puts her arm around you. "Christ, Vittorio, be serious. What if they catch us?"

"Who?"

"The police, who else?"

"Naah, relax. Remember, they're just cops. If they knew what they were doing there wouldn't be any crime, right?"

"Come on, joking aside."

You can feel her body right alongside yours. You shiver. "Cristina, your concerns are my concerns, and I have the same fears. But I'm an optimist, I think everything will go fine, and in any case we've got no criminal records and even if they do catch us we won't spend a single day inside."

She looks into the distance, towards Monte dei Cappuccini. "Yes, but if they do catch us, our lives will become hell just the same."

"Come on, they're not going to catch us, Cristina, they won't. And Grissino's a master, we're safe with him."

She shakes her head. "Sure. Grissino's not a man. He's a ticking bomb."

"And even if you're always arguing with him, he does know what he's doing."

"I know. And it's true I'm always arguing with him, but actually I like him a lot," she reflects. "In some ways he's a remarkable man."

You look at her, puzzled, pick up your bottle of beer and gently tap it against hers.

"Come on, let's have a toast."

"To what?"

"Anything."

Cristina puts her mouth a millimetre away from your ear and you shiver, like when the hairdresser touches your ear with his scissors. "Why do I feel so close to you?" she whispers.

It seems impossible that this sensitive and affectionate girl could be the same as the one who throws hardbacks in her fiancé's face and argues with Grissino at every opportunity. But the situation is bothering you, you don't know what to do, so you suddenly stand up. You walk the thirty-odd paces to the bar, go up to the cash desk and ask a guy with dyed hair if he can change a hundred-thousand lire note. He looks at you like you've asked him to donate a kidney and says, "Sorry, can't help you."

An hour later you're drinking vodkas at a table outside a little restaurant in Piazza Carlina and Cristina is saying she shouldn't drink this much because when she was sixteen she was admitted to the Amadeo di Savoia Hospital with acute hepatitis. She got it on holiday in Santo Domingo with her mother, she tells you, and when she got back her doctor mistook the symptoms for influenza, so that by the time she got to the hospital she was given only four days to live. But within a couple of weeks she was out of danger.

Through one of time's windows, you see her laid out on a hospital bed.

"It was weird, you know, Vittorio," she says. "For a long time afterwards, I woke up every morning with the feeling that each new day was a gift, I thought happiness had entered my DNA for ever. Really. For months, when I got up and when I went for walks in the park, I felt happy. I saw a tree and I was happy. I breathed and I was happy. I was happy to go to bed and happy to get up in the morning. Happy to feel my legs walking and my arms moving and my eyes seeing. Happy to laze around, study, listen to a record, happy to be alive."

"And now you don't feel like that any more?"

"Yes, sometimes. Even now I wake up and I tell myself I'm young and healthy. That my evening classes bring in enough for me to share the rent with Milo. That I've never gone hungry in my life. And I remember I have many years to meet people I like, who make me smile, from whom I can force a smile. But I know I'll never again be able to feel like I did when I left the hospital. I've forgotten what it was like. It's normal: I've forgotten all the cuts and scrapes I got playing as a little girl. I wouldn't even be able to show you where they were on my body."

You stare into space. "That's right. Everybody says one of the most fascinating things about the human brain is its memory, its ability to remember, but maybe what should be fascinating is actually the exact opposite: its ability to forget. Its ability to wipe out. To think about someone you spent years of your life with and realize a few years later that you can hardly remember anything about him, you can't remember his words, his movements, you just have a few vague physical images, nothing mental. Nothing."

Cristina glances at you sadly. "Who are you thinking of?"

You shrug and take a sip of ice-cold vodka.

Cristina seems to be cheering up gradually; she's being friendly and inclusive, and after a while you start joking around again and she looks you in the eye with an expression that is, to say the least, questionable. "Let's play a game: we each have to name our greatest desire. You start."

You look at her for a moment. She seems too sure of herself, too sure that she is your greatest desire. You feel like putting her off her stride. "Okay.... My greatest desire? Hmm, let me think.... Okay, I've got it. I'd like to start a new global revolution."

Cristina pretends not to be surprised—or maybe she really isn't surprised, who knows?—"Wow! And what's it based on?"

"Simple," you improvise. "There are five points. Okay, point number one: no more consumerism, buying anything useless is forbidden.... Point number two: selling stuff with brand names and logos is forbidden, also wearing stuff with brand names.... No, hold on: the second point is just that: no more brand names. That's to stop us being the most vacuous younger generation in the history of the world.... Then...."

Cristina laughs. "Stop, you're making this up as you go along. You've got a case of Grissino Syndrome. Besides, what kind of a programme is that? It's banal: who decides what's useful and what's useless? It's all a matter of opinion. And brand names? Everything has a brand name, how can you say that? And anyway, if no one bought anything any more, if your revolution was a success, it would kill the economy and we'd all be unemployed. I wouldn't back it. Yes, we're slaves to consumerism, but in spite of everything I think that's better than being slaves to hunger. Or just being slaves, period."

You pretend to be utterly serious. "Hmm," you think, "when

you put it like that it does seem a bit of a dead end…on the other hand, you don't seem much of an expert on the problems of the world…. But you're right. I was joking: I wouldn't start a revolution. I don't have enough faith in the human race: what's the point of tearing down fences if the cows just stand there chewing their cud and don't even notice?"

"Well," she smiles, "now I know you've got Grissino Syndrome for sure."

"Anyway, now it's your turn, what's your greatest desire?"

She makes a mischievous face and says, "Right now my greatest desire is to go dancing!"

So you get back into the BMW and go to the Murazzi, which is crowded with people, and while you're rolling a couple of joints by the banks of the Po you invent a really stupid game you call "spot the double"—you have to find someone who looks like a famous person among the people around you. During the next half hour you shuttle back and forth three or four times, from the riverbank to the bar opposite and back again, you drink enough vodka to put a Moscow after-hours club to shame, you invent the first Caribbean-Italian cocktail (rum and chinotto) and spot only one interesting double, a perfect Mario Andretti, the great Formula One driver of the 1970s—which starts an animated discussion on John Player Specials, the ones with the black and gold packs; whatever happened to them?—as well as a few vague resemblances such as a guy who looks to you like the lead singer of Dream Syndicate (but Cristina says he doesn't count because she's never heard of them).

Thinking about it now, it was obvious even then that things were shaping up really nicely for you; you were both laughing, saying silly things like, "What's your sign?" "Me? Piranha," and joking with the barman. "Another vodka for me and a glass of blood for the lady…." In short, everything seemed to be heading in the right direction. You were making a lot of cynical, sneering comments— "Look at that lazy bastard there…and what about that one over there, dancing like a dead duck"—and bitching about the cashier.

"They're fake; she's had a boob job."

"Yup."

"And a nose job."

"Yup."

"And a lip job."

"Maybe a little."

"And a hand job."

"A hand job?"

"Yes, they used to be webbed."

True, every now and again, for a fraction of a second, it occurred to you that you were fooling around with your best friend's fiancée, but it was a hateful thought and you were able to banish it instantly: behaving like a bastard sonofabitch is the easiest thing in the world. It must be, because there are tens of millions of us in the world.

Suddenly Cristina grabs your arm. "Listen to this song. It's fantastic, I absolutely have to dance to it," and she drags you inside.

Okay. Right now it's all about to happen, but thinking about it now—I swear, gentle readers—I didn't want it to happen. It's just that this damned instinct we have inside us is a thousand times more focused than any rational thought; it's so clear, so pristine, that it overcomes everything and annihilates your conscience; it doesn't make distasteful or disagreeable things happen, it just makes things happen. I think you'll understand, because it could have happened to anyone. Because none of us live in a rational world; we all live in a complex, emotion-filled, emotive world in which instinct doesn't give warning: it simply bursts in. Luckily. Sure, I was a bit far gone, and as we danced we brushed against each other and Cristina was wearing this lovely little tight-fitting tee-shirt and it was a pleasure to look at her and at one point I mumbled into her ear, "God, Cristina, when you look in the mirror before you go out, how do you manage to keep your hands off yourself?" and she laughed and squeezed my hand as we danced, and then it happened, which is to say I didn't make it happen and nor did she, it just happened. What happened is that she, with her forehead dripping with sweat and her clothes sticking to her because of the heat, amid the loud music and the flashing lights, well, she put a cigarette in her mouth and signed to me to light it and I, I don't know what came over me, I got out my lighter and put my hand up to her lips, but instead of lighting the cigarette I removed it from her mouth and kissed her right then and there, and she kissed me back and then she stopped and went and sat outside by the riverbank, and I followed her and said I was sorry and all around was the moist, dark night and the street lights and the cool air. She said she hadn't come across the cigarette trick before, that she hadn't been expecting it, that she wouldn't have kissed me back otherwise, but she didn't seem annoyed and I swore—I swear to you too, gentle readers—that the cigarette business wasn't a trick, I just didn't know what had come over me, so she just said "Let's go" and we went back to the parking space and the brown BMW and as soon as we were inside she said again, "Why do I feel so close to you?" and kissed me, and we kissed for a long time. I worried about the vestigial red spots I still had on my chest for a second and then I forgot about them and we kissed enthusiastically, for minutes at a time, without saying a word, we kissed passionately, the way you only do when you're kissing for the first time. We kissed the way you sometimes see two kids kissing in the street, and you envy them a little but then immediately think, in your superior way, that if they're kissing like that they must be just starting out, they don't know anything about love, it's obvious. And, some time later, I thought of Milo, I pictured him asleep in front of the Playstation, so I said "Let's go." Just "Let's go," not "Take me home" or anything like that and Cristina whispered "You drive," and we stopped at an all-night stall along the way to buy two bottles of beer and I drove gently and we moved through the night without talking, the news on the radio.

Then the other thing happened.

So, you turn on to Corso Marconi.
> You stop at a red light.
> You glance at Cristina.
> You tune the radio.
> No cars in sight.
> Fine rain begins to spot the windscreen.
> A man is pushing a market barrow along the opposite lane.

Somewhere in Italy the temperature is nineteen degrees.

Oscar Luigi Scalfaro is the chilling President of the Italian Republic.

You half-close your eyes.

You reopen them, but the light is still red.

Another quick look and you go.

The next thing is a raised baton and that faintly spiteful expression you often see on the faces of those who consider themselves the Guardians of Order. You stop twenty or so metres beyond the road block and size up the situation: you're drunk as a lord, the dashboard clock says 05:03, you've just gone through a red light and in the rear-view mirror you can see an enormous *carabiniere* coming closer. Not to mention the two empty beer bottles rolling around on the back seat.

"This car has no registration document and no insurance," says Cristina laconically, looking straight ahead through the glass.

Oh shit. You glance in the rear-view mirror again. The *carabiniere* arrives, he leans in the open window and looks at you. You look at him. In silence. He really is huge.

Then something happens that you would never have anticipated.

"Do you speak English?" he says.

Of course, it's obvious: your car has German plates, it so happens that your seatbelts are fastened, you both have light brown hair and pale complexions. He's taken you for a textbook pair of German tourists.

"*Sprichen Deutsch, ja, no Englisch,*" you improvise on the spur of the moment.

The *carabiniere* glances at Cristina, muttering curses under his breath, then looks at you with hatred and orders, "Out of the car, get out of the car."

By now, though, you've slipped easily into the role of an innocent, perhaps slightly obtuse, German tourist, so you look at him inquiringly.

"Get out of the car," the Huge One repeats, backing it up with broad gestures.

Now, slowly, you undo the seatbelt and get out of the car. "Follow me," he says.

It would be funny, except that by driving without registration or insurance you're risking serious trouble. On top of which you guess that pretending to be German, if you're caught out, might make the position worse, so you go quietly and start walking towards the road block. After a few steps, the Huge One takes you by the arm, but gently, with the deference many Italians instinctively show to Germans. You try to appear more sober than ever and walk alongside him in an orderly manner, towards the confiscation of your licence for driving while intoxicated, driving an unregistered car without insurance and, in addition, impersonating a citizen of a European Union country, a crime which will be invented specially for you.

When you get to the police car, the Huge One leans down to the window and you hear him say to his partner, "A couple of German tourists. I'll handle it." You stop, but he comes alongside you again and gestures for you to go on down the street. At this point you begin not to understand. Where's he taking you? Is there a police station in Corso Marconi? Are you under arrest? Is he going to take you to a dark corner and beat you up? Did the Nazis commit some kind of brutal war crime against his great grandmother, for which you're going to pay? Despite your fear, in short, you find it impossible to stay serious, you're in an alcohol-induced state of hazy indifference, you're remembering Cristina's kisses and you're feeling good. But now the Huge One is stopping suddenly, raising his arm and pointing at the red light, saying, "Red. The light is red. So you must not pass. *Nicht pass.*"

Now you feel really embarrassed and you say, "*Ja!*" spreading your arms and indicating good comprehension. The Huge One gives you a gentle shove and says, "Now go away, go away. And don't let me catch you again."

You pretend not to understand, so he gives you another push and gestures that you can go now, and you leave, walking quickly, and a few seconds later you're passing the police car and you turn and say: "*Danke! Danke!*" and you think, Up with the *carabinieri*, Up with the *carabinieri*, and woe betide the next person who tells a joke about them.

When you get back in the car and start it up, Cristina is incredulous. She says, "Where did he take you? What did they do to you?" but you put the car in gear and get going, joking: *"Gott mit uns, Fräulein, Deutschland über alles!"* and you laugh to yourself and dawn is breaking but it's much more than just a dawn and you see it as more like the dusk of the night.

A warning, gentle readers; owing to its explicit nature, the following paragraph may offend those readers who are particularly sensitive to descriptions of sex in books. Such readers are advised to skip the following few lines—the plot will not suffer—and go directly to the next chapter.

So, gentle readers, what should I put in this paragraph? I'm one of those people who get bored to death when they watch sex scenes in films. Unless it's hard-core porn, obviously. You know what I mean: soft lighting, special music, the couple rolling around in the bedclothes suggesting intercourse, glimpses of skin, buttocks, breasts—a load of balls, in short, but nothing you can get your teeth into (I mean this figuratively). That's why, although the note above might make you think otherwise, I'm overcome by a sort of modesty; or rather, by the fact that I'm supposed to be telling you about something extremely intimate, yet, I hope, profoundly familiar to most of you. So there's nothing I can add, is there? Would you like something in the style of a romance novel (along the lines of: he settled between her legs with the tenderness and irresistible power of the rising tide), or something more new age (still nautical: it was like great waves breaking against a cliff, and if there were no cliffs, as we know, the waves wouldn't reach so high)? No, I don't feel like it. I could be a bit frivolous instead, or edge over into pornography, but even then it's hard to say anything that hasn't been said before. In short, gentle readers, I'd like to keep this experience for myself. I don't want to say any more. Try to understand and, if you can, please support me in my choice and allow what has to take place between me and Cristina to take place. If you really want to know what it was like, take hold of your partner, and go about it sweetly and in a frenzy.

Chapter thirteen

In which our subjects are bulls on wheels, homicidal charity, and the public sector; and in which the thought of Cristina torments Vittorio.

B ow? As in B-O-W?"

"Yes, BOW. Bulls On Wheels," Luca Martini repeats.

It's the first time you have invited anyone to your headquarters, and you note with pleasure that both Scarro and Martini were impressed with your stylish offices. The conference room is the crowning glory; inlaid parquet floor, nineteenth-century prints on the sand-coloured walls, a vast oval table in polished glass, surrounded by eight leather chairs, aluminium bookshelf, projector, video recorder and stereo system. All with that shiny new look unique to things that are fresh from the factory. A terrific effect, especially since the entire furnishing of the office has only cost a tiny deposit.

You and Cristina are sitting at one end of the table. Grissino, who has introduced himself as the chief executive of the company, is between you. Scarro and Martini are seated at the other end. They're presenting their launch proposals for your express courier service.

"Bulls on wheels," Grissino repeats doubtfully.

"That's right, Bulls on Wheels," says Martini enthusiastically. "That's the name." Upon which he stands up, opens a huge black portfolio on the table and takes out a printed sheet. "And here's our idea for the logo," he goes on. "See, it's a stylized B-O-W in blue and red, slightly curved. At the top we've put this motif, which looks like a bow on its side, but also a pair of horns...bull's horns, of course...a play on words, you see."

Grissino picks up the sheet of paper, examines it carefully, then comments, with a puzzled expression, "Looks like the logo for a steak house."

"No, no," Martini exclaims with his usual enthusiasm, "think about it a minute, we have a good name, BOW. Simple, short, easy to remember...immediately you think wheels, motorbikes, but also the bull, the symbol of Turin.... And B-O-W spells *bow* too...so you also think arrows, swiftness, movement, hitting the target, scoring a bull's eye (forgive the pun).... To sum up, this logo embodies all the associations and concepts we want to bring across."

Grissino picks up the sheet again and examines the logo with revived interest. Ever the consummate actor, he plays his part. "Hmm," he says, sounding unconvinced. "Even supposing you're right, how do we use this symbol to make an impact with our communications?"

Martini was expecting this. "That's the best thing about it, sir, I hope you don't think we stopped here. Here, look at this, this is our proposal for billboards."

Martini opens up the huge black portfolio again and takes out another sheet. It's a very colourful computer-generated image of a friendly-looking bull on a motorbike: he has a crash helmet on and an envelope clenched between his teeth. He's wearing a bib with the BOW logo and the slogan: BULLS ON WHEELS: STEERS AT YOUR SERVICE. And below this: THE NEW EXPRESS COURIER SERVICE WITH UNBEATABLE PRICES. And then, smaller: FOR FURTHER INFORMATION, CALL FREE ON....

Scarro looks at you complacently.

Martini explains, "As you can see, the idea is to use computer graphics for the billboard campaign. Images of bulls in helpful poses, images that foster the perception of bulls as loyal animals, domestic animals, like the dog that brings his master the newspaper or his slippers. That's the concept: that the bulls on wheels are obliging creatures, at the customer's service."

"And this will be the image for your mailshot too," he adds, "seeing as you're putting together a mailing list."

Before the meeting, Grissino had warned you and Cristina to let him do the talking, to say as little as possible and under no circumstances to show any enthusiasm, but by now this is proving a difficult task: this image has a significant impact. Trying not to be affected by Martini, you concentrate on Cristina instead. For the last few days you've been busy, separately, entering data on hundreds of potential customers into the computer, and your paths have only crossed for a few seconds at a time, during which she has been cold and businesslike. Her mind seems to be somewhere else, as if she regrets what happened between you, and she's so distant you don't know how to behave, so you've buried yourself in your work and banished all thought of her. As for Milo, you can hardly look him in the eye.

Serena—your receptionist, hired by Grissino the previous week—comes in with Milo; she gives the "CEO" some papers to sign and leave the room. Scarro, who has been very subdued till now, takes over. "Our idea is to make about fifty six metres by three posters and place them in the central zone of the city.... Later, if we increase the budget a little, we could 'sponsor' a bus. Just imagine the effect...."

Grissino looks at him condescendingly. "What about doing something on local radio instead?"

Martini's ready for this too. "You're right. We thought of that too. We have an idea for a radio spot. You hear the bell at the door, it's a delivery...you hear a voice saying, 'Who's there?' and the answer is the bellowing of a bull...then a voice-over saying, 'For express deliveries in town, come to BOW, Bulls On Wheels, steers at your service....'"

At this point Grissino gets up and starts speaking, smoothly. "Qoèlet, a very subtle writer and poet whom I always recommend, says in one of his most famous texts: there's a time to throw stones and a time to gather them, a time to embrace and a time to abstain from embracing. A time to seek and a time to lose, a time to conserve and a time to throw away. A time to tear up and a time to sew up, a time to be quiet and a time to speak. Well, now's the time to throw stones, so that we can gather them later. Let's get going right away, with everything, there's no time to lose."

Martini and Scarro are almost speechless with surprise.

A little before dawn, a violent downpour hit the city. You were awakened by the thunder, as well as a monotonous roar, like rain in the tropics, as if someone had left the tap running in the bath. You looked around your dark room and thought about Milo and Cristina, you saw them together in bed, you tried to erase the image and then, soothed by the background noise and the rapidly cooling air, you went back to sleep.

Now it's nearly ten and the sun is shining in the middle of a bright blue sky, but the air is cool and seems clearer and cleaner than ever, as if no one has ever breathed it. You and Grissino are walking beneath the colonnades of Piazza Carlo Felice, on your way to the headquarters of the postal service. At the entrance to Via Roma, a filthy little boy pushes through the passers by and appears in front of you. "A thousand lire," he says, holding out his hand.

You move a bit to the right and pretend not to see him, but Grissino stops and you have to stop with him. He looks the boy in the eye and says, "Go get your father."

The boy doesn't bat an eye. He just says "A thousand lire" again.

But Grissino insists. "Bring your father here."

So you go and grab Grissino's arm. "Come on, don't make a scene," you say. "We've got things to do." But he shrugs you off. Then he crouches down until his face is level with the boy's.

"Your father is a bastard of the first order," he says.

The boy spits in his face, then stands there with a defiant look. Grissino stands up, pulls a handkerchief out of his pocket and wipes the spittle off his face. Then he puts the handkerchief away and gets out his wallet. He gives the boy ten thousand lire. "Buy yourself a knife and kill the man who's turned you into a slave," he says.

The boy snatches the note from his hand and runs away. You don't say anything. The man's mad.

"Good morning," you say to the clerk at the booth. "We're interested in sending a large number of letters within the Turin area and we'd like to know what we need to do."

The postal clerk has a pair of glasses with pink frames and seems friendly. "What you need to do? That depends. Are the letters identical?"

"Yes, absolutely identical," you reply.

"And do you have a defined list of addresses?" the clerk asks.

"Yes, most certainly," you reply.

Grissino interrupts, "Look, we've got a few thousand letters, all the same, and we need to send them within the city. What we want to know is how much it's going to cost. In particular, we want to know what we have to do so we don't have to stick stamps on them all, one by one. We understand there's some kind of bulk rate?"

The clerk nods. "That's right. If the letters are identical they count as Printed Matter and there's no need to stick stamps on them one by one. You need to go to the second floor and ask for Printed Materials, a Mr Bucossi. It's that way."

You and Grissino thank him and head for the inner staircase.

"You see," you say as you approach the stair, "some people preach sermons in the park about how public sector workers don't want to work...then you come here and find courtesy and efficiency...."

Grissino grumbles, "It's not work, what they do. It's public service. There's a difference, subject, a big difference. Look around you now."

In fact, the room in which you asked for information was clean and brightly lit, whereas now, on your way up, the walls are a dirty green and you feel like you're in an abandoned school. On the second floor, four men are sitting around in a cubicle drinking coffee and smoking. They're carrying on an animated conversation, and half a minute passes before one of them gets up and comes to the window where you're waiting. "Whaddaya want?" he says irritably.

"Simple," says Grissino, looking daggers at him, "we're looking for Mr Bucossi's office."

"Right-hand corridor, seventh door on the left," the man mumbles as he turns his back on you and goes back to his seat.

"Thank you so much," mutters Grissino, giving him the finger behind his back. You look at him disapprovingly and he smiles with satisfaction. You go down the right-hand corridor, carefully counting the doors in your head, until you reach a cream-coloured door with three nameplates, one of which is engraved with the name 'C. Bucossi.'

"Good. We seem to have found it," says Grissino, knocking loudly.

You wait a few seconds and then, since there's no answer, Grissino opens the door and you go into a grey and dirty office with a linoleum floor and three rickety metal desks. A man in a mustard-coloured turtle neck is eating a sandwich, with a greasy sheet of paper laid out on his desk as a tablecloth. Another man is sitting at the second desk, almost hidden behind a copy of *Tuttosport*.

"We're looking for Mr Bucossi," says Grissino loud and clear.

The man with the sandwich points his chin at the empty desk, on which you notice a nameplate with 'Carlo Bucossi' written on it.

"Has he gone out?"

The man with the sandwich shakes his head.

Grissino goes up to him: "Do you happen to know where he is?"

The man with the sandwich shakes his head a second time. Grissino glances at you, perplexed, then goes up to the man with the newspaper: "Do you happen to know when he'll be back?"

The man lowers his newspaper crossly and, with an anger out of all proportion to the situation, starts shouting, "I KNOW NOTHING. NOTHING AT ALL. NADA!" and raises the newspaper again.

You are stunned.

Grissino takes a deep breath, adjusts the knot of his tie, incinerates the man with the newspaper with his eyes and then goes back to the desk of the man with the sandwich. "Excuse me," he says cautiously, "we're here to—"

"Can't you see I'm eating?" the man says shortly.

"But the office is open for visitors now, isn't it?" you ask, trying to calm him down.

"Yes, but when I'm hungry, I'm hungry. That's my business."

You look at Grissino. He takes a deep breath, adjusts his tie again and takes another breath, then taps his foot on the ground irritably and throws you a look that's difficult to interpret. All of a sudden, with all the strength at his disposal, he bangs his fist on the desk of the man with the sandwich, making him jump out of his seat.

The other man immediately lowers his newspaper and says indignantly, "What manners!"

Grissino starts staring at them fiercely, first one, then the other, muttering "worthless, lousy layabouts" through clenched teeth.

And he goes on, raising his voice, "You shameless parasites, you disgusting worms."

And raising it some more, he starts yelling, "YOU INCOMPETENT PETTY-MINDED ARROGANT BASTARDS."

And then, screaming at the top of his voice, "YOU UNBELIEVABLY FUCKED-UP CONSTIPATED MORONS! YOU COULDN'T EVEN PRODUCE SOME DECENT FERTILIZER THROUGH YOUR ASSHOLES! IT'S NO WONDER A PAIR OF SHIT-FOR-BRAINS LIKE YOU CAN'T ANSWER A SIMPLE QUESTION!"

Half an hour later you're sitting on a bench in Piazza Castelli. You're talking to Milo on the mobile, relaying what you hear to Grissino.

"Okay," you explain to Grissino, "he says the free phone number has been activated, Serena's very good, she's really getting down to it...and he's recruited our first, and last, motorbike courier."

"Good," murmurs Grissino. "What about the letter? And the addresses?"

You put the phone to your ear again. "Milo? Are you still there? Good. Listen, your uncle is asking if you've heard anything from the agency about the letter, the one introducing our service...."

Ah, good…. It's ready, being typeset…. Good…. And the mailing list of potential customers? Ah, good…. Cristina's on the computer sorting all the data we've entered…. Yes, excuse me a second…. What is it, Grissino?"

"I can't remember: ask him whether the list includes self-employed people."

"Milo, did you hear that? Can you confirm it? Yes, all potential customers in the Turin area are there…all the private companies, all the limited companies, all the branches of all the banks, all the insurance companies, businesses, notaries, law firms…and—"

"Ask him whether the residents' associations are in there."

"Milo, did you hear that? Yes…. Okay," you say to Grissino. "He says everything you could possible want is in there, even hotels and travel agencies, we've even put fortune-tellers and tarot readers into the database…."

"What's that? How did it go at the post office? Well, there was a bit of a problem…. No, unfortunately not. I don't think it can be solved…. What are we going to do? Hey, don't you worry: we'll just stick stamps on everything by hand…. Yes, he's fine, do you want to talk to him? Yes, he's in a good mood…. Of course not…. All he's done today is incite a little boy to parricide and have us thrown out of a post office…. What more do you expect? Here he is…."

You live behind the Lungodora, just beyond the Rossini bridge, in a flat you share with two students from Palermo: one room each plus shared bathroom and kitchen. They're tidy young law students in their first year of retakes. Every year they disappear back to Sicily at the end of May, except for a couple of visits to Turin in July—a couple of days at most, just enough to take an exam during the summer term and disappear again—and turn up again in the autumn. So right now you have the place to yourself.

The flat is on the fifth floor, which is the top floor of an old building inhabited almost entirely by immigrants. Your neighbours across the landing are Romanian: you often bump into them early in the morning as they go downstairs, six or seven of them in single file, each carrying a bike. You don't know exactly how many there are, at least ten. They're completely silent all week and then let their hair down on Sunday afternoon: you can hear the sound of violins and accordions through the walls, and they dance and make a hell of a racket.

On the next floor down there are another ten or so Nigerians, black as crude oil: you often bump into them talking on the landing or in the entrance hall. They always wear loud new tracksuits, except at the weekend, when they put on bright green or orange embroidered tunics. The rest of the building is inhabited mostly by families from Abruzzo, people who work in the markets: if you go by after six in the evening you see a row of seven or eight identical vans parked in the street outside, each with a huge roof rack and a gigantic umbrella, folded up and fitted alongside the roof rack like a pen in the pocket of a diary.

The building is old and poorly maintained. It's nothing special—in fact it's one of the worst places you've ever lived—but it has fantastic inner walkways: five quadrangles of peeling railings, one above the other, all screaming out *life*.

On this particular boiling hot Sunday at the end of June, the Moroccans who live on the floor below, to the left of your bedroom, have created an honest-to-goodness piece of theatre.

It all started around ten in the morning. You woke up, enraged by a muffled metallic thumping coming from outside, opened the window and looked out into the airshaft. On the floor below, to the right, you could see three Moroccans trying to attach a satellite dish to the railings. They were taking risks, leaning out and holding one of their number by the hand as he perched on the outside of the banister with his feet on the cornice. They were moving the dish by tapping its iron support with a hammer, orienting it millimetre by millimetre, according to a series of commands being shouted from inside. They were at it for a couple of hours and then, finally, they fixed the dish in place with strips of metal and wire and all the noises stopped. But at lunchtime they started making a racket again, singing in their guttural language and shouting and then, after twenty-odd minutes, there was a roar and they all came out on the balcony, waving the Moroccan flag and shouting "Goal! Goal!" There were at least a dozen of them, taking it in turns to wave their red flag with its green star, and they were hugging each other and throwing up their hands with happiness; anyway, you worked out that there was a football international on and you were happy for them and even the people from Abruzzi came out onto their balcony—widows in black, plump children, men in their undershirts—and some of them looked on disapprovingly, unhappy about the noise, but most played along. Then, after another half an hour, the other team must have scored because you could hear a few swear words and then nothing, and nobody came out with a flag and you felt sorry. Who would have thought it: you didn't even know who was playing.

And so you spent the whole afternoon lazing around, leafed through a couple of comic books, ate a whole packet of crackers, listened to the radio, dozed, tolerated the heat, read ninety-odd pages of volume two of *War and Peace* (which, at this rate, will take you precisely eleven months to finish), read every single article in some old magazines left behind by the two Sicilians. You learned that the Moscow public library contains forty million, seven hundred thousand books; you learned that in Sri Lanka a worker who complained about a defective piece of machinery which sliced a fellow worker's finger off had been executed along with the lawyer who tried to defend him; that the human heart beats one hundred thousand, eight hundred times a day on average; and that the percentage of Italian students who have used drugs at least once in the preceding year is forty-three. Most of all, you thought about Cristina.

In the evening, you switched on the TV and watched several programmes, skipping from one channel to the next, unable to settle on anything for more than ten minutes, until you came upon a programme about the villages in the oil-producing areas of Nigeria on RAI 3 and saw poverty and filth and forests destroyed by oil and polluted rivers and locals denouncing Shell and Agip—awful stuff. Then you tried to go to sleep but couldn't, and you lay on your bed with your eyes open in the darkness, still thinking about Cristina.

In the middle of the night, having tossed and turned for a couple of hours, you went out onto the balcony, and everything was peaceful and quiet, there were no electric lights, just the glimmer of the moon and the cool air, and you smoked a cigarette or two, leaning over the railing, and your mind was filled with worries—about the future, the Big C and Cristina—but you drove them away and finished a half-empty but well-stoppered bottle of Nero d'Avola left behind by the Sicilians. A fabulous wine, which made you feel better: you relished the cool night air, humming Carole King's 'It's Too Late' in a version all your own, less sad and suggestive than the original, more bouncy, more pop. You remembered the faces of the day, all at the same time: the Nigerians on the floor below and the ones on the TV, with their anti-Agip and Shell placards; your magico-animistic demons; the characters in the Napoleon cartoon; Cristina and Grissino and Milo; the Moroccans and their satellite dish; one of the Abruzzo kids, cheerful and chubby, with whom you often kick a ball about in the courtyard; and you thought, with a little help from the wine, that none of these things would exist if you didn't exist and that being alive is the most amazing thing in the world and that out there there's work and money and you're reasonably capable and you've always managed somehow and you don't see why you shouldn't manage in the future; and then you made yourself some camomile tea and had a wank and, finally, went to sleep.

Chapter fourteen

In which our subjects are a hot July sales season, human stupidity, cartridges in pneumatic tubes, and building managers, and in which someone finally reveals how to bring quality tourism to Italy.

All of a sudden one day, as you and Cristina are walking along Via dei Mille, a very blonde little girl comes running out of a doorway and wraps her arms around Cristina's leg, seeking protection. "Help! Help! Sebi's trying to spit on me," she whines, twisting her head round to look into the doorway.

You both look over and see a little boy with puffed-out cheeks watching you from the other side of the courtyard, unsure what to do. At this point the little girl looks up, but the expressions on your faces are so bewildering that she lets go of Cristina quickly and runs back into the hall.

"You don't scare me, Sebi: if you spit at me one more time, I'll hit you," she shouts menacingly.

Sebi waits patiently until she's level with him and unleashes a stream of water in her face, then they start chasing each other and disappear from sight.

You look at Cristina and say, ironically, "Look what we've

become; we scare small children. They'd rather be spat on than stay anywhere near us."

It must be said that you look more like a pair of ruthless killers in a Hollywood movie than a pair of salespeople: you're both wearing black suits, black shoes, dark glasses and carrying brand new, still shiny leather briefcases. On top of which, the suffocating heat and the fact that Cristina is answering your every question in monosyllables have put a sinister frown on your face.

This time, too, Cristina limits herself to a polite smile and doesn't say a word. You know very well that when a woman behaves like this it means there's something behind it that a man is incapable of understanding, but you hope this behaviour is just down to the fatigue and overwork brought on by the great success of the publicity campaign. The intense barrage of billboards, radio spots and direct mail has resulted in a remarkable number of calls to our free telephone line, testing Serena to the limit: everyone wants further information on Bulls on Wheels' rates. That's why you've been visiting potential customers for the last three days, and the number of visits converted into orders is incredible. Grissino has instructed you, for the first week, to go to every meeting in pairs and to swap around as much as possible so as to learn from each other. But for the coming week there are as many as thirty appointments a day, so all four of you will have to work alone, and fast: there will be plenty of hard work to do.

You and Cristina arrive at a big wrought-iron gate and stop by the intercom, above which there is a sign: Pablo de Sarasate Institute of Music. You ring, and the answer is the metallic click of the lock; you open the gate and walk down a long gloomy passage which opens into a small, rather cloister-like courtyard. On your right you notice a small dark green door, ajar. As you go in, the air conditioning assaults you: you find yourselves in a spacious, brightly lit reception area with spotlessly white vaulted ceiling, walls, furnishings and decorations. A secretary politely asks whom you wish to see and Cristina answers that you have an appointment with the director, Mrs Conde.

"Please take a seat in the waiting room," the secretary says, directing you to a room on her left.

You go into a second room, also white, and sit down in an

armchair. You watch Cristina as she walks over to the window, her manner suggesting that she's annoyed to be here with you; you follow the outline of her slim, pale legs through the skirt of her suit, then you look away and pick up a magazine. Somewhere in the world the average salary for a man is five dollars a month. If all of humanity were to experience the same standard of living as the rich countries, it would be necessary to have seven planet Earths to use as sources of raw materials and repositories of waste. There are children of ten who work in shoe factories from six in the morning till five in the evening in return for one meal a day and two dollars a month. It seems, however, that the top story of the week is the release of a new handbag by the Fendi sisters: it costs several million lire and is available only in the most exclusive Milan boutiques. Apparently there are American women who are willing to fly across the Atlantic just to get hold of this valuable novelty. You hope the taxis that take them back to Malpensa blow up on the way.

Cristina moves away from the window, comes over to you and strokes your hair. She looks at you tenderly, as if apologizing for something. Just then, a heavily made-up woman appears in the door and says shrilly, "Here I am, here I am!" She comes over to you and, as you get up to shake her hand, adds formally, "Marisa Conde, Marisa Conde. Thank you for coming."

She is a very tall woman, pear-shaped, about fifty, designer labels from top to bottom. Maybe you know the type, gentle readers—star sign Prada, with Armani in the ascendant, Mercury in Valentino and Venus in Gucci. She shows you into her office, a masterpiece of international minimalist furnishing, everything spotlessly white, needless to say. She sits down behind the desk and gestures for you to sit in the two chairs in front of her. Then she starts talking: a torrential flow of foolishness, delivered with disarming naïvety and given added spice by a ridiculous nervous habit that often makes her repeat the first part of a sentence.

To begin with, she talks about the Institute of Music and tells you its entire history, from its founding to the present day, including the most recent events, "Even though I know you young people are only interested in rock...." Then she starts talking about Turin,

"It's become, it's become so vulgar, so dirty, thanks to all these Arabs. Think of me what you will. I'm all for a multi-ethnic society, but I'd rather it was with Germans and Swedes, not with these people who call us infidels and consider us women not much better than camels." Then she goes on to talk about her career, "I started, I started as a housewife, but, you know, my husband was in politics;" about her son, "Oh, he's thirty years old but he doesn't do a thing: the hardest thing he does all day is press the button on his shaving foam before he shaves;" her job, "This, this is a good job, you know. Some mornings, if I need it, I call my husband's driver and have him take me all the way home;" her office, "Do you like it? Do you like it? An architect friend of mine did it for me. And ikebana? Do you like my ikebana? I arranged it myself, with my own hands. I did a course in Japan, last month...." But above all she talks about herself and her interests, "You see, you see: I love Gucci. More than anything. I love Gucci. Everything he makes, every dress, every accessory gets me going: my heart races when I'm in front of a Gucci window display...."

Half an hour later, fortunately, she gets to the point. "The point, the point is, I called your free number because I got your letter. Well, first of all, thanks: it was very kind of you to write to me. How did you know we needed you?"

You and Cristina, in turn, start to enumerate the benefits of your service; lower prices than the competition, efficiency, the chance to buy booklets of a hundred delivery vouchers in advance, at a fifteen per cent discount. Mrs Conde stares at you, motionless, her eyes empty. She seems more like some kind of prototype robot, equipped with only basic gestures, than a human being: you can tell when she's thinking because she nods and her eyes squint. But she doesn't seem to understand much: if there were a digital panel on her forehead it would probably display "syntax error, repeat input" continuously. Then it's like she wakes up, and she starts asking a series of incredibly stupid, exasperating questions. You and Cristina answer patiently.

"But it's absurd to have to pay in advance," she objects at one point, squinting. "We pay everything in arrears."

"That's not quite right, madam. In the courier business payment is always in advance: when you send a letter you have to buy a stamp beforehand. In the same way, when you want an express delivery you have to buy a book of vouchers."

"Yes, that's true. It's like stamps. I hadn't thought of that."

She squints again, for a long time, and finally asks another question. "And how do you make these deliveries? On mopeds?"

The only way this woman would notice she had a brain would be if she suffered a stroke. You look at her without betraying any kind of emotion. You want to play a joke on her. "Actually," you answer sweetly, "we've adapted the existing sewer network to interconnect the whole city by means of a system of pneumatic tubes and cartridges: we put our deliveries in these big suppositories and shoot them around with compressed air at six hundred kilometres an hour."

Cristina glances at you with some hostility, but Mrs Conde, who has been listening distractedly, squints in bafflement and finally comments, "It's quite amazing what they can do with technology nowadays."

The days go by monotonously and arduously. Every morning at seven o'clock sharp, all four of you meet in the conference room to share out the day's appointments. You're generally out on the street by eight, and you go on paying visits until late at night. No big deal: it's what any half-way decent salesman does as a matter of course, but you're not used to it. You're tired, irritable, stressed out. Within a few days you look different: Cristina has huge bags under her eyes and Milo's face is drawn, his eyes permanently bloodshot, like someone who's been through some kind of smog therapy.

Grissino, on the other hand, is in his element: he flatters you, tries to buck you up, digs out prospects and notes, explains that everything is going very well. "Subjects, we're working like stars: in these first few days we've managed to make about twenty personal visits a day. In money terms, that's about thirty million a day, an unbelievable average, a million and a half per visit. Considering not every visit results in a sale, that's a fantastic result. Next week, as we agreed, we'll start working on our own: Serena's setting up thirty appointments a day, seven or eight each. That's a lot, and it'll be demanding, so I'm asking you not to go out at night, to go to bed early and look after yourselves. If one of us falls ill and spends three days in bed, we could lose forty or fifty million."

And it's Grissino who sets up the pairings every day and organizes the visits, sorting them according to their difficulty and earning potential. For each customer who calls the free number, Serena prepares a file containing every bit of information and a symbol showing what Grissino calls, American-style, a "ranking": the letters A to E, in descending order, indicate the level of difficulty of the visit, while the numbers 1 to 5, also in descending order, indicate the earning potential. A meeting with the buyer for a bank is ranked A-1, because the type of person in question is hard-nosed but the chances of closing a substantial deal are high. The ideal customer, of course, is an E-1—an easy mark with a high earning potential—but you've never yet managed to assign this ranking to anyone.

Your first appointment today is an A-1 and you're with Grissino: the annual Building Managers' Association convention is taking place at the Lingotto, and the treasurer of the Turin branch has asked to meet you there because he wants to place an order for five hundred vouchers.

Sitting in the taxi on your way to the Lingotto, you're not in the best of moods and you don't say a word; through the window you look at the passers by, the shop windows, the other cars baking in the sun. Last night you tried to call Cristina at home, since her mobile is permanently switched off, but Milo answered and told you they were already in bed and worn out. You asked if everything was all right and he snorted, "Are you kidding? Everything's great! We're making millions!"

So you went out for a ride on your Vespa. You went round the Murazzi and then the Roman quarter, but it was a strange evening: there weren't many people about and you didn't feel like staying in any one place. You went home but couldn't get to sleep, so you surveyed the programmes on television and settled on a film in which Christophe Lambert hung about in the Paris metro in a dinner jacket with some kind of neon tube in his hand.

You thought what might happen between you and Milo if he found out you had slept with Cristina. You thought about all the things you'd been through together, how this was a real betrayal, how he was one of the few people in the world you really cared about. You felt like a worm. You tried telling yourself that he had cheated on Cristina too, after all; that if something happened between you and her, it wasn't just your fault, it was their fault too, his for cheating on her, and hers for fooling around with you—but they were just excuses and weren't good enough. You also thought about what you would all do, once the money had been shared out. Grissino would go his own way, of course. But the three of you? At first you think you could go somewhere in South America together. And then what? How would things turn out? How would the trio hold up together? Sooner or later it had to split up, no question about it. Milo would never accept it if Cristina swapped his arms for yours; at the very least, he'd go off on his own. And you'd have Cristina, of course, but you'd lose Milo, and just thinking about it makes your stomach churn. On the other hand, how long could you bear being with the two of them after what happened? Not long: you'd go off on your own, and you'd be alone. Alone. It would probably be best if Cristina left: you and Milo would be unhappy, but it would be just the two of you, ready to start afresh, this time with money, and in fact this idea gives you some comfort. But Cristina would never leave; she's in the best position. She can choose to stay with him or take up with you, or even choose to leave things as they are and stay with him but fool around with you. All in all, you don't see a way out. Maybe you should just be content and concentrate on the fact that you're earning millions, but instead you're here, thinking about it.

Once out of the taxi, you and Grissino walk across the spacious square in front of the Lingotto, heading towards the conference centre. Just before you reach the glass doors, you pass two kids sitting at a table collecting signatures. One, wearing a white tee-shirt with the peace symbol on it, steps forward. "Are you against war?" he asks Grissino.

Grissino walks by without stopping and says, "Everyone's against war. You're wasting your time, subject."

The kid takes a couple of steps and stands in his way. "If you're against war and against world hunger, you have to sign," he orders him.

Grissino smiles mockingly. "Hey, subject, aren't you being a bit aggressive for someone who's against war?"

Then, without leaving time for him to answer, he goes on. "Look, I'm against war, I'm for peace on earth and goodwill to all men, I'm for jobs for all, I'm for a global minimum wage of five thousand dollars a month. But I don't know how to achieve it. Do you?"

The kid hesitates, then says, "No, I don't. But that's not up to me."

Grissino: "Of course not: you don't know, and it's not up to you. Well, I've had it up to here with people who say peace and prosperity for everyone, and when you ask how, they say, I don't know, it's not my job, but I want honour and glory for proving my heart's in the right place. I want to hear some plans, some serious proposals, I'd like to discuss the Tobin Tax and, to begin with, how to overthrow all the dictators lining up to get the money...."

The other kid comes over and says to the first, "Forget it: look at their clothes. They're just bourgeois shits."

Grissino looks at him sweetly. "Help me out here. What kind of pacifist are you? The kind that's against uniforms but thinks anyone not wearing his should be ignored? I don't think you know anything about pacifism. And you're not here to collect signatures. You're here to collect money for yourselves...."

At this point you grab Grissino by the arm and drag him away while the two kids hurl various terms of abuse at him.

You're furious. "For Christ's sake, you need help: you've got a case of Preacher's Syndrome. Must you pick a fight with everyone you meet?"

Grissino wriggles free and straightens his jacket.

"Those two are con men," he huffs, "not pacifists. I was just trying to provoke them."

When you enter the hall, the Building Managers' convention is still in full swing. A stocky speaker is inveighing against the secretary of a political party, slipping in pearls like "...and when this man is no longer in place, things will go better for us building managers." His mouth contains four or five cartridges of adverbs, which he machine-guns at his audience: every phrase begins with a "without further ado" or a "duly" or a splendid "graciously." You and Grissino are the only people in the room listening. Thirty-five per cent of those present are talking aloud; two per cent are asleep; twenty per cent are reading the newspaper—some blatantly, some with varying degrees of furtiveness; the remainder are outside the hall, talking into their mobile phones. Sitting in front of you, in the last row but one, there are two men, one very old, one middle-aged, who look like they've stepped out of a film by Totò. The older man must be half deaf, because every thirty seconds he asks the younger one what's being said, pointing to the podium, and the younger one says, "Nonsense, dad, just the usual nonsense."

Finally, the speaker comes to a close "without further ado" and "graciously" hands over to the next speaker, a short, plump man, completely bald, who steps up to the podium, adjusts the microphone to his height and gets out a small sheet of paper. He starts to read out loud, so quickly you can't understand a word he's saying, but then he has a panic attack and starts trembling and stammering. The microphone screeches, causing much of the audience to stop reading their newspapers in irritation. The man's contribution turns out to be brief, fortunately, and just as he closes, looking like he's about to have a heart attack, the lights suddenly go out. It's half past ten in the morning but it looks like a gala evening: a spotlight illuminates the stage with a cone of light and a presenter in a dinner jacket appears. "And now, friends, a short break. While coffee is being served at the back of the hall, Tonio Banco, a very special musician and a cousin of the vice president, will entertain you on the piano with some pieces by Liszt."

There is some discreet applause, and the old man in front of you asks, "pieces by whom?"

"Prinz, some kind of musician," replies the son, with a long-suffering air. Then they both get up and walk over to the tables at the back of the hall, where a couple of timid-looking waiters are trying to cope with a full-blown siege.

Grissino stays in his seat beside you, shakes his head and starts philosophizing. "The thing is, subject, Marx was wrong. He believed in the proletariat. Not enough to acknowledge the son he had by his housemaid, but still...he believed in it. He thought the differences between people were all down to money, and once that had been redistributed, everyone would be cultured and educated...and the world would be a better place. But if Marx came back today, I'm sure he'd be dismayed: in this part of the world we're all well off, we have compulsory schooling, we study...and yet we're more ignorant, greedy and selfish than ever. The truth is, Marx greatly over-estimated mankind."

"Maybe you should start sermonizing in the Valentino again," you mutter. "I get the impression you can't do without it. But I must say your view is rather simplistic: I don't think people are so easy to pigeonhole and judge, they're not baskets of fruit, oranges here, bananas over there...."

Grissino smiles. "Come on, let's use the break to find this treasurer."

You've spent the last half hour on a secluded sofa with the treasurer, outside the conference hall, where the work of the convention goes on. He is a thin, dry man with frog-like eyes hidden behind a pair of round glasses. Grissino has explained, carefully and patiently, all the benefits of using Bulls on Wheels' services, but the man is still behaving very coolly. Finally he asks you to excuse him for a moment and gets up to greet a colleague, so you take the opportunity to murmur to Grissino, "I don't get this. He called us, but he doesn't seem at all interested."

"Uh-huh," says Grissino pensively. "Now watch and learn."

The treasurer comes back and sits down again. Grissino starts up. "To sum up—I imagine you're already using a courier service you trust?"

"Yes," the treasurer confirms.

"But I imagine our prices are lower?"

"That's right. That's why I asked to see you."

"I imagine, too, that changing suppliers is always a bit difficult, not just a financial calculation."

"That's right," the treasurer agrees.

Grissino lowers his voice and goes on, conspiratorially. "I see. Well, the thing is, we...we wouldn't want to disturb the present, shall we say, status quo...and whatever benefits you enjoy of a, shall we say, personal nature...from your current supplier...well, you can rest assured that we'll match them."

The treasurer brightens. "I see we understand each other," he says. Then he scribbles something on a business card and holds it in front of your eyes for a second. You read "15%."

Grissino touches the knot of his tie and his face opens into a broad grin. "No problem. You'll have it with every order, at the same time."

So the treasurer pulls out a federation cheque book and quickly writes a cheque for four million, two hundred and fifty thousand lire. He hands it to Grissino, then stands up and shakes your hand. "It's a deal," he says. "I'll expect a delivery from you within two days: five books of a hundred vouchers each, and a plain brown envelope containing my cut in cash."

The days go by quickly and you work continuously, rushing around the city all day, from one appointment to the next, without a moment's rest, not even time to think, and inside you there's a hard core of exhaustion, a kind of blurring at the edges, but also a sense of deep satisfaction because things are getting better and—I know it sounds silly, but still—*you're doing a good job.*

By now you and Milo are consistently paired up with each other, because Grissino always wants Cristina with him, and in fact she is a big help in the A-1-type meetings—Grissino prefers to manage these personally—since she distracts the male clients and acts as a sort of universal open sesame. You haven't been paired up with Cristina since the meeting at the Institute of Music: you see her fleetingly at the morning meetings, but you never manage to talk to her. From time to time you try calling her on her mobile, but it's always switched off and in the end you tell yourself that in some ways it's probably just as well you have to put off explaining things to each other.

"I can't wait for the weekend, so I can get some rest," says Milo as you walk beneath the arcades on Via Nizza.

"Are you joking?" you retort. "Grissino's already told us we have to be in the office on Saturday and Sunday: we need to go over the week's meetings, do the books, work out how much we've brought in...."

"Christ," he says. "I'm worn out. I'm not used to working like this."

He pauses, then says, "Though I must say I'm enjoying it. Last night I had an amazing idea."

You look at him questioningly.

"I was thinking," he continues. "What if we took on a few couriers and actually started to do some deliveries in September? We'd have found ourselves a real job, no?"

You look at him, stunned. Milo bursts out laughing and claps you on the shoulder. "Gotcha, subject," he says, mimicking Grissino, then abruptly looks up and stops. "Here it is, number twenty-nine. Let's go in."

You're beginning to learn that the entrance to a business is often a good indicator of the atmosphere in all its departments. The offices of Dahl Limited (industrial lubricants, annual turnover forty billion) have a vast entrance, at the back of which, behind a reception desk that wouldn't look out of place in a five-star hotel, you can just make out two receptionists at work. The atmosphere is rarefied, like in an aquarium, and the two women move in slow motion, speak in hushed voices, and handle faxes delicately, as if they were soap bubbles.

When you go up and ask for Mr Rinaldo Dahl, the two receptionists look horrified. "*Doctor* Dahl," one of them emphasizes.

Then she leads you over to a half-concealed door and asks you to wait in a small windowless lounge with pale red walls and diffuse lighting. You and Milo joke a bit about how it feels like a crypt, then you notice that there's a water cooler in the corner, the standard white column with the large plastic container on top. Since you're hot and don't feel very well, you take a beaker of water and drop in an aspirin. Just then a man comes in, fortyish, tanned, gleaming white teeth and a pair of deep grooves running between his nose and cheeks, making him look like a boxer dog.

"The gentlemen from Bulls on Wheels?" he asks overbearingly.

You nod, and he says, "Good morning. I'm Doctor Dahl."

He shakes your hands as you introduce yourselves, then, noticing that there's something fizzy in your beaker, he asks, "Is that to calm you down? I see you've been warned about me." He looks pleased with himself.

Where did this idiot come from? Where do people like him get the idea they're so important that people need a sedative before talking to them? Really, gentle readers, what sort of a world do we live in?

"No, it's just aspirin," you say, shrugging and looking at him like he's mentally defective.

He frowns and says, commandingly, "Come to my office."

You think it will be a real pleasure to cheat someone like this.

You follow him down a narrow corridor lined with doors and awful pictures until you reach an office at least fifty square metres in size, with an enormous desk and some antiques behind a protective cordon of brass and velvet rope. Standing behind the desk is a broomstick-like figure with a straw-coloured wig which Dahl introduces as his wife; it promptly vanishes. Then he sits down at the desk and indicates that you may sit down. "You may be surprised to find yourselves talking to the most senior person in the firm on such a simple matter," he says pompously, "but I trust no one here and I handle all the buying personally."

You hold back from reacting by looking down at your feet, then you look up and manage to say, in a very serious voice, "It's an honour for us to be talking to you."

Dahl beams with self-satisfaction and starts telling you the story of his life—where he was born, where he studied, what he learned, how he started out, why he is where he is now, how he is a self-made man and so on: an exhaustive account of how anyone lucky enough to have capital, ambition and guts can achieve anything. Here's a list of things you think about while he's talking: how long it would take for his body to decompose in this office; that Giorgio Gaber song in which he says God is as precise as a Sweda watch; that bit of Descartes where he argues (him too) that life is a fraud; the fact that our ruling class is blind and deaf, but unfortunately not mute; the DJs at Docks and their psycho-delicatessen; the question: What if God were a fat black momma?; your magico-animistic demons; Cristina's ass; the fact that love encompasses many ways of winning—winning by running away, by coming back, by laughing, by crying, winning by telling lies, by staying sincere—but the point is: what wins? There's no sign of intelligence in this office, and yet Milo and you go on taking notes.

Dahl notices you're not paying attention, stops talking and looks at you instead. "Ah," you improvise. "Of course."

Just then the telephone rings. He answers, then stands up and disappears, saying he has to leave us for a minute. Milo looks around for a minute and you whisper, "The man's a worm."

"But when it comes to money, he's a giant," he reflects.

"I don't care: when it comes to humility, he's a midget," you reply.

He smiles. "So, to sum up: the man's a giant when it comes to money, a midget when it comes to humility, and a worm when it comes to manners. So what's new? A good proportion of the people who make the world go round are like that, Vittorio. Get used to it."

At this point Dahl comes back in, but he doesn't sit down; instead, he goes over to the window and starts looking out. "Do you know the difference between people like me and ordinary people?" he asks, seriously.

"That you're an asshole?" you think, but instead you put on an interested expression and ask, "What is it?"

He points at a group of high-rise blocks visible through the window. "Look at that," he says. "There are plenty of people out there with dreams in their desk drawers, saying they'd like to do this or that. But they don't do it. They don't do it. Do you understand? That's the difference."

Milo seizes his cue and puts on a dreamy expression. "You know, perhaps you don't realize it," he says ingratiatingly, "but you've just given me a wonderful gift. You could say you've opened my mind.

Allow me to give you an extra five percent discount on top of the offer we're about to make you."

Barely twenty minutes later, you're leaving Dahl's office with his "No thanks, I'm not interested" still ringing in your ears.

"You know," you say to Milo as you go back down the corridor with the awful pictures, "when you think about it...well, everyone who's ever lived in this world since the beginning of time, like, they're all dead."

"Brilliant insight," Milo replies sarcastically. "Must be Shakespeare, *King Lear*, Act Four, Scene One. So?"

"So? Well, after meeting an asshole like that, it's an insight that helps me rest easier."

The next day you're in a charmless and crowded bar in the city centre, sitting among the tables that divide the bar itself from the lottery machines. Grissino is sipping his "barley coffee in a large cup with brown sugar" and going on about how pleased he is and how things are going even more smoothly than he expected, and you're listening distractedly, looking intently at a man sitting next to you reading the *Gazzetta dello Sport* with as much satisfaction as if it were a will making him the sole heir to two hundred billion. Suddenly, he looks up from his newspaper and gets a mobile phone (on vibrate) out of his jacket pocket. "Hello.... Yes.... Ah, hello Doctor Passo.... Of course... whatever you want... but I can't right now, I'm with some customers.... I'll call you back in about half an hour."

He puts the mobile back in his pocket and buries himself in his newspaper again.

"I like him," says Grissino, who has noticed the whole scene. "He's one of us."

Your appointment with the purchasing manager of a bank, which could result in a record order worth six million, is in a magnificent building a couple of blocks away. You're a bit on edge, but Grissino's calm reassures you, he doesn't stop talking for one moment along the way. "You see, subject, the job of a purchasing manager is an interesting one: they don't know anything about anything, but they have to buy everything, from generators to toilet brushes. Some-times they're agreeable, open-minded people; other times they're very shrewd assholes, paid according to how much money they save. But don't worry, even they are human beings like us."

You walk by three kids with extensively pierced faces standing at the bottom of the stairs leading to the entrance of the best-known private boarding school in the city. They're talking among themselves, and as you go by one of them raises his voice: "...and not like those slaves of the system there, with their jackets and ties."

You turn to see which of them might have uttered this banality, but Grissino has already stopped. You stare him down immediately and decisively. "Don't you dare! Leave it, for chrissakes, it's already hot enough, who gives a shit about three kids spewing out commonplaces? Come on, we've got a tricky meeting ahead of us." But he's not even listening, he goes up to the three and, with his usual calm, looks at the one who spoke. "Are you talking to me?" he asks.

The boy, who looks surly and whose forehead is peppered with spots, turns and spits to his right, then looks at Grissino and says sullenly, "You and all the other slaves of the system."

You look at your watch and call Grissino again, telling him you have more important things to do, but he doesn't answer. He puts one foot on the first step and goes down on one knee, looking at the boy, then says, "Yes, it's true, I'm a slave of the system and I wear a jacket and tie. And do you know why?"

The boy looks over at his friends, amused, then shakes his head and says defiantly, "You tell me, slave."

You're fuming, you can't bear Grissino's posturing, his way of attacking everyone he meets. You weigh whether it's going to come to blows, you'd like to see how Grissino would perform—he's tall and hefty and looks like someone you'd better not argue with—but who knows.

"You see, subject," he explains gently, "I'm a slave of the system because the best jobs have all been taken by people like you, with parents who pay six hundred thousand a month for them to be educated. In a democratic country, you would be a cleaner on the railways, but unfortunately, this fuckawful system, of which I am a slave, will allow you, by dint of kicks in the ass and your family's money, to get a degree by the time you're thirty and get a better job than mine."

Then he gets back to his feet and says, "So what do you three really think? You think you're rebels because you've got a couple of earrings in your face? Do me a favour! Is that it? The sum total of your rebellion? Get out of here: I've seen thousands of rebels like you, whole herds of rebels like you."

One of the boys flanking the first one sniggers. "What the hell's your problem, old man? Piss off!" but the first one doesn't say anything.

You grab Grissino by the arm and say, "Come on, let's go."

So Grissino turns round and comes away.

After a few yards you explode. "Jesus! It's like a joke! We've got important things to think about and without fail you get involved in these ridiculous situations.... You've got Preacher's Syndrome. You need help.... Are you quite satisfied, now you've sorted those three children out?"

"Yes," he answers imperturbably, "and I hope to swindle that particular one's father and see him in a few years, selling encyclopae-dias in a jacket and tie. I can't stand listening to such nonsense."

You shake your head. "But they're kids, Grissino, maybe fifteen years old: that's what we were all like at that age. You know what they say; if you weren't an anarchist at fifteen you were never young."

"You just don't understand, subject," he sighs. "These are the important things in life."

The headquarters of the bank makes its presence felt with a huge marble lobby designed to make you feel inferior. As soon as you get to the reception desk, Grissino whispers: "Don't trust these people, subject. There are posters all over the place saying they're entirely at your disposal, and yet, look around, the pens are chained down."

You smile at him. And your smile contains something you wish you could tell him. You smile and your eyes light up; you smile deeply, magically; you smile a smile that moves you from head to foot; you smile a smile that enters into your guts, a smile that instantly sweeps away your recent irritation; you smile a smile that makes you understand the real reason you're here with Grissino; you smile because you remember that passage of Kerouac's, which you've read and re-read so many times you know it by heart, the one in which he says: "...because the only people for me are the mad ones, the ones who are mad to live, mad to talk, mad to be saved, desirous of everything at the same time, the ones who never yawn or say a commonplace thing, but burn, burn, burn like fabulous yellow roman candles exploding like spiders across the stars and in the middle you see the blue centrelight pop and everybody goes 'Awww!'"

Grissino asks for Doctor Lasdalle, the manager of the purchasing department, and a brunette with honey-coloured eyes immediately leads you upstairs to an elegant waiting room, where she asks you to wait for a few minutes. The room is rectangular, with milky-white walls, furnished with a dozen dark leather chairs and a low table on which a few business magazines have been placed. The usual antique prints hang on the walls and, at the end, there is a large fish tank which you instinctively approach. Dozens of tiny silver and orange fish are swimming around inside, the biggest no bigger than a cigarette end. You watch them in silence for a while, fascinated.

"Quite a big tank," you say to Grissino, just to say something.

"Yes," he says, "and the fish are tiny."

You go back to watching the tank like children.

"I wonder," you say aloud. "They're so small: maybe they don't even realize they're enclosed in a place with no way out."

Grissino puts his right index finger on the glass, in front of one of the little fish, which goes into reverse with a single stroke of its tail and disappears into the background. He says: "Maybe there's someone up there watching you and me and saying the same thing to someone else."

You're sitting in the office of Giovanni Lasdalle, manager of the purchasing department, and you are struck most of all by his nose, which in profile presents a precise quarter-circle, huge and perfect, like one of Jacovitti's cartoon characters.

Lasdalle has asked you to sit down, but then his telephone rang and now he's involved in a conversation which is profoundly embarrassing for everyone sitting there listening. You'd think it would be embarrassing for him too, but since he shows no sign of being embarrassed it becomes embarrassing for you.

"Yes, my little sea-green-eyed pussy cat...yes...all right...yes, I understand, but...listen kitty-cat...yes, but wait...listen to your own true love...you're right, you're right, but...but we have to decide what to do with the little one in August...no, not in the boat with us...well yes, if you'd let me finish...yes, you're right...wait, let me think...wait a minute...what about if we sent him to Courmayeur with the Philippina? Eh? Not bad from your own true love, eh? What do you think, my little grass-green-eyed pussy cat? What do you mean there's a problem? Yes, it's true, you're right: if we leave him there he'll eat the whole carpet...listen, kitty-cat, let's give ourselves a bit of time to think about it, okay? We could ask Lucilla...yes, okay...I have to say goodbye now, I've got some suppliers here.... Love you...love you...yes, okay...love you, bye... kiss kiss...bye."

At last it's your turn. Grissino starts describing the Bulls on Wheels service, explaining the benefits in detail, comparing the prices with the competition's, overwhelming Lasdalle with his eloquence, passing the baton to you so that you can supplement, polish, intervene, comment, the end result being that you come off as a pair of true professionals and make a brilliant impression.

"In the case of an order of a certain size, since we're dealing with a customer of your calibre," Grissino says in conclusion, "we'll make an exception to our policy. As you know, our competitors all require cash on delivery of their vouchers. That's our policy too, but in your case we're offering thirty days' credit. Bearing in mind, as I explained to you earlier, that the Bulls on Wheels service won't be launched until the first of September, for organizational reasons."

Lasdalle now calls in a colleague, and together they fill out an order form, then the colleague takes the form away and comes back about ten minutes later to tell you that everything is in order: the administration will sign it and send it on by fax. At the end, for some reason, Lasdalle feels obliged to take you to lunch. He's very insistent and you can't get out of it, but when you finally accept he remembers he has a previous engagement. He won't hear of your leaving and leaves you in the hands of another colleague. It's an absurd situation: Lasdalle goes off to the lunch he wants but you, who would like to go off to the lunch you want, are forced to have lunch with this colleague of his, who would presumably have liked to go off for the lunch he wants.

So you and Grissino end up at a table in a restaurant with this young functionary in a very smart chalk-stripe anthracite suit much more suitable for a wedding. The last button on the cuff is undone, which is code for tailor-made, but apart from the suit, the problem with this young man is that he has a cherry instead of a brain.

His hair is black, fine and curly and his manner is conceited. His opening gambit is particularly striking: "This is my fifth job in four years, you know, but I went to the Bocconi University and job rotation is very important for us Bocconi graduates."

Then he starts telling you all about his experiences as a student and employee, and as he talks his Adam's apple goes up and down: the boredom level rises and rises and the only way you can resist it is by ordering the most expensive dishes on the menu.

"You know," he says after a while, "I'm from Milan and I like Turin fine as a city. It's the people who leave something to be desired."

Then he asks if you're from Turin and you nod, somewhat ironically, and he flounders around, trying to recover from his blunder. "No, you can't be one hundred per cent Turinese, not through and through. There are very few real Turinese."

Grissino rises to his feet and says, rather formally, "No offence taken. Personally, I can't stand the Milanese, but then I also hate Milan."

There you go. And you were just wondering how he had managed to go almost an hour without attacking anyone. The result is three minutes of frosty silence, broken, mercifully, by the waiter bringing the first course. Grissino joins his hands and starts praying aloud. "Bless us, O Lord, for these Thy gifts which we are about to receive from Thy bounty, through Christ our Lord, amen."

The Bocconi graduate doesn't know what to do. He starts eating and, after a while, tries to get the conversation going again, remarking that the people at the next table are speaking English. "I'm sure you'll agree that tourism in Italy is a remarkable phenomenon," he says, gulping down a glass of Barbera.

Grissino utters his splendid "True," the word he uses any time he doesn't know what to say, and then looks at him as if encouraging him to go on. The young man does go on. "But I don't think the problem is tourism itself, so much as how to bring quality tourism to Italy."

"True," says Grissino again.

The young man becomes enthusiastic: he probably hasn't had two consecutive expressions of agreement with two consecutive statements since his university days. "And do you know why?" he asks excitedly.

"Why what?" asks Grissino distractedly.

The young man is annoyed. "Do you know why there isn't much quality tourism in Italy?"

You are hanging on his words. "Why?"

"Simple. There aren't enough golf courses in Italy."

You are stunned, and you ask yourself, how come so many of the people in this book are such assholes?

Chapter fifteen

*In which our subjects are hotel breakfasts, work, game,
how men and women really only understand each other
in short bursts, and in which homage is paid, in a small
way, to a sixteenth-century work by Gian Giorgio Alione.*

The following Wednesday, by which time you've become accustomed to going to all your appointments by yourself, a customer calls Cristina in the office—while you're all in a meeting—and postpones her first appointment of the day, so you suggest the two of you have breakfast and go on to your first appointment together. Surprisingly, she accepts, and you leave the office together.

Being dressed up like a manager from dawn to dusk has some notable advantages, among the best of which is that you can enjoy fabulous breakfast buffets, free, in the best hotels in the city centre. You usually attract less attention if you're alone, but after a brief discussion you agree it should work for two as well, so you walk a few blocks towards the railway station and a well-known four-star hotel in that area. Cristina doesn't stop talking as you walk: she inundates you with words, all unfortunately to do with sales problems or difficult situations during meetings with customers. You'd like to talk about the two of you, but you can't get a word in edgeways. You listen unenthusiastically until your attention is drawn to the sight of all the people stuck in their cars in the traffic, and notice how rarely anyone sounds their horn with real malice. Their reflexes are still half asleep, the beast within is still snoozing. You take pleasure in seeing how traffic lights allow a continuation of the morning toilette, providing pauses to relish: rear-view mirrors are turned towards faces, women brush their hair or put the finishing touches to their lipstick or mascara, men adjust their ties or comb their hair. You feel a general sense of complicity and brotherhood, a kind of wordless solidarity, the sensation that you're all marching towards the same scaffold. Cristina shakes your arm. "Hey, are you listening to me or what?"

You start, then look at her and calmly say, "No."

She mutters, "You're not very kind, you know." Then, absently, "I like that in a man."

You go into the lobby of the hotel, mingling with a group of conventioneers, from whom you quickly separate, and follow the signs marked 'breakfast' down the corridors. The dining room is chaotic: there are forty-odd tables laid in the usual way, with dozens of people sitting at them, and a long buffet table laden with a cornucopia of goodies; croissants, all kinds of doughnuts and pastries, crackers, brown bread, fresh white bread, toast, little packets of butter, jam, honey and Nutella, jugs of orange and grapefruit juice, fried eggs, bacon, cheeses, cold cuts, frankfurters, yoghurt, bowls of fresh fruit, cereals, muesli, milk—enough to feed an army. Cristina takes a seat at an empty table while you head for the buffet, quickly load two plates with treats and join her.

You start eating, slowly, and she goes on asking you questions about work, how you respond to certain objections, how you get round others. You don't let yourself get involved, you answer without enthusiasm, but after a while you realize that perhaps she's only asking all these questions because she's afraid you'll change the subject, so you interrupt brusquely. "Why don't we talk about us instead?" you ask.

She looks down at her plate abruptly.

You glance around the room, as if someone might be listening. "I don't know whether I have a right to an explanation or not," you insist, "but it seems pretty silly if I can't even talk to you."

She looks at you for a long time, right into your eyes, then says, "You're absolutely right, Vittorio. I'd just like you to give me a little more time. Wait until we've finished this month's work. Please."

She pauses, then goes on. "Act like time is suspended, hanging in the air, don't ask me any questions. Trust me. Please."

You don't know what to say, so you look over at a group of English tourists in shorts and T-shirts.

You change the subject. "How's it going with Grissino? You're with him all the time now."

"Well, we're starting to get along. And we're closing a lot of orders. I must say I'm starting to like him, he's a real character."

She looks at you. "You're not jealous too, like Milo?"

You don't say anything for a moment, thinking about how to respond, and a middle-aged waitress, blonde, comes over to your table with pen and pad in hand. "May I have your room number?" she says politely.

You smile at her and nod. "Hold on, I've got the keys right here."

You start searching your jacket pockets, in vain of course, then your trouser pockets, then you make a funny face at the waitress and say to Cristina, "Didn't you lock up, darling?"

She looks at you adoringly, nods and rifles through her handbag.

"I can't find them," she says.

The waitresses is looking impatient now. "All I need is the number," she says.

So you make something up. "Two hundred and twelve."

She writes the number down on her pad, thanks you and disappears.

As you enter the headquarters of the award-winning firm of Ettore Schmitz & Sons, the first thing that strikes you is a strange smell of old age, subtle at first, like the smell of a well-thumbed phone book, but then stronger, until it smells like *minestrone*. The lobby is a large grey room, and the first thing you notice is a marble column bearing a bronze bust of the founder: Ettore Schmitz, as the notice underneath explains. The three receptionists behind the desk, who all look well over sixty, greet you with kindly smiles. When you tell them the reason for your visit, one of the three stands up and takes you directly to the office of Ettore Schmitz III, where she asks you to wait for him.

The room is medium-sized, austere, the antique walnut furniture shiny with the patina of long use. Behind the desk there's a map of Italy, studded with pins bearing little red flags, and a narrow frame with a striking motto: *"Man is only possible as a predator.* Friedrich Dürrenmatt."

After a while, a little old lady appears at the door. She's about seventy, and covered with ribbons and bows. Speaking with difficulty, she asks you to wait a few minutes. When she is sure you've understood her words, she limps off.

"Well," says Cristina somewhat maliciously. "It seems the fountain of youth has temporarily dried up."

"Seems so," you laugh. "I remember her in *Whatever Happened to Baby Jane?*"

"Yes," she smiles, "in the role of Whatever Happened."

Christ, you think, this awful bit of repartee is the first joke you've exchanged in two weeks. Just then, Ettore Schmitz III arrives. He is a fine, healthy-looking sixty-year-old, slim, with a well-groomed moustache and intelligent eyes. He introduces himself quickly and, as he sits down, notices that you're looking at the map of Italy. He grins broadly. "Don't be alarmed by the flags," he says. "They don't mean we have tanks in those places."

Upon which he takes a letter out of a drawer, and when he opens it on the desk you recognize it as one from your agency.

"So, you are Bulls on Wheels," he says. "Bulls on Wheels," he repeats, with a touch of irony, looking you in the eye. "Right. Tell me everything I need to know."

You and Cristina start with the usual explanation. Meanwhile, he starts cleaning the inside of the middle drawer of his desk with what looks like a make-up brush. Then he cleans the telephone receiver, the photograph of his wife, his desk diary, his calculator, a pile of timesheets, his pens, the tape dispenser, a pair of scissors, the ruler and the lamp. When you stop, he says, "Go on, I'm listening. It's just that the cleaners do such a terrible job."

Cristina finishes describing the advantages of your service. "Basically, we're a new agency for private deliveries. We're young and dynamic. We can guarantee swift delivery of correspondence on excellent terms. We guarantee delivery within three hours, anywhere in the city, and we're available twenty-four hours a day."

The man interrupts. "Fine, I understand: you're the best. Like everyone else. But let's talk money."

Having said this, he places a blank sheet of paper on the desk, then gets an electric pencil-sharpener out of a drawer and positions it on the edge of the desktop, tightening up the clamp. He inserts a new pencil into the hole and you hear an electric buzzing sound. Satisfied, he removes the sharpened pencil as you start to explain. "What we do is sell deliveries in booklets of a hundred vouchers. Once you have the vouchers, all you do is stick one on the envelope or package you want to send and call our number: within an hour, one of our motorcycle couriers comes and collects the consignment and delivers it to its destination. Each voucher, or each delivery, costs ten thousand lire, so a booklet costs a million. But there's a fifteen per cent discount or, if you prefer, we can give you a block of fifteen extra vouchers free."

The man looks at you doubtfully. "That's a lot of deliveries for us. A hundred and fifteen in a year...."

You hold his gaze. "Well, it's one every three days."

The man looks at Cristina. "Suppose we're interested. When does your service begin?"

"Well," answers Cristina, "our service begins on the first of September, for organizational reasons. In practice you pay now, in July. As soon as your payment clears, one of our couriers will immediately deliver your booklet of vouchers, but you won't be able to use them until the first of September."

"All right," the man answers. "So come back in September."

"As you wish," you say quickly, "but in September you won't get the fifteen free deliveries."

The man seems to think for a minute. He puts the pencil back into the sharpener, waits, then takes it out again exactly as it was. He says, "I understand. That makes your offer more interesting."

Then he adds, "Do you mind if I smoke?"

"No," you answer in unison.

He gets out a fat cigar, snips off the end with a pair of scissors and lights it, inhaling deeply. He takes a couple of puffs and then says, "I understand, and I want to help you out. Really. I want to help you. And do you know why?"

"Why?" asks Cristina.

He takes another puff and gestures broadly with his arms. It's like he can't be still for more than ten seconds.

"Because," he replies, smiling, "your prices are better than what we're paying now, so I save money."

Then he adds, with a new smile, "But also because you're young and clever. And I'm sorry to see you caught up in the system so early. You look tired, I think you're working too hard."

You look at him, taken aback. He takes another puff and goes on. "Take some advice from an old man: watch your quality of life. Nowadays, work and deadlines take it away from you."

God help us, here comes another string of banalities.

"It wasn't always like this," he goes on. "Once upon a time, and I often think about this, our ancestors would spend a week at a time hunting, but afterwards they would spend three weeks resting, roasting their kill over the fire. Nowadays, we work, we work and then we work some more. Nowadays, every day is a hunting expedition, every day we come home loaded with game, but there's no time to enjoy it by the fire."

He takes another puff of his cigar and stares into space. His voice takes on a more confidential tone. "It's amazing, but now that we've finally won our freedom, after years of struggle, we're just slaves again. Slaves of the office, slaves of work. Listen to this: our sales director wants twenty per cent more every year, but everyone knows the growth rate in our sector is only three per cent. Which means we have to take market share from our competitors, or else go out and steal. The only way to get that twenty per cent has nothing to do with raising ourselves but everything to do with crushing everyone else...."

188

You look at him without saying anything. You wonder whether some terrible illness is going around, making everyone preach sermons about society.

"On the other hand," he sighs, "our competitors are out to crush us. There's a vicious war going on in the world, but no one notices because people are killed without any blood being spilled.... But I want nothing more to do with it. I've sold everything. I'm here to run the purchasing department, but I want nothing more to do with it.... I retire in November. I can't stand it any more, seeing these aggressive young recruits, slaves to themselves, stressed, anxiety-ridden, eaten up by ulcers, chasing absurd targets."

You wonder what he's referring to: this picture doesn't match the old ladies you've just seen. He seems to read your mind. "Oh, I'm not talking about the receptionists, I'm talking about everyone upstairs," and he points to the ceiling. "Their offices are like command posts: telephones ringing off the hook, faxes, people running up and down, but for what? This firm was established a hundred and fifty years ago and it's always been healthy. It's only now that its rhythms have changed. We've invented all these infernal tools—mobile phones, e-mails—which are supposed to make our work easier but just speed it up; we're always available, we've always got to give someone an answer.... Ah, our stupidity is incredible.... We should all step aside from this process... but when it comes to our wallets, the truth is that we all want twice as much. The truth is, we're all greedy."

You smile understandingly. Just as well Grissino wasn't with you or you'd have been there all night.

And that, gentle readers, is how the days go by, as we work round the clock and all four of us are more and more exhausted and worn out, and we only see each other for a few minutes in the morning, after which it's every man for his own customers, with seven or eight visits a day.

Don't take it as a sign of disrespect, but I'm now going to sum up a typical day from the point of view of my ass.

"After I woke up I sat on the edge of the bed for a few seconds, then on the toilet—my boss likes to be comfortable when he has a pee—then on the kitchen chair, waiting for the water to come to the boil for tea, then on the chair in the hall, while my boss did up his shoelaces, then on the saddle of the Vespa, then on the revolving chair in the meeting room, where I was cheek to cheek with the rather nice ass of Serena, the receptionist—today's look, by the way, is Hospital Porn, which she alternates with Scarlett O'Hara and Roman Gladiator (complete with robe and strapped sandals)—then I was on a seat in the bar, where I had a brief chat with the Bulls on Wheels courier—a remarkable man, who manages to deliver as many as forty booklets a day—then again on the saddle of the Vespa, then in the uncomfortable waiting room at Cluster's offices, and finally in a soft comfy armchair for more than an hour, while my boss smiled to himself as he talked to a guy who looked like a cowboy, and his secretary, who looked like a Romanian javelin thrower and repeated everything the cowboy said like a parrot; then again on the Vespa and then in a soft chair in the waiting room at Beltrami and Beltrami, saddle of the Vespa again, another four offices, all very similar (three hard chairs, one comfortable one) and the office of Marlene the Soothsayer, who needs to deliver urgent talismans—a colleague of my boss', in a manner of speaking. Lunch break on a bench in the Parco del Valentino, then a chair at Swift Travels, a travel agency, then the saddle of the Vespa again, a waiting room at Lumol Limited, then a comfortable armchair in front of the purchasing manager, the saddle of the Vespa again and the office of Signorina Paola of GSCT Limited, another five forgettable offices, then saddle of the Vespa, kitchen chair, toilet, armchair in front of the TV and, finally, mattress."

Chapter sixteen

In which matters come to a head, and our subjects
are whisky, sexpot Japanese waitresses, inappropriate
enthusiasms, mental dilemmas, anxiety and breathlessness.

The situation unexpectedly comes to a head on Thursday the twentieth of July.

You arrived at the office at seven o'clock in the morning, you're in the meeting room checking the accounts. You gather together all the appointment sheets and orders and match them up with your courier's deliveries of voucher booklets and transfers to the bank account. Then you switch on the computer and enter the data, updating the spreadsheet that contains your projections. The results are excellent, but lower than you expected: between the beginning of the month and yesterday you've had more than four hundred appointments, an enormous number, a very high percentage of them being successful; you've banked three hundred and ninety-eight million and there's another twenty million or so to be banked at the end of the month—special deals, made by Grissino, for a couple of customers who've placed the biggest orders. The figure is substantial, but now you have only seven more working days before the August holiday period, and at best that means another hundred and fifty or two hundred million—much less than the figure you had planned, but still a tidy sum: divided by four it's not bad at all.

At eight o'clock sharp, the doorbell rings. You get up and walk out of the office, you go the few yards down the corridor to the door and open it without checking first, curious to know what Serena's wearing today and where she left her keys. But instead you find three middle-aged men, wearing jeans and T-shirts, looking at you.

"Can I help you?" you ask, noticing that all three have mobile phones clipped to their belts.

One of the three, the one closest to the door, squares up to you and says, "Who are you?" His manner is tremendously overbearing, but you find you can't match his arrogance when you reply, "And who are you?"

Unmoved, he gets a green identity card out of his pocket (it has a photograph of him in uniform) and waves it in your face. "Revenue," he says.

You try to hold back the panic welling up in you.

"And wh-what do you want?" you stammer.

"We're here to carry out an audit," says one of the men standing behind the first one, walking in confidently and showing you a piece of paper. You let them all come in. You're incapable of any kind of reaction. Your heart is pounding like mad.

The first agent glances down the corridor. "Are you alone here?" he asks.

"Er, yes. Th-the others haven't come in yet. Th-they usually come in at about eight thirty."

The three men start walking down the corridor, then they hesitate, glance enquiringly at each other and split up, each going into one of the rooms. You try to keep your cool, but you can't do it, your brain is firing out a rapid series of images; yourself in handcuffs, Cristina and Milo lying on a beach in the tropics, drinking orange-coloured cocktails, the striped shadow of the bars on your face, Grissino laughing as he lights a cigar, you sitting in a corner with your head in your hands, Milo rolling a joint in the bright sun. You feel a void in the pit of your stomach. You try to stay in control, you're breaking out in a cold sweat, you think you might pass out.

You take a deep breath: what kind of a con man are you, if you give in to panic at the first sign of difficulty? Come on, it'll all be over in ten minutes. But your brain keeps on firing out images: your photograph in the newspapers, Grissino in a Hawaiian shirt coming out of a bank with a briefcase, the three Revenue agents dragging you down the stairs, Cristina diving nude into crystal-clear water. You feel faint. You take another deep breath, you try to control the terror that's overwhelming you: what on earth could they find? So far, you haven't cheated anyone, have you, you tell yourself, but it's hopeless: your heart goes on pounding furiously, you can even feel it in your temples, the panic is intolerable. You glance down the corridor: one of the agents is coming out of Grissino's office. He comes up to you.

"Look, do me a favour," he says, not bothering with niceties. "Order up some coffee. We're going to be here for a while."

"Okay," you agree as he turns his back on you.

You fling yourself at the exit and start running down the stairs, two at a time, as if you're escaping from a fire.

Once out on the street you stop on the pavement—what the hell are you doing? you ask yourself for a moment—but then you look quickly left and right and start running again, as fast as you can, pushing through the passers by, past the shop windows, slaloming between the parked cars like a man possessed, and by the time you stop, leaning against a wall and gasping for breath, you've done three whole blocks. You frantically get out your mobile and look for Cristina's number in the list. You press the call button and wait a few seconds, but it's switched off; you try Milo's home number and when he answers you tell him everything without pausing for breath. "Milo—it's Vittorio—they're onto us—I was in the office and the Revenue turned up—I, I, I don't know what came over me—I didn't know what to do—I ran away—we've got to disappear, all of us—don't go to the office—we've got to warn Grissino."

Milo listens without saying anything, so you start again. "They're onto us, Milo. I'm not kidding. The guys from the Revenue came. Are you listening to me?"

Milo's silent for another second, then says, "Come over to my place, right now," and hangs up.

You switch off your mobile and put it back in your pocket. You lean against the wall and breathe deeply, through your mouth, trying to reduce your heart rate—you can still feel it in your temples. A taxi is passing by on the street and you almost throw yourself under it to stop it. You open the door and jump in, you give the driver Milo and Cristina's address and add, "Make it fast, please."

The taxi sets off into the traffic, tyres squealing, and you collapse on the back seat, out of breath, your eyes wide open. You take a deep breath. The taxi driver makes a joke—in a hurry, eh?—but you pay no attention: you're suddenly overcome with a sense of satisfaction that you've got away with it, but it only lasts a second, just long enough for you to realize what will happen to Grissino if he sets foot in the office, or what will happen to Serena if she's the first to arrive and finds herself alone with the three Revenue agents. You try to calm yourself down, telling yourself that even she doesn't know your real names, and then the thoughts come one after the other: you were a coward to run away like that, you should have controlled the situation, Grissino would have handled it better; no, you were right to disappear, it's better that way, no risk; but the three agents have seen your face, for chrissakes; the money should be safe, because Grissino transfers it to another account every two or three days; but if Grissino's arrested, none of you know exactly where it is.... Christ! You clench your fists, you'd like to be somewhere else, you close your eyes.

Within a few minutes you're at Milo's. The meter shows eleven thousand six hundred lire; you give the driver two ten thousands and run out without even shutting the door. You fling yourself upstairs and, when you reach the second floor, attack the doorbell. Milo opens the door immediately: he's wearing a jacket and tie and seems a bit out of it. He closes the door behind you and turns the key in the lock three times.

"Try to stay calm," he says immediately, dragging you towards the living room. "No one has our real names." You go to the window and instinctively part the curtains to look down onto the street. There's nothing to worry about: men on their way to the office, women with shopping bags, children with backpacks. You take a deep breath and ask for a drink.

Milo prepares two neat whiskies, then points at the telephone on the floor and says, "I tried calling Grissino twice, but the answering machine's on. I've left a message."

You look around and suddenly remember. "Where's Cristina?"

Milo shakes his head. "She didn't sleep here last night."

You stare at him, wide-eyed.

"Yes," he says. "She went back to live at her sister's a week ago."

Only now do you notice that the room is a pigsty: boxes, pizza crusts, McDonald's bags and empty cans all over the place.

"Have you called her?"

"Sit down," says Milo gently. "Sit down and try to calm yourself."

You collapse into a chair. You grab the glass of whisky and swallow it in one go. You feel the liquid go down and burn in your stomach.

"So where is she now?" you ask, more and more worried.

"Everything's okay, Vittorio. Try to calm down. I've spoken to her and she says she's coming over. Try to calm down: no one has our real names and the money we've taken so far should already be safe...."

"Oh, for Christ's sake!" you interrupt. "How can I calm down? They're onto us...and if Grissino doesn't know and is on his way to the office he's going to walk right into their arms."

"Grissino's not a child, he can look after himself, you'll see. Now try to calm down. Remember that we have the money and it's safe. All we have to do is sit tight here and wait. Do you want to play Playstation? It'll help you relax."

Christ, how can he think this is a good time to play Playstation, you think.

"Why not?" you say, breathing hard through your mouth.

You are a sexpot Japanese waitress, squeezed tightly into a black miniskirt with a little white apron and high heels; Milo, on the other hand, is a sort of Nazi warrior in camouflage, and he's hammering away at you like a blacksmith while you punch keys at random, trying to guess the right commands. You can't concentrate much at first—your stomach is burning and your hands are shaking—but then, as you gradually gain confidence and learn the keystroke combinations, the battles on the screen become less ferocious and chaotic, more graceful, the moves and countermoves are no longer random but deliberate, balletic, a more violent version of chess. In short, you begin to be distracted, helped by the fact that Milo plays with an enthusiasm that seems inappropriate, given that he doesn't know what's become of his uncle, his fiancée and his money. About twenty minutes later, after he's beaten you for the sixth time, you get up and look at your watch. It's ten past nine.

"Christ, Milo, where's Cristina? She should have been here long ago."

Milo glances at his watch, then gets up calmly and goes over to the telephone. He dials a number, and after a few moments you hear him say, "Hi, Valeria, it's me again. What's happened to Cristina?"

Milo listens to the answer and then says, "Right, thanks. Bye."

He hangs up and smiles at you. "Everything's okay. That was her sister. She says Cristina just left and is on her way here."

You pace nervously around the room a couple of times, open the curtain again and check the street, then you go over to the telephone and pick up the receiver. "I'll try Grissino again," you say.

You dial the number and wait. First ring, no answer; second ring, no answer; third ring, no answer; fourth ring, no answer; on the fifth ring, the answering machine clicks on. "Hello. This is Grissino. I'm not at home. I've gone out to beat up a few policemen, get a fix of heroin and pick up some thirteen-year-old girls."

When you hear the tone, you start in anxiously. "Grissino, it's Vittorio, hi, I'm at Milo's, get in touch as soon as you can...."

A dry click interrupts you, then you hear Grissino's voice. "Subject," he says, "hasn't it occurred to you that our phones might already be tapped?" and then he bursts out laughing.

From your expression, Milo grasps that Grissino has answered, springs across to you and grabs the receiver out of your hand. "Christ, uncle, are you at home?"

Grissino says something you can't hear, and this time it's you grabbing the receiver out of Milo's hand. "The Revenue came to the office this morning and—"

Grissino interrupts. "You're talking like Huey, Dewey and Louie."

Then he adds, "I know everything. I heard Milo's message while I was in the shower. Let's all keep our heads. I know exactly what to do."

He pauses, and you take the opportunity to share the receiver with Milo's left ear.

"So," says Grissino, "let's go over this carefully. First of all, Vittorio, you shouldn't have run away like that, your reaction was irrational—"

"You're right, but I didn't know—"

"Be quiet, what's done is done and there's no point in talking about it," he interrupts immediately. "So, to begin with, it's unlikely the Revenue was there because of our scam. It's a crime for which you don't just issue a summons, you need a specific complaint...and, since none of our victims can predict the future, there can't have been a complaint.... Besides, if that were the case, it would probably have been the police or the *carabinieri*...."

He pauses again, then goes on. "So I suspect these agents were sent by someone who smelt a rat somewhere or, probably, they came for a routine audit. It's unusual for a newly formed company, but it happens."

"That's exactly what they said this morning: we're here for an audit," you say apologetically.

Grissino seems to be thinking about something else. "In any case," he continues, "it doesn't matter. What we know is that as soon as they get their hands on the company documents—not to mention the accounts—they'll find a series of infractions, each more serious than the last. And if they go in at all deeply, they'll find that something smells bad, starting with our false names.... Conclusion: the Big C is over today, and never mind all the money we might still have made. Let's enjoy what there is and count ourselves lucky."

"But the money's safe?" asks Milo immediately.

Grissino pauses before he answers. "The money's safe. Fairly safe. As you know, every two or three days I transfer it to another account…and, whatever happens, it'll take the Revenue a few days to get permission to check out the banks. But I don't want to take any risks: I'm going to go down there right now and transfer the loot to a third account, after which, tomorrow morning, we'll withdraw the whole lot in cash and share it out—"

"Can't we do it right away?" asks Milo, snatching the question from your lips.

"Yes," answers Grissino, "we could. But you two are too upset and you'd make any cashier suspicious. We're talking about withdrawing four hundred million: they don't just hand that over in a couple of minutes. They have to go through all the right checks. You need hours, and the signatures of all the branch managers. You have to be calm and relaxed and patient. We'll do it tomorrow, don't worry: the money's safe."

You look at Milo unhappily.

"Go on then, Grissino, go there today, on your own," suggests Milo.

"Nah," he says, "don't be in such a hurry. I have no intention of wandering around on my own with a briefcase filled with four hundred million lire."

"We can be your escorts, and wait outside," you say quickly.

"Be patient," says Grissino, "trust me. If I say we'll do it together tomorrow it's because it's better to do it together tomorrow."

"Okay, uncle," says Milo grudgingly, "we'll do it your way."

"And what do we do now?" you ask.

"You stay at home and behave yourselves. I'll join you in an hour or so. We'll lie low all afternoon, then we'll order a pile of pizzas for supper, we'll eat, we'll go to bed and tomorrow at half past eight we'll be outside the bank. We'll take our hundred million each and then it's every man for himself. And now I'll say goodbye. See you later."

You say goodbye in unison and hang up. Milo goes over to the sofa, pushes aside a couple of dirty plates and an empty beer can and drops onto the cushions. He stays there a while, staring absently into space, then says, unexpectedly, "Four hundred million. A hundred each. And we thought it would be three or four hundred each, at the beginning."

You shrug.

Neither Cristina nor Grissino has arrived by half past twelve. Now Milo is behaving like a crack addict who's taken an overdose; eyes staring, he scratches his nose, gets up from the sofa, paces nervously around the room, goes over to the window, opens the curtains, looks out at the street, scratches his nose, pours himself a whisky on the rocks, sits down, takes a gulp, gets up again, turns on the radio, goes over to the window, opens the curtains, looks down at the street, shakes his head, paces nervously around the room, looks at you with fear in his eyes, takes another gulp, turns off the radio, sits down again, scratches his nose, checks the time, shakes his head, gets up again, goes over to the window again, opens the curtains, looks down at the street, scratches his nose, takes a gulp, shakes his head. Just watching him is a nightmare.

You're making call after call to all the numbers you can think of: Cristina's mobile is switched on, but there's no answer. There's no answer at Valeria's house either (Cristina's sister), but that's to be expected—you tell yourself—she's probably at work. There's no answer at Grissino's, not even the usual answering machine. Even when you take a chance and call your office there's no answer. And, while your ears are hearing nothing but the sound of telephones going unanswered, your eyes are seeing Milo getting up, sitting down, getting up, checking the time, shaking his head, going over to the window, opening the curtains, looking down at the street, taking gulps of whisky, pacing nervously around the room, sitting down, getting up and so on.

"What are we going to do?" you ask, finally. It's nearly two o'clock in the afternoon and you try to gather the various thoughts that have passed through your head in the last few hours.

"Where can they have got to?" you ask. "Suppose Grissino did go to the bank and he's been arrested. It's a remote possibility, but it's the only one I can think of. Okay? In which case, what's happened to Cristina? She was out and about, no one could have caught her. Where's she got to? And why isn't she answering her mobile? Maybe she's been run over. Okay? In which case, where's Grissino? Is it possible that both these things happened at the same time? It's strange. I don't understand. I can't make sense of it."

Milo comes over, grabs your arm and says, "Let's go out. Let's go to Grissino's."

You think about this for a moment, then say, "What if they turn up and we're not here?"

"Hmm," thinks Milo. "You're right. One of us had better stay here."

"Okay," you agree. "I'll go to Grissino's and you wait here. We'll be in touch as soon as anything happens."

You're about to leave when he comes over to the door and gives you a big hug. "We're a team," he says. His eyes are shining and his breath smells of whisky.

Nobody answers Grissino's intercom. You're hovering indecisively by the door when, after a minute, a woman comes out with a poodle. You take the opportunity to go in. You go up the stairs cautiously and unhurriedly and, when you reach the right floor, step up to Grissino's door. Before ringing the bell, you put your ear to the door and listen. You don't hear anything for a while. So you ring the bell, insistently, and put your ear to the door again. You don't hear anything. You wait another minute, ringing the bell a couple of times, then you hear two buzzing noises inside and recognize the sound of the intercom. You rush down the stairs, certain that it's Cristina, but when you get to the bottom and throw the door open you see two faces you have no trouble recognizing: Barbie's grandparents, the couple that came to see the apartment. You slip past them, pretending not to recognize them, and walk half a block before you cross the street and go into a bar from which you can watch the whole street. You order a cappuccino, get out your mobile and call Milo.

It rings once and you hear his voice. "Hello?"

"It's me, Milo. What are you doing?"

"I'm doing a whole bunch of things at the same time," he says sarcastically. "I'm smoking, drinking and talking on the telephone. Amazing, huh?"

"Well, not everyone has the gift," you remark. "Any news?"

"Christ, no, and you?"

"There's no one at home at Grissino's."

"Christ, Christ, Christ," Milo curses, and you hear a dull thud, as if he's beating his fist on the ground. The line is silent for a while, then you say, "I don't get it. What the fuck's going on?"

Milo doesn't say a word.

So you try another possibility. "What if they've gone off together, with all the money?"

"Impossible," he retorts indignantly. "Cristina's my fiancée. And Grissino's my uncle. They'd never betray me."

Chapter seventeen

*In which our subjects are a letter, what Milo and Vittorio
do a few days after receiving this letter, the Old Wolf
and the Young Wolf, style, and how life is cyclical.*

The letter arrived at Milo's the following morning. Express
delivery, ironically.

> *Dear Milo, Dear Vittorio,*
>
> *As you have had occasion to notice on several occasions, some people
> have rather outlandish tastes. Oboists, cricket lovers, poets, necrophiliacs,
> collectors of telephone cards or racing cars. Body builders, shoe fetishists,
> gossip addicts. There are Amedeo Minghi fans, readers of romance novels,
> enthusiastic shit-eaters, religious nuts.*
>
> *Among these various human types we may find the most outrageous
> of all: con artists. And this last group shows the most skill in amassing
> various and strange vices. I have personally known con artists who are
> evil, devious, grasping, untrustworthy and selfish. I wouldn't wish to press
> the point, but I combine several of these characteristics myself.*
>
> *However.*
>
> *However, in the last month I have come across people who are
> far worse.*

I have come across senior executives who have asked me: this service that's starting on the first of September, when does it start exactly?

I have come across executive secretaries with the arrogance of generals and I have come across clerks/salesmen/advertising agents/purchasing managers whose eyes give away what they're thinking: you don't know who I am. Whereas I did and do know. And they could know too. All they had to do was stretch their arms out to the sun to find out who they were: mouse turds in the bilges of God's ships.

I have seen all kinds of morons, driven, like us, by just two motives.

I have seen Cristina absent-mindedly undoing a button of her blouse and suddenly awakening the interest of a bored manager, thus closing a contract worth more than three million.

I have seen people who wouldn't listen until I mentioned plain brown envelopes.

I have seen too many fellows, which made me think a man a worm (Shakespeare, King Lear, *Act Four, Scene One).*

I have seen, for the thousandth time, a world that is rotten and disillusioning.

But I'm losing the thread. Let's get back to us.

So, let's think about this: you decided to carry out this con with me and now I've disappeared. Or rather: we've both disappeared, Cristina and I.

I imagine you're a bit annoyed with us. On the other hand, we all choose our teammates on the bobsleigh, and there are always a few nasty surprises on the way down.

As for the money, don't waste time wondering who has it.

As you will have noticed from the postmark, we're taking a convenient flight out of Milano Malpensa, and covering our tracks will be child's play. I'm sorry to tell you that it's unlikely we'll meet again in this life. Four hundred million, combined with my savings, adds up to a sum which in some countries really is a fortune.

You must have a lot of questions running through your heads, but the answer is very simple: we've ripped you off. The details are unimportant: be certain in the knowledge, though, that you're in no danger because your real names don't appear anywhere. Of course, the loot's not there any more, but is it worth your freedom?

You know, I'm reminded of the story of the Old Wolf and the Young Wolf. I'd like to tell it to you.

So: the Old Wolf and the Young Wolf come to the top of a hill and in the valley they see a flock of sheep. So the Young Wolf pipes up: let's run down and bag us a couple of sheep. And the Old Wolf answers: no, let's go down nice and slowly and bag all of them.

That more or less summarizes the relationship between me and the two of you.

As for the aspect which, I'm sure, amazes BOTH OF YOU, which is to say my liaison with the attractive young lady—right now she's about ten metres away from me, waiting in a line at the bar, and I can assure you she's looking stunning—it doesn't take long to explain: I attribute 40% of the blame for what has happened to me and 40% to her. But the remaining 80% I attribute equally to the two of you. Well done, you're saying, you're quite the mathematician: that makes 160%. And that's exactly how it was: there was 160% of blame—unbelievable, a real surfeit of blame.

I leave you with this thought on your share in the blame. And in any case, if you had paid more attention, you would have tried to guess James Addison Reavis' third lesson: if you want to be happy, look for your "fifteen-year-old Mexican girl." She's out there somewhere.

And now I must leave you, my friends, they're calling our flight. Be good, but not too good.

F.G.

P.S. for Milo: Give my love to the family and tell them they'll probably never hear from me again. They'll be pleased.

P.S. 2: Consider the enclosed twenty 500,000-lire notes a kind of reimbursement for expenses. You've certainly earned them.

❧

You look at the people around you. It's like being in the bar in *Star Wars*: the only thing missing is the freaks with the blue faces and proboscis-like noses; actually no, when you look more carefully they're here too. Beside you and Milo, sitting on the stools at the bar, two guys with faces like road signs are talking loudly to each other. The first, who's wearing a sleeve ripped off a wool sweater as a hat, is saying to the second, "I had to take the dog to the shrink because every time Daniela came in the house he pissed on her."

The barmaid is graceful as a sapling. You stare at her long, graceful neck and its snowy skin, then look up at the ceiling, which is covered with fake starfish made of red plastic. You're communing with your usual rum and Coke, but Milo is silently drinking a big glass of red wine and Coke.

"That's disgusting," you say. "I don't know how you can drink that muck."

Milo shrugs. "At least I change from time to time. You've always got the same old rum and Coke in your hands."

"Of course," you answer. "A glass of rum and Coke satisfies all six senses."

"There are only five senses," he grumbles.

"Listen to me," you answer, without acknowledging that he may be right. "Think about it: a rum and Coke satisfies all the senses."

Then you raise your glass, take a sip, close your eyes and go on. "Right; it satisfies the sense of smell with this ultra-sweet caramel scent. It satisfies the sense of taste with this wonderful flavour of alcohol and sugar flowing down your throat. It satisfies the sense of touch with this magical sensation of ice-cold glass and moisture under your fingers. And it satisfies the sense of sight: look at this range of colours, from black to brown…and the different levels of transparency of the glass and the ice cubes…. Ah, it's magic."

Milo looks at you, puzzled, than takes a cigarette from the pack on the bar. "And hearing?" he asks with a sly smile.

You answer with an identical smile, raise your glass to his left ear and clink the ice cubes. Somewhere in the world, in the People's Republic of China, a woman is holding a plastic bunny rabbit between her thumb and forefinger. On her other hand she has five thimbles, one on each finger. On the tips of the thimbles there are five tiny paintbrushes, each a different colour, which the woman is using, in a single swift movement, to paint the plastic bunny rabbit. The plastic bunny rabbit will be a surprise inside a little chocolate egg. Somewhere in the world, someone collects plastic bunny rabbits. Under Pol Pot's Khmer Rouge, one million seven hundred thousand Cambodians disappeared, wiped out by summary executions, famine, exhaustion and war. Benin has some six million inhabitants: about half a million workers are underage, and eighty per cent are illiterate. In the poorest countries of West Africa (Benin, Togo, Burkina Faso, Mali), more than two hundred thousand children a year are sold and sent to work in the "richer" countries (Nigeria, Côte d'Ivoire and Gabon). Somewhere in the world, a *sadhu* is saying: we are in the era of Kaljuga, the cosmic era of decadence and attachment to appearances and material things. Your mind wanders here and there, unable to concentrate. God wants three things: your mind, your words and your eyes. But your eyes look elsewhere, your mind goes off on its own and your mouth says other things.

Milo says nothing for a long time. He looks defeated, and so do you. You stare at a phrase scratched into the bar in small letters: "I love fishing rods but I don't go fishing," and the bar is half empty, the two guys next to you are leaving, and this silence is killing you.

"What time is it?" you ask.

"I don't know," answers Milo.

And then he adds, "But it's night time."

"Thanks for the reassurance," you answer.

Milo smiles.

He keeps quiet for a while, staring into space, then he sighs, "Anyway, he who lives by fraud will die by fraud."

"Come on, Milo," you say quickly. "Let's not dwell on it any more: let's forget the whole thing. It's just you and me. Again. With no one else in the way. And we never expected to go through life without any low blows, or disappointments. So let's forget all about it—Cristina, Grissino and the Big C. We're here, we're free and we're friends. Remember our motto: you and me a thousand percent together, always."

Milo stands up and gives you a bear hug.

"You're right, Vittorio," he says with shining eyes. "You and me a thousand percent together, always."

Then, moved, he sits back down.

"Besides, if you think about it, we're better off like this," you go on. "Those two have gone off with the money. But we know that right now they're on some beach in the tropics, getting bored, while we're still here, back to making plans and feeling alive."

Milo gives you a nasty look to point out the silliness of what you've just said, then orders his fourth wine and Coke and your fourth rum and Coke. You drink two thirds of yours with embarrassing haste. You wonder who's going to throw up first. Your internal bookies give the following odds: Vittorio evens, Milo eight to one: you've never seen him throw up.

"Okay, Vittorio, at the end of the day you're right," he says. "Let's forget it. It's you and me again, a thousand percent, and this world is full of rich imbeciles. And we're here to fleece them."

"Yeah. And there are lots of ways to do it, if we work on our style."

"Work on our style?"

"Yes. If we want to be better con artists, we have to work on our style. If you've got style, you can make rich people believe any old crap...I mean, just look at an art gallery, for example."

Milo smiles at you. You finish off the rest of your rum and Coke in one gulp and he does the same.

"And most of all, never forget," you say, half drunk, "money isn't the point."

"Shakespeare, *King Lear,* Act Four, Scene One?" he asks, looking at you with bloodshot eyes.

"No. And I'll give you an example."

You pause for breath, then go on. "Okay, sometimes a guy comes up to you and says: Look at that girl over there, she's a knockout. Is she with that other guy just because he's rich? How can she stand it? But in fact, if you look closely, there's no discrepancy—the truth is that a mediocre knockout is going out with a mediocre rich guy, so it's not about a knockout going with a rich guy, but two mediocrities sticking together. It all makes perfect sense."

Milo, red-faced and sweaty, raises his empty glass and repeats, "It all makes perfect sense," and you both laugh and feel good. Then his mood plummets again momentarily. "What do you think?" he asks. "Were they in it together from the start? Would they have gone off together even if the Revenue hadn't turned up?"

You order some more drinks and then say, "Look, forget about it. I'll tell you what we're going to do. We're going to spend a few months on holiday in Cuba. Free."

"Oh yes?" he says, coming closer. "How?"

"Listen to this scheme I've just dreamed up. Pay attention. First we take the ten million Grissino left us and buy two tickets to Cuba—"

Milo interrupts: "I thought you said it was free?"

"Listen to me. We go to Cuba. A cousin of mine lives over there. She works in a local travel agency. Before we leave, we take out an insurance policy and then, when we're in Cuba, we fake a car accident or something. We have my cousin help us with medical certificates from some hospital or other—it won't be a problem, everyone over there can be bribed. Then we come back to Italy and report the accident, backing it up with our excellent certificates, which they'll never be able to check. Result: they reimburse our tickets and pay compensation on the spot."

Milo looks at you happily: "Superb, Vittorio. It's a brilliant idea, and—"

Just then a kid interrupts him, resting a hand on his shoulder. You turn to look at him: he can't be more than sixteen years old.

"Guys," he murmurs, looking around timidly, "do you by any chance know where I could get some... like... some tablets."

Milo sobers up instantly, gets down from his stool and says to the kid, "Follow me," as he heads for the exit.

Really, gentle readers—isn't it amazing how dazzling and miraculous it is, this reality ticking away from one second to the next?

Acknowledgments

Thanks to Valentina, for what has happened, what is happening and what is yet to happen.

Thanks to all those who have framed the last six years. Thanks to my colleagues at Soco and We&Media. Thanks to Lutèce and all the life to be found there. Thanks to Motel Connection, Tiziano Lamberti, Subsonica, Sushi, Mau Mau, Mambassa and all those who are giving new sounds and colours to this city.

Thanks to Luca Ragagnin for the next story.

Thanks to the Civette sul Comò and the Osvaldo Soriano Football Club.

Thanks to Luca Bertini for the idea of "Bulls on Wheels."

Thanks to Elena, Giovanna and Eugenio for their valuable suggestions and thanks to Alessandra and Rita, my most ruthless readers.

Thanks to all those who have written and continue to write letters and e-mails about *Rossenotti*: particular thanks to the ultra-nice Barbara Bussoli and Marco Schiavone (who have been 'sampled' in a few exchanges in this book). Thanks also to those very few readers (Gabriella, Luigi and Carlo) who have discovered the second plane on which to read that book (there's fun to be had there too, but the story is even more complicated). By the way, thanks to Ben Harper &

the Innocent Criminals for the most blatant of the fifty-six quotations here.

Thanks to all those I thanked last time: feel your presence here.

Thanks to Shakespeare, and of course, to *King Lear,* Act Four, Scene One.

And my thanks to you, gentle readers, who have made it this far. If you have any comments on the affair, you can write to me at ziogrissino@virgilio.it.

Lots of love.

About the Author

Enrico Remmert

Enrico Remmert was born in 1966 in Turin, Italy, where he still lives and works. He has published numerous stories in literary anthologies and magazines in Italy and abroad. His first novel, *Rossenotti*, won the Tuscania and Chianciano prizes and has been translated into several languages. *The Ballad of the Low Lifes* is his second novel.

The fonts used in this book are from the Garamond family